Missing Dixie

Missing Dixie

A NEON DREAMS NOVEL

CAISEY QUINN

WM
WILLIAM MORROW
An Imprint of HarperCollins*Publishers*

MISSING DIXIE. Copyright © 2015 by Caisey Quinn. All rights reserved. Printed in the United States of America. No part of this book may be used or reproduced in any manner whatsoever without written permission except in the case of brief quotations embodied in critical articles and reviews. For information address HarperCollins Publishers, 195 Broadway, New York, NY 10007.

HarperCollins books may be purchased for educational, business, or sales promotional use. For information please e-mail the Special Markets Department at SPsales@harpercollins.com.

FIRST EDITION

Library of Congress Cataloging-in-Publication Data has been applied for.

ISBN 978-0-06-236686-3

15 16 17 18 19   OV/RRD   10 9 8 7 6 5 4 3 2 1

For you, because you shattered me into a million pieces and forced me to put myself back together again. I would've given you anything—but I will give up my dreams for no one.

"In the end, we are all just humans . . . drunk on the idea that love, and only love, can heal our brokenness."
—F. Scott Fitzgerald

Missing Dixie

Prologue | Gavin

"I NEED A MICHELOB LIGHT, TWO JACK AND COKES, A BOURBON on the rocks, and a Sex on the Beach," a waitress named Kimberly calls to me over the crowded bar.

"Yes, ma'am!" I shout over the din while filling the order quickly, tossing an umbrella into the fruity drink and briefly wondering what the hell kind of group orders such random drinks. It's an odd number, so probably not a double date.

Once Kim's tray is full, she takes off into the crowd and I take a few more orders from patrons sitting at the bar. The house band announces that they're taking a break and I'm grateful that the bar is full enough to keep it from being quiet.

Silence has always been my enemy. Hence why I play the drums, the loudest, most deafening musical instrument in existence. They're the only things that drown out the sounds in my head. Once my customers and waitresses have been taken care of, I do a quick wipe-down of the bar and restock the highball glasses.

It's in the brief moment when the raucous chatter dies down enough that pool balls can be heard knocking together that the music begins.

Someone is playing the piano, the old Wurlitzer that sits abandoned in the back corner of the Tavern. It's not the music itself that stops me where I stand. It's the way it's being played. Effortless yet meticulous, a combination that I've only known one musician in my entire life to be capable of.

Glancing in the direction where the melody is drifting from I notice I'm not the only one mesmerized by the sound. Half the bar has made their way to the back corner to get a closer listen. My boss, a perpetually red-faced man named Cal, is going to kill me, but I have to see. I have to know if it's her. My body propels itself around the bar just as a voice from my right calls my name, startling me out of my trance.

Turning, I look directly into a pair of gleaming green eyes beneath a perfectly even bob of blond hair.

Ashley Weisman stands across from me in her pencil skirt and oxford dress shirt with two too many buttons undone to be here for professional reasons.

"You've been avoiding my phone calls," she says evenly.

"Been busy." Huffing out a breath, I place my hand gently on her elbow and attempt to steer her toward the exit.

Stilettos planted firmly on the liquor-sticky floor, she purses her full red lips at me and glares into my eyes. "You can't ignore me forever. I'm your attorney. Besides, what's the rush, Gavin? Not even going to offer me a drink? What kind of bartender are you?"

"One who doesn't have time for this right now. I'll call you tomorrow."

I can't explain it, but deep in my soul—if I have one that is—I know exactly who's playing the piano behind me. I don't know why she's here, I don't know if she knows I work here, and I sure as hell don't know if she'll want to see me. What I do know is that she and

Ashley cannot cross paths right now. Not yet. Not before I've told her everything.

"I think I'll take the drink now, thank you very much." Twisting out of my reach, she hops up onto a bar stool and steadily ignores the scowl on my face.

The music continues swirling around us and all I know is right now, I need to know who is playing that damn piano.

Clenching my fists, I walk around behind the bar and wait for her to tell me what she wants.

"I'll have a Screaming Orgasm, please." Her eyes gleam and I meet her interested gaze with a dispassionate one. "Multiples, actually."

I barely suppress a loud sigh and grab the Baileys, Kahlua, and a top-shelf bottle of vodka. Once her drink is mixed I set it down in front of her.

"On the house. Feel free to take it and go."

A frown mars her attractive face. "I don't think I've ever seen you in such a hurry to get rid of me. You have a hot date later?"

I can't help it—I glance over toward the piano. The music speeds up and so does my heart rate. The notes call to me like a siren song and I know I won't be able to keep myself from barreling over there for much longer.

"The piano player? I saw her when I came in. She's pretty."

"You done?" I nod to a newbie barback named Jake to come get her empty glass and he does.

"Oh, I see," she says evenly, watching me carefully. "It's her, isn't it? The one you're so eager to get your shit together for, huh?"

"I need to get my shit together regardless, Ashley. You know that. How about helping me do that instead of causing more trouble?"

She frowns as if I've insulted her. "I'm not trying to cause trouble. I'm curious. Pretty sure curiosity isn't a crime."

Closing my eyes, I inhale through my nose and exhale out my mouth like the meetings have taught me. "You know what they say about curiosity."

Cal walks by and I call out that I'm taking my break. Without waiting for his response or approval, I move out from behind the bar and make my way through the sea of bodies separating me from the girl behind the piano. Once I've navigated the treacherous waters, I see her.

It's smoky in here tonight and several women I'm not familiar with are surrounding her but I see her sitting there—playing her heart out—and all I can do is watch.

She doesn't make music, or create it. She is music. It flows through her as she plays and it's an incredible sight to behold.

There she is. My beautiful bluebird.

My stomach tenses and my throat constricts.

She shouldn't be here.

I shouldn't be here.

Seeing me here will hurt her and there is nothing I wouldn't give to prevent that.

Before I can even begin to formulate the words in my mind that I should say to make this okay, to make it somehow hurt her less, the music stops and she turns as if she can feel me standing there. Applause breaks out around us but it fades into background noise.

There isn't a name for the emotion that crosses her face, darkening her eyes and causing the fire in them to flare at me. It's part shock, part betrayal, and complete pain.

My jaw clenches and I force my eyes to remain on hers even though mine would prefer to close and block out the sight of her wounds deepening.

"Taking requests?" Ashley's voice calls out from beside me. Her expression says she's genuinely impressed by Dixie's talent but I can guess what my temperamental Bluebird will see.

Dixie Leigh Lark arches an eyebrow at her and then shoots me a scowl of pure disgust before answering with a short, "Not at the moment."

"Too bad," Ashley answers with a shrug.

I step closer to Dixie just as she shoves the piano bench backward, scraping it across the hardwood floor. Before I can blink, we're face-to-face and if looks could kill, someone would be performing CPR on me in a matter of seconds.

"Hey . . . I thought you might've gone on back to Houston. Or I'd hoped—"

"Go to hell, Gavin," is all that escapes her beautiful mouth. Her rage hits me with the force of a ten-foot plate-glass window shattering over me.

I turn to watch her storm out, as I run a hand over my head and feel the heat of several angry glares from other women around me.

Ashley smirks from behind her glass as she polishes off another drink I didn't realize she was holding. "Well that escalated quickly."

Yeah. It did.

I am so fucked.

1 | Dixie

"SON OF A BITCH," I BITE OUT AS THE TWISTED METAL TEARS INTO my skin.

"Jesus, Dixie. What the hell?" Jaggerd McKinley glances up from under the hood of a 1968 Mustang Fastback and narrowly avoids slamming his forehead into it.

Before I can stop him, he's around the car and grabbing a clean rag from a tray beside me.

"Be still," he commands, using the cloth to blot at the blood on my hip. I tug the waistband of my jeans down a little lower so he can press it against my flesh wound. It's not huge but feels deep and raw. Kind of like I just walked too close to a piece of gnarly metal sticking out from under a tarp, which is precisely what happened.

"What the hell was that?" I nod toward the tarp. "What's under there?"

Jag's eyes resemble the color of whiskey in the sun and tighten when they meet mine. "Nothing," he mumbles under his breath.

"Sure as hell didn't feel like nothing." I lift his hand gently and peer at my wound. I can handle just about anything except the sight of my own blood.

I feel my eyes rolling back and Jag's firm arms around me.

"Still squeamish about that, huh?" His breath tickles the side of my face and I am suddenly acutely aware of his proximity.

"Yeah, apparently," I say, feeling the edges of my vision fade.

"Easy, girl," he says with a laugh, wrapping his arms even tighter around me and leaning me gently on the passenger door of the Fast-back. "Take a few deep breaths."

"I'm fine. I promise." I run a hand through my wayward curls before wiping the sheen of sweat from the back of my neck. "It's just been a long week."

"I heard Dallas was back. I'm glad the scare overseas turned out okay."

I nod. I had every intention of staying angry with my brother for not telling me Gavin wasn't on tour with him but then he went and disappeared for almost forty-eight hours, scaring me half to death and forcing me to forgive him. "Me, too. The wedding is this weekend."

Jag busies himself wiping his grease-covered hands on his jeans. "Guess it really does work out for some folks."

The cocktail of emotions behind his statement twists around my insides like twine. "Guess so."

"Robyn seems like a great girl. Glad they were able to get their second chance."

The constant heaviness I carry in my heart lightens a little. I am happy for Dallas and Robyn. I'm excited to be a part of their big day and literally ecstatic about becoming an aunt to my future nephew. But . . . something about the anticipation of it all, the impending burden of necessary smiles and laughter in the midst of my complete and utter devastation about having to face Gavin Garrison for the first time in months . . . It's like getting the worst news of your life on the brightest, sunniest, clearest day of the year.

I'm a walking, talking, living, breathing storm cloud waiting to burst and rain on everyone else's parade.

But I won't. Because I can't.

I had my chance. My one night. And even a little more than that.

"Wait for me, Bluebird," he'd said.

Apparently I should've asked for the specific details of just how long he intended to make me wait. I thought he meant wait until he got back from being on tour with Dallas. Too bad he didn't go on tour with Dallas. Lucky me, I got to find out the hard way.

I have seen Gavin Garrison a grand total of twice in the past three months. Once at a bar he apparently worked at, unbeknownst to me. And then again when my brother went missing and he stopped by to check on me—as if he actually cared. He didn't even come inside, just stood on the porch and asked me to keep him posted about Dallas.

Adrenaline courses through me like an electric current at the memory of seeing him at the bar with another woman. Her perfectly manicured nails skating up the skin on his arm.

"You sure you're okay?" Jaggerd's voice yanks me from the past.

I swallow hard as he takes a step back. "Yeah."

"When was the last time you had a tetanus shot?"

I try to recall if I've ever had one. I have. Once. "Pretty sure I was a kid. Thirteen or so. I cut my hand on a rusty car rim when Dallas and Gavin let me go to the junkyard with them to find a side-view mirror for Dallas's truck."

Jaggerd mumbles something unintelligible under his breath.

"What'd you say?"

His eyes lift to mine and something unidentifiable flickers in them before he blinks it back and answers. "I asked if you had any memories that didn't include him."

There's a challenge in his tone, as if he already knows the answer and is daring me to deny the truth.

It irritates me—the unnecessary shade he's throwing, the male macho bullshit, game playing of any kind. I've had enough of that for one lifetime. After years of letting my older brother and Gavin Garrison—and even Jag in the year that we dated—dictate my life, my feelings, and my mood, I'm finally in a place where I am my own damn person. A few months on the road alone and coming home to have my heart broken have helped me to grow up a bit. Turns out I'm perfectly capable of making decisions all on my own and one of them is not to tolerate being condescended to on any level.

"Why don't you just go ahead and say what you mean, McKinley? Save us both the time and trouble of trying to decipher your double-speak?"

Surprise widens his eyes, then he smirks at me with a look of slight approval in them. "Sorry. Old habits die hard."

"Old habits?"

Jag shrugs. "I always felt like third runner-up. Hell, I *was* third runner-up."

I frown because now I'm lost. "Meaning?"

"Meaning music will always be your first love. Gavin Garrison is your second and the one you've always wanted. I was more of a consolation prize—someone to kill the time with until he took notice of what was right in front of him."

"Jag—"

"Don't bother lying, Dix. I may just be some dumb mechanic but I know you and you have a terrible poker face."

Sadly, I've heard that before.

"You were never a consolation prize." This is true. Jaggerd McKinley was a little rough around the edges from a distance, but up close, he was genuinely a sweet guy. He took my virginity and he was kind and gentle about it. Granted he didn't make my heart race or my entire body light up the way a certain someone else did, but he was a good guy and I cared about him.

"Uh-huh. What was I then?"

I rack my brain for an answer that's honest but won't hurt his feelings. "You were a very sweet guy who treated me with respect. And you're still my friend and honestly, I could use a friend right now."

He's still standing close enough that I can feel the breath released by his sigh. "Oh, the friend zone. Guess I might as well get comfortable there, huh?"

The silence stretches out long and awkward between us. Jaggerd has thick, auburn hair that's always about two weeks past needing a cut. It matches the scruffy beard that's typically a few days past needing a trim. Beneath the rough exterior, though, he has bright hazel eyes, flawless skin, and a full masculine mouth women would stand in line to kiss if he'd pay more attention to them. He really is a beautiful guy. He's just not *my* guy.

"What do you want me to say?"

His shoulders relax and he removes the cloth from my hip. "Nothing. It is what it is." With a lingering glance at my bare hip, he shrugs. "I think you're fine but go to the bathroom and rinse it out, then check the cabinet for some Neosporin. Last thing you need is an infection before your brother's wedding."

His words remind me why I came by. "About the wedding . . ." I sink my teeth into my lower lip and look up at him expectantly.

Jaggerd's eyebrows lift noticeably. "You're not serious."

"It doesn't have to be a date *date*. I just don't want to go alone."

"Because he'll be there?"

I sigh harder than necessary. "Yes and no. He's in it. And I imagine he'll have . . . someone."

Jag studies me for a full minute as if I am a complicated creature he can't seem to figure out.

"Tell you what, I'll come to the wedding," he tells me on a sigh. "On one condition," he clarifies when I grin at him. I nod and he continues. "We can ride together but if either of us decides to leave with someone else, no hard feelings."

"So I'll be your wingman?" I can't help but laugh.

"More like a wingwoman," he says, nudging me gently. "But I'm betting it will be you I lose to someone else—not the other way around."

There is disappointment etched into a forced smile on his face. "Jag," I whine softly. "Please don't—"

"I'm not," he says, holding both hands up. "Just be careful, please. Garrison is trouble and he'll never be good enough for you as far as I'm concerned. But I'll mind my own business." He nods toward my hip. "Except about that. Go clean that up, please."

"Going," I say, tossing the bloody rag in the dirty pile before I head into the bathroom.

While I'm cleaning out my wound and trying not to pass out, I think about what he said. Why is it people are always telling you you're too good for the one you can't have? I've never thought of Gavin as someone I was better than—for that matter, I've never considered myself better than anyone. We're all made of the same stuff—just some of us were dealt different cards. Gavin got a shitty set of cards and my deck wasn't all that great, but somehow, when we're together, none of that matters. Dallas, Gavin, and I have always been a family. Now that Dallas has Robyn and a baby on the way, he has his own family and I feel like I'm just . . . existing. Being with Gavin was the last time I felt truly alive—like I finally belonged where I was meant to be. In his arms. But like all happiness, it was fleeting.

He was here. Right down the street and he didn't even bother to call me. Maybe I'm being overly sensitive, but maybe not. It hurts. A lot. And it makes me angry as hell. After everything we've been through over the years he still didn't deem me worthy of a call? A text? *Hey, Bluebird. About that whole waiting-for-me thing? Never mind. I'm home but I have zero interest in seeing you. Take care!*

Ugh. None of it makes sense. Only after I busted him in a bar with some blonde did he start calling and texting asking for a chance to explain.

Too little, too late, drummer boy.

I probably would've given in eventually, though. Maybe he knew that, because after a few days, his calls and texts stopped.

I've analyzed and overanalyzed every moment we spent together in Austin, everything he said before he left me in Amarillo, and each message sent since then. I've yet to reach a conclusion about the motivations and intentions of Gavin Garrison.

Papa used to say living your life was like driving a car. While it's necessary to glance back every now and then, it's much more important to watch where you are going than dwell on where you've been. I won't be that girl anymore, the one that determines her self-worth or lack thereof based on one guy's ability to notice her.

I glance up into the hazy mirror and look at my own faded reflection.

Gavin Garrison is so much more than just a guy I like—more than an infatuation or an addiction. In my heart, he's my past, present, *and* future. I just don't know if he wants to be. Or if I'm willing to put myself out there again and ask him to be.

I lost a lot of time focusing on the pain and the past. But when I stopped letting it consume me, I found myself in the same place where I always find myself. In music.

When I stopped moping and feeling sorry for myself, I made some changes in my life. I've found happiness and joy in giving piano and violin lessons to underprivileged local kids and it's been such a successful program that I had to get a business license and name it. Over the Rainbow is my passion project and I've formed friendships with many of the parents of the kiddos I teach. Maybe it's not performing onstage or coming to life beneath the lights, but I love it just the same.

If there is anything I've learned about gifts, like the gift of being able to play an instrument, it's that they should be shared with the world one way or another. I also learned a valuable lesson from my grandparents that it took traveling around the country living their dream to fully comprehend. They didn't get to live their dream but it didn't mean they weren't happy. Together they lived a full, satisfied life and they had plenty of love leftover to give to the two orphans they ended up raising. Life doesn't always turn out how you expect and sometimes parts of you get broken along the way, but there is always hope and even broken pieces can be rebuilt into something beautiful. My heart is a piece of mosaic art at this point.

Standing there, staring at myself in the glass, I vow to focus on the music, on grabbing hold of what joy I have in my life and not letting go.

Most important? I vow never again to hand my heart over to Gavin Garrison.

At least not until he hands me his first.

2 | Gavin

BAND MEETING. TODAY. REHEARSAL SPACE. 4:30. DON'T BE LATE.

That's all the text from Dallas says. Kind of odd since we're not "technically" a band anymore, but that's Dallas for you. No more explanation than he feels is necessary. I'm too tired from working a late shift to text back a list of questions.

His text is the first thing I see when I wake up and check my phone out of habit on a random Thursday afternoon. I worked late last night, so even though it's nearly three in the afternoon, this is basically breakfast time for me.

For months I've checked my phone day and night. Part of me was waiting for this, the opening, the opportunity to see her again and show her that while I'm still a work in progress, I'm trying, improving, and growing closer to becoming the type of man she deserves. The other part of me is dreading it.

After our band sort of unofficially broke up after Austin Music-Fest, Dallas went solo, Dixie went home, and I went straight to my probation officer to find out how I could right my many, many wrongs.

Trouble is, I didn't exactly tell Dixie that. I let her believe I was on tour with Dallas.

When I saw Dixie Lark three months ago, she used her last words to me to tell me right where to go. I've left her voice mails, sent texts, asked repeatedly for the chance to explain what she saw—what I did and why I didn't contact her sooner. When Dallas went missing in Rio, I stopped by to check on her but she didn't look at all happy to see me in her time of grief. So even though I wanted nothing more than to hold and comfort her, I saw McKinley there and decided it would be best if I kept my distance. Christmas and New Year's came and went and they were the first ones I didn't spend with her and Dallas since I met them ten years ago. Dallas invited me to his and Robyn's place but I declined, choosing to work instead. If it had been her asking me to come, then I would've quit my job to be there if necessary, but all I've gotten from Dixie Lark is radio silence.

I don't even blame her.

Groaning, I stretch as far as my back will allow and lumber out of my bed. After a quick shower, I throw on a T-shirt and a clean pair of jeans and step into the lace-up work boots I rarely bother to lace.

Glancing at my reflection on my way out, I note that I should have shaved my face, but I would've been late and I'm not really in the mood for pissy Dallas at the moment.

I glance down at the kitchen table and see a notice about the rent on the trailer being overdue. Usually I scrape up enough to keep it paid on time, but I've been saving my money lately. My mom is rarely even here and this isn't where I plan to spend the rest of my life.

My plan for becoming a worthwhile human being has three major components.

The first is paying for all past mistakes in full so those fuckers don't sneak up on me. I'm fulfilling all the requirements of my probation to a T. The second is making a regular effort to reach long-term goals involving the things that matter, like money, music, and my life. The third is finding a way to be completely honest with Dixie—about everything.

It's the third one I'm struggling with the most.

The rehearsal space isn't too far away but it's beginning to mist outside so I walk to the truck stop a few blocks down the road and check for Mr. Kyung. He's on the phone, speaking Korean with an earpiece in, when I step inside.

Without even acknowledging that he sees me, he tosses a pair of keys into the air—lobbing them in a perfect arc into my hands.

"Komawoyo," I call out as I turn to leave. "Bring her back before closing."

He waves me off while continuing his conversation.

He's one of the very few people on the planet who actually trust me.

When I was nine I got caught stealing a pack of cheese from Kyung's. He took one look at me, saw that I was filthy and most likely starving half to death, and told me he wouldn't turn me in if I would work off what I owed and promise never to steal another thing. Most days I swept the floors, restocked drinks, and delivered groceries and food orders to nearby houses I could reach on foot. Every time I walked in the door his seventy-something-year-old mother insisted on making me enough food for two meals. Now that I'm older I'm pretty sure it was just his way of providing for a kid he felt sorry for, but I still appreciate that he did it without making me feel ashamed. He made it clear that in his family a man is nothing without his pride. I have always been thankful that he allowed me to keep what little bit I had.

When I was sixteen and still "working" off a five-dollar seven-year-old debt, Mr. Kyung bought an old red Isuzu pickup and hired me officially as the delivery guy, but it was also officially under the table.

In some ways, the man of small stature and few words is like a father to me. I never stole another thing. Since getting the job at the Tavern I haven't needed the extra cash but he still lets me borrow the truck and come by for a meal now and then. No questions asked. His mother passed away a few years ago and his wife started doing the cooking.

"It's not as good as my mother's was," he told me quietly in his still slightly broken English over some type of dumpling soup he called *manduguk*, "but if you stop coming by it will hurt Lin's feelings and I'll have to hurt you."

Again, I don't know if he was just worried I wouldn't eat otherwise, or if it really would have hurt his wife's feelings or what, but I still come in every now and then.

I drive the barely running truck back to my place, load up my kit just in case Dallas has more than a simple meeting in mind, then head to the rehearsal space in downtown Amarillo. I listen to my favorite rock station on the way, concentrating hard on the music and wishing I had the drumming chops of Keith Moon or John Bonham, while trying to keep the anxiety over seeing Dixie at bay.

It works for a little while, right up until I pull behind the building and see EmmyLou parked beside Dallas's truck. She's already here then.

Dallas will be glad she wasn't late. Whatever it is, for him to call an emergency band meeting the same night as his rehearsal dinner, it must be important.

I pocket the keys to the truck and make my way to the back door of the repurposed storage building we used to rent out to rehearse in. When I open the door she's the first thing I see.

My adrenaline, testosterone, and heart rate all rise immediately at the sight of her.

Dixie sits cross-legged on the couch, Oz in his case beside her. Clearly she had the same inclination I did about the purpose of this meeting. Dallas is standing across from her but his guitar is nowhere in sight.

"Now that you're both here," he begins as soon as the door is closed behind me, "let's get right to it. We all have to be at the restaurant in about two hours so we don't have time to waste."

Dallas continues before I have time to check if any sign of comprehension registers on Dixie's face.

"There is a battle of the bands at the Tavern two weeks from now and I went ahead and signed us up before the list was full. We haven't played together in months and I know I should've talked to you both first, but time wasn't a luxury I had."

Dixie's mouth opens slightly and I can tell this is the first she's heard of this. Dallas puts his hands up and continues.

"I'm proposing that we give Leaving Amarillo one more shot, rehearse as soon as I get back from my honeymoon, play a warm-up gig next weekend, and perform in the battle." He pauses, glancing briefly at both of us before going on. "But Austin MusicFest was like herding cats with the two of you and I won't do that again. We all three have to want this equally, have to be ready to give it all we have. Otherwise, we can say to hell with it, and I'm going to see if Afton Tate wants to work together on writing and hope I can make a living writing songs for other people. This isn't just about living my dream anymore," he tells us on a heavy sigh. "I have a family to support now, one who I would do anything for—same goes for you two. Don't say yes for me, say yes if and only if you really want this. If it's your dream, too. If it's not, I'll have us taken off the list. Drill Sergeant Dallas is retiring so either you're in or you're out."

He huffs out a loud breath and my eyes dart to where Dixie sits, still as stone with only her side profile visible to me. When neither of us answers right away, Dallas looks ready to throw his hands up.

"Well . . ." he prompts.

"I'm in," I choke out before clearing my throat. "I'm with you. All in."

I've been hoping for this moment since I saw the flyer in the bar, not that I was hoping for Dallas's solo career to fail by any means, but I'd be lying my ass off if I said I didn't want to once again be a part of the only thing that has ever mattered to me. I'm done lying, to them and to myself.

The silence takes on a sort of self-awareness, as if it's as much in the room as we are.

"Dix," Dallas says quietly. "I know it's been a tough year. I know you've dealt with a lot on your own and whatever you decide, I will be okay with. I mean it."

My heart feels like a lead weight in my chest when she stands. She lifts Oz but doesn't remove him from his case and I can feel that she's going to pass. On this. On me. Because of the pain I've caused her.

When she turns to face me I do my best to give her a "what do we have to lose" look and a hopeful shrug, but she barely registers my presence. There's blind drive in her eyes; I just don't know what it's driving her to do. I don't have to wait long as she starts to make her way to the door.

Her voice is soft but clear when she faces Dallas. "Is that all you wanted?"

He nods. "Yeah. Mostly. I had a request about the wedding but we can discuss that tonight at the rehearsal dinner."

She frowns and I cross my arms and wait for her to pummel my already fucked-up heart with blatant rejection.

"I need some time . . . to think . . . about all of this," she says carefully. "I'll let you know something when you get back from your honeymoon. That okay?"

Dallas's shoulders sag slightly and his face shows his disappointment, but he doesn't look surprised by her answer. "Of course. I understand. I want to say take your time but I'll need to know something soon."

She nods. "I know. I'll have an answer as soon as possible. If that's all, I'm going to head on home. There's a little boy who keeps showing up for lessons, and I haven't ever met with his parents, so I'm going to try and catch them before they drop him off. And I still need to get ready for the rehearsal dinner."

Dallas gives her a quick one-armed hug and the next thing I know she's breezing right out the door. Lessons?

"Guess you don't get a goodbye," he says evenly. "I'll take that as a bad sign on the current climate between you two. I think it just lowered a few degrees in here."

I don't answer. Instead, I just sit back down on the couch and place my head in my hands. There has to be a way to help her understand why.

"She'll come around, man," Dallas tells me. "Enough to at least hear you out, I hope."

I glance up at him. "And the band? You think she can really put what happened behind her and forgive me?"

"I think she can try."

"Hope so," I answer dejectedly. "Hey, how long do we have the space for?"

Dallas checks his phone. "About another half hour. You gonna stay and play?"

I nod. I need to work off all this amped-up energy before going to his fancy, formal sit-down dinner.

"Later, man," he calls on his way out. "Don't be late tonight. In fact, I'll pick you up in about an hour or so."

"Got it."

Drill Sergeant Dallas may have retired but he's still Dallas. Dude will probably make a damn good dad.

Once he's gone I set up my kit and play until my arms ache. I'm sweaty and tired and I still have to return the truck and shower, but knowing I'll get to see her again, even if only for a little while, even if from a distance, keeps me motivated.

I return Mr. Kyung's truck and purchase the few groceries I need for the week, basic stuff that fits into one bag. I practically jog home knowing I need to shower again, but I stop short when I see the front door isn't closed all the way.

I closed it when I left.

I know I did.

Locked it, too.

"Hello? Someone here?" I practically yell as I pull open the screen door. "Something I can help you with?" Like a busted fucking face. My arms are tired but they aren't *that* tired.

When no one answers and I don't hear even the slightest sounds of movement, I head into the kitchen figuring my mom came by and raided her stash before leaving again. I shift the bag of groceries to my other hand but they fall to the floor when I step into the kitchen.

My mom's here, all right.

Unconscious on the kitchen floor.

3 | Dixie

"HE'S NOT COMING," DALLAS SAYS AS HE HANGS UP THE PHONE. I knew when he arrived at his rehearsal dinner without Gavin that something was wrong.

"Everything okay?" Robyn asks and I'm grateful she begs the question before I do. Every time I so much as mention Gavin's name I get the pity look, and frankly, it's getting old. I smooth the black knee-length dress I'm wearing and strain to hear Dallas's answer. All I catch is "had to work," so I'm guessing that explains Gavin's absence. Or is a lame attempt at explaining it, anyway. Dallas didn't sound too convinced and the line between his brows has made an appearance.

I barely made it on time myself—practically had to sprint inside after my lesson with the troubled little boy whose parents I have still yet to meet ran a little long

"The wedding coordinator is ready for y'all," I tell them when I see the gray-haired lady motioning maniacally. "Like five minutes ago."

"You first, Maid of Honor," Robyn tells me with a tense smile.

The wedding isn't huge but it's in a huge place. A property Robyn has dreamed of getting married on since we were kids. Photographers are everywhere and *OK!* magazine is here doing an exposé on Dallas Walker and the love of a lifetime who led him to walk away from the fame.

Part of me wondered how my brother would be when he got home. I was expecting him to be forlorn or sullen or something. He had everything he'd ever dreamed of as far as music was concerned—well, everything except his band. But Dallas Walker the solo act decided he'd rather come home and marry his pregnant girlfriend instead of continuing on tour. The press is having a field day—proclaiming Dallas and Robyn's relationship the stuff fairy tales are made of. Dallas says give it a week and the tabloids will be screaming that they're done forever and Robyn is pregnant and alone.

Life sure is funny sometimes.

I can't help it, I check my phone to see if there is anything from Gavin. I've been doing this for far too long and like always, there isn't a peep.

A few of the moms of the kids I give music lessons to have messaged me back saying they don't know the little boy I've been asking about and don't recognize him from my description.

Liam is his name and every week on Tuesdays and Thursdays he arrives like clockwork at five on the dot. He doesn't seem to enjoy learning to play piano or violin but he keeps coming, so I keep trying. I just wish I could talk to his mom or dad about his behavior and how to reach him. So far all he's said out loud to me is his name.

"You. Come. Now," the wedding coordinator from Heritage House hollers at me. I began a slow march down the aisle with a fake version of my bouquet. The spray on the fake flowers makes me sneeze and the woman looks at me like I'm intentionally pissing her off.

"Sorry," I tell her as I continue my stroll to the altar. Once I'm down I see Robyn's friend Katie and our mutual friend Cassidy coming down as well. They're escorted by two of Dallas's friends. I was supposed to walk with Gavin, but as per usual, he is missing and I am alone.

Once we're in place the music begins to play. Dallas has taken his place beside the blank space where Gavin is supposed to be and I give him an encouraging grin. I'm proud of him, happy for him, and all-around ecstatic about his upcoming nuptials, but Gavin's absence is weighing on me heavily.

Maybe he really did have to work, but it felt to me like Dallas wasn't buying it and I'm not, either.

When Robyn's mom begins coming down the aisle, we all giggle a little as Mrs. Lawson takes her arm looking proud as a peacock. Apparently it's bad luck for the actual bride and groom to rehearse before the wedding, so Mrs. Lawson volunteered to stand in— bless her.

Once they arrive, the pastor reads his part of the vows, has Dallas and Mrs. Lawson repeat after him, and then pronounces them man and wife. We all make our exit to a small smattering of applause from the members of Robyn's family that are in attendance.

I glance around to see if Gavin made it but see no sign of him. It's a mutual gut punch of welcome relief and disappointed concern that he's not here. Seeing him earlier in the rehearsal space was like watching the color coming back into my life. All while feeling like someone was ringing out my intestines like dishrags.

"He better not bail tomorrow, Dallas. I told you about him. You know how he—" Robyn's sentence cuts off abruptly when I whirl around. There's no need to ask who she's referring to. Our perpetually troubled drummer friend who specializes in disappearing and reappearing at will.

"Missed you at rehearsal dinner," I text to his number. "Hope everything is okay."

We do two more walk-throughs, me with my invisible Gavin, before heading into a formal dining room for dinner.

I check my phone several times, finding exactly what I expect to time and time again.

No new messages.

This past year, traveling on my own, meeting new people, coming home, and establishing a life for myself—one that didn't include my brother or Gavin or the band—it hasn't been easy but it has made me a stronger, more independent version of myself. I have grieved the loss of my grandfather, met new people, seen things I never thought I would, started a successful music instruction business, and moved on from the pain of knowing Gavin didn't want me the way I wanted him. All of this I've done *alone*. No overprotective brother giving orders or watching my every move, no broody drummer distracting me at every turn, and no one to answer to except myself.

I didn't reach out to him, even when I knew he was home. Because one thing I decided over these last few months is that I did the reaching in Austin. It's his turn. He has to decide if he can do this—us, me and him, the band, all of it—for real this time, not with only half his heart.

I'd be lying if I pretended that part of the reason I haven't answered Dallas yet about rejoining Leaving Amarillo wasn't Gavin. I'm not saying I wouldn't just because Gavin doesn't want to be with me, but I would need a definite answer from him before being able give it another shot with the band. I am strong, stronger than I thought, at least. I can handle it if he doesn't want me or isn't able to give himself to me the way that I truly need. Completely.

Once dinner is over, I give in and check my phone for the final time before heading home, and the sting of what I see is a real physical thing in my chest. In a way, it feels like Gavin's lack of response is the answer. For now at least.

No new messages.

What else is new?

4 | Gavin

IF THERE IS A GOD, HE'S NOT A BIG FAN OF MINE. I DECIDED THIS AS a kid when my mom was strung out for days and there was no food in the house, but as if I needed further proof, I'm currently in the seventh circle of Hell. Wearing a tux.

"Missed you at the rehearsal dinner last night," Dallas says as we pose for another round of pictures. "Hate that your boss wouldn't let you off."

"Yeah. He's a real dick." And I'm practically a professional liar. "Sorry, man."

"No worries. You're here now. That's all that matters." He claps me quickly on the shoulder, before grinning once more for the photographer.

As if dealing with what I thought was my dead mom passed out on the kitchen floor last night wasn't bad enough, lying about it to my best friend is somehow worse. Somehow my mom has always managed to turn what should be her shit into mine. Pushing the image of me shaking her awake and screaming for her to regain consciousness out of my head, I do my best to force a smile toward the camera.

The bridal parties didn't mix before the wedding and for that I'm grateful. At one point the groomsmen, me and Dallas's friends Levi and Alex, stepped outside to take a picture with the bride. So far I've only seen hints of Dixie, caught the faint scent of her, and heard a chiming laugh down the hall that might have belonged to her.

Heritage House is an interesting mix of elegant and rustic. The property isn't far from Hamilton Pool, where Dallas and Robyn met. According to Dallas, Robyn has always dreamed of getting married here. I feel out of place surrounded by so many smiling faces full of love. There are mirrors reflecting everything all over the damn place. Everywhere I look I see a reflection of a man I don't recognize. A man pretending to be something he isn't.

Beneath the monkey suit, the tattoos, and the freshly shaven face, I am still a wreck of a human being. I'm still a lost, hungry, fucked-up kid confused about the way the world works and where I belong in it. My adrenaline spikes when we line up to enter the atrium-style room where the wedding is being held. My teeth are even on edge when Cassidy nearly bumps me on her way to the room where the bridal party is getting ready.

"Sorry, Gav," she mumbles quickly as she scurries past.

I grunt and nod, noticing a disheveled-looking Jaggerd McKinley staring dazedly after her.

Ah. Slutty wedding sex. I'm familiar with it. While I've fooled around with a bridesmaid or two in my day when we played gigs at weddings, I don't recall ever hooking up with a girl I actually knew or one who was friends with my ex. Not that I ever technically had an ex. Whatever.

I don't know how Dixie will feel about this or if it will even matter to her, but the thought that it might bothers me on multiple levels. I have so many questions and no right to ask her any of them.

Did she get back with McKinley when she came home?

Would she care if he hooked up with Cassidy?

Is she hooking up with McKinley—or anyone for that matter?

Is she still pissed I didn't tell her I was home?

And the biggest one of all, if I tell her everything, will she ever be able to forgive me?

Judging from the icicles that formed around her when I looked in her direction at our band meeting yesterday, the outlook isn't looking so great for those last two.

Only one way to find out, I suppose.

The wedding coordinator decided to make a slight change, apparently, and I can't help but wonder if Dixie asked her to or if my not attending the rehearsal caused it. Instead of walking Dixie down the aisle, something I was both terrified and excited about, I will stand with Dallas and Dixie will walk alone.

While Dallas and I walk to the front of the altar, I try to visualize telling Dixie everything, the same way Dallas visualizes us having an amazing show before we perform. I can see myself talking but I can't hear the words.

The small chapel is quiet while I shake Dallas's hand and congratulate him one last time. There's a sacred sort of silence surrounding us. Robyn's family isn't huge but her side is still much fuller than the Lark side. I glance out over the crowd, seeing only a few familiar faces. I grin at Dallas while fighting the urge to loosen my tie.

"I'm nervous," he whispers. "This isn't like playing music. What if I'm a terrible husband and father? What if I—"

"Relax," I tell him. "Robyn seems really set on sticking with you now that you knocked her up and all. So I think it's okay even if you suck at it." But he won't. I watch him sometimes with her, the adoration in his stare, the slight gleam of amusement in his eyes as if he still can't believe she actually picked him.

He's a lucky guy—but he's a good guy, too, and he loves the hell out of her, so Robyn could've done worse. I want to ask them both, no, *demand*, to know what the secret is. How do you give yourself to someone—flaws and all—and expect them to just love you for the rest of your natural-born lives?

Before I have time to contemplate these burning questions any further, the doors in the back of the room open and Dixie stands there in all her perfect glory. Her dress is strapless and dark blue, a midnight-sky shade of silk that falls just below her knees and wraps her body lovingly. My Bluebird even has a feather in her hair and I nearly get hard at the sight of it barely restraining her wild curls. She holds a small bundle of white flowers and her ink shows on her arms. Everything about her is vibrant and breathtaking.

She is perfection personified and in my heart she's mine. Always has been, always will be.

Except . . . she isn't.

I am a statue as she comes down the aisle toward me. I stand un-blinking, immovable, unwilling to miss a single second of this sight. As much as I wish I could, I can't picture us having a day like this. A traditional Texas wedding, her in a white dress and me in another stifling monkey suit—but I also can't deny that in this moment, my eyes locked on hers as she comes closer, I'm pretending and wishing like hell.

At the last second before she reaches me, she averts her gaze and winks at Dallas before turning to stand on the other side of the altar.

I thought seeing her yesterday was tough, but this is a wrecking ball to my chest. She isn't a girl anymore, isn't my girl. She's a grown woman who owns me whether she wants to or not.

I release the breath I was holding captive and take in fresh air so I don't pass out. Her wildflower and vanilla scent wafts toward me and it's a struggle not to toss her over my shoulder and carry her out of here.

The other two bridesmaids come down the aisle escorted by Levi and Alex and I can't help but wonder why Dallas would choose me as his best man. Maybe because he's known me the longest, but in all of my twenty-two years, I don't think I've ever been the best man at anything. Except maybe the drums. God, I need my drums.

I haven't been with anyone in months and the sexual frustration and proximity to Dixie Lark, the last woman I've laid a hand on and the only one I wasn't supposed to, are about to do me in.

Just before I completely lose my waning grip on my sanity, a piano begins to play and Robyn makes her grand entrance. Dallas pales and then smiles so wide he looks like he's about to burst a blood vessel at the sight of her.

Robyn's always been attractive but today she literally seems to be glowing, radiating a light all around her that's almost too intense to stare directly at. Her smile matches Dallas's and my throat constricts.

A chill hits me hard when Dixie's voice fills the air around us. I'm not the only one in shock as she uses her sultry sweet voice to sing "Marry Me," a Train song I never paid much attention to. Dallas and Dixie were apparently in on this one together. Dallas is practically vibrating with emotion and I pull my eyes from Dixie's surprise performance at the piano to where the bride and groom are now lost in their own world, in which the rest of us do not exist.

This is Dallas's first priority now, not the band. Without him playing drill sergeant, I don't know if Leaving Amarillo will stand a chance. But I can see in his face that it doesn't matter; any sacrifice he has to make for this woman will be worth it.

When Dixie finishes, she takes her place across the altar and I can't tear my stare from her. Her sapphire eyes shine like diamonds with the promise of tears.

I wish I could give you this.

Right as I'm about to look away, her gaze collides with mine. My heart swells in my chest. I have so much to say and no words to say it.

I'm sorry.

I'm trying.

I love you.

She doesn't even flinch at the turmoil I know is probably apparent on my face. She just gives me a confident smile and a knowing look as if to say, *One day.*

One day that will be us.

A future.

A forever.

I fucking hope so.

I just have no clue how we'll ever manage to get there.

5 | Dixie

I GOT THIS.

Right up until I had to be this close to him. Seeing him across the altar was hard; seeing what my impossibly hopeless heart thought was a wistful look in his eyes nearly broke me.

Now I'm sweating, nervous, and my heart is threatening to make a break for it straight out of my chest for all to see.

I so do not got this.

"Smile," Robyn says quietly to me after the third flash of the camera. "I love you, babe. And you nailed the song and made my wedding the most special day of my life. But you're making my wedding photos look like mug shots."

"Sorry," I mumble under my breath.

I switch the small bouquet of calla lilies I'm holding to my other hand and tuck a wayward curl behind my ear.

I can feel him watching me—he has been since I first made my way down the aisle. He held his breath for a full minute when we had to stand beside each other for pictures and now I'm holding mine.

Dallas and Robyn kiss again on the photographer's command and I have to look away.

I can't explain it, but it hurts to see such blatant displays of affection when I'm consumed with this longing for a man who keeps his heart so closely guarded from me in particular. A man who is so close I can inhale him, smell him, and practically taste him. The heat radiates from his body and warms mine. If I leaned back a few inches I would be resting on his chest, a tempting thought that makes me hate myself. But I need the . . . contact.

I clench my hands around the neck of the bouquet and focus on smiling. On breathing. On keeping myself still where I stand and not dragging Gavin into a back room to force him to give me what I need.

Answers. Explanations. Himself.

"Okay, I think we're good for now," Jacqueline, the photographer calls out, finally allowing me to relax a few fractions of an inch. "We'll get a few more at the reception and some as you leave for the honeymoon."

So much for relaxing. I haven't had time to mentally prepare myself for the reception. Dancing. Touching. Other women. Single women who will want to take their turn on the dance floor with Gavin so they can slip him their numbers while I watch.

I am better than this. I am not this girl anymore.

No one else has ever had this effect on me and it infuriates me that he does. Still.

It also doesn't bode well for my ability to play music on the road with a single Gavin Garrison whom I bear no claim to. I nod and force a smile for Robyn and my brother before heading around behind the chapel and into the sprawling backyard, where guests are already mingling at the reception.

Robyn's mom waves from the middle of a group of ladies about her age and I wave back, but I keep walking. What I need is in the back corner of the barn in Jag's pants.

Once I reach the table where he's sitting with his dad and his dad's girlfriend, Gina, I set my flowers down and hold out my hand. With an eye roll I ignore, he hands over the shiny, silver flask.

"Pace yourself, crazy girl," he warns low under his breath as I take my first swallow of gloriously burning liquid fire.

"Pacing is for sissies," I mutter back before taking another drink. My heart pounds hard in my chest but the sweet burn distracts me from my oncoming anxiety attack.

"I'm guessing pictures went well?" Jag retrieves the flask of what I'm pretty sure is Jack Daniel's from my reluctant hands.

"Fabulous."

"The ceremony was beautiful," Gina says softly. I recognize the way she's looking at Jag's dad. She's wondering if they'll ever have a ceremony like this one. I know the feeling. Maybe this is why so many people have sex at weddings—it makes you slightly desperate and strangely turned on.

"It was," I say, because saying thank you feels like taking credit for something I didn't really have much to do with. I didn't actually pay much attention to the décor because I was busy keeping my shit together, but I did see tears in Dallas's eyes when Robyn promised to make his dreams as important as her own.

Watching those two be so deeply in love is probably going to kill me. Particularly since I'm just a few strays away from becoming a lonely old cat lady at the ripe young age of twenty.

Or a groupie of a member of my own band.

Fuck.

Levi's band launches into a song called "Love You Like That," by Canaan Smith, and Gina drags Jag's dad off to the dance floor.

"Don't be stingy, McKinley," I practically growl once our company is gone.

"Don't get wasted, Lark," he answers while handing the flask to me once again. "I'm serious. Your brother will be pissed and nothing good will come of you getting hammered and making decisions you'll regret." Jaggerd's eyes drift over my shoulder and I follow his gaze.

Cassidy is dancing with Gavin and doing her best not to look this way. I return my attention to the flask.

"Okay, party girl. That's enough. Let's dance." Jaggerd pulls me up by the hand and maneuvers us entirely too close to Gavin and Cassidy.

"I don't want to dance." I'm pouting. I know it and I can't even stop myself. Damn Gavin Garrison to hell.

Jaggerd snorts out a laugh and draws me closer to his chest. "Maybe you just don't want to dance with me, huh?"

Leaning back, I sway a little from the potent mix of liquor and adrenaline before looking into his eyes.

"Not true. I just don't want to be here right this second. Not this close to . . ."

"Him," he finishes for me with a tilt of his head.

"Everyone," I correct. "Right now I'm tired, these shoes are killing me, my boobs are squished together like sardines in this dress, and I've had my fill of lovey-dovey mushy mess for the evening. Thank you."

"You're full of shit, Lark. But I still like you. And for the record, you look beautiful in that dress."

I glance down at the midnight blue silk wrap and I nudge him hard with my hip, forgetting it's the one I cut a few days ago while helping out in his garage.

A hiss escapes my lips and the pain sobers me instantly. "Ugh. Ouch."

Jag's eyes widen and he glances down to where my hand has gone.

His hand meets mine. "Your hip still hurts? You need to get that checked out."

"You're probably right. I didn't realize it—"

"You step on her toes or what, McKinley?" Gavin breaks in.

"What? No. She hurt her hip in the garage a few days ago and—"

"I'll check it out for her. Here." Without warning, Gavin passes Cassidy off to Jaggerd and pulls me into his arms as if they planned the switch ahead of time.

"Let's go," Gavin says, taking me by the elbow. "I'll look at your hip and we need to talk."

Yanking out of his grasp, I walk off the dance floor only to come face-to-face with him as he turns abruptly around in front of me. It would be nice if for one damn second he weren't so freaking gorgeous.

"Excuse me? Are you a doctor now? Guess you've been busy these past few months." The liquid courage is in full effect.

"What the hell happened to your hip? I thought McKinley fucking broke you. Your face just went completely white."

You're the only one with the power to break me, I think but don't say. A few more sips from Jag's flask and that one might have slipped out. Gavin reaches for my hip and I flinch, wincing at the reminder. "Nothing. My hip is fine."

"Bathroom. Now."

No, he did not just order me to the bathroom.

"Gavin Garrison, you know as well as anyone that I do not take orders. I'm sure as hell not going to start now."

"Fine. If your hip is in such great shape, you can dance with Robyn's uncle Elvis then." Gavin tugs me to where Robyn's uncle Richard, the Elvis impersonator who came dressed in full white sparkly jumpsuit getup, is stepping all over Robyn's mom's toes and wiggling his own hips for all he's worth.

"Wait." I dig my heels in and plant myself on the edge of the dance floor. "Might not hurt to at least take a quick look."

"If you insist." Without allowing me to argue any further, Gavin slips his warm, supple hand into mine, threading our fingers together and leading me into a back hallway.

I follow him, allowing my eyes to roam from thick dark hair I want to slide my fingers through, down his thick muscular neck, broad shoulders, to his perfect backside. He can rock a tux, that's for sure. A pang of longing shoots through me when we step into the bathroom and he closes the door.

I'm trapped, in a small, enclosed space with a man who smells like Heaven and tastes like sin.

He removes his jacket and slings it over the counter. His white dress shirt is fitted tightly to his muscles, hugging and caressing them in ways I've been dreaming about for months. He unbuttons his top two buttons and I can't stop staring at his neck, his fingers, his mouth. All of it.

"Gavin," I breathe, prepared to beg him to open the door and let me out because I can't do this.

"Let's see it, Bluebird."

He drops slowly to his knees, never once breaking eye contact. Other than a slight trembling in my hands and legs, I remain still—entranced and completely paralyzed by his proximity.

I swallow to make sure I can still function and then lift my dress one inch at a time until the gash on my hip is revealed to him.

"Jaggerd McKinley had sex with Cassidy before the wedding. You have any feelings about that?"

I shake my head even though it's swimming from having him this close. "Um, yay for them?"

Gavin doesn't even flinch at the sight of my black lace thong. Nor does he touch me in any way that even borders on inappropriate, which is almost brutally painful.

Smooth fingers graze the area just below my still-healing wound.

"It's bruised pretty good and a little inflamed. I'll check for a first aid kit with antiseptic wipes but you should probably get it checked out. Mind if I ask what happened?"

Come to me, words.

I fumble over my tongue for a second and take a deep breath.

"I ran into something in Jag's—um, the McKinleys' auto body shop. Sometimes I help out over there. Answering phones and stuff."

Jesus. I sound like a nervous teenager. Which I no longer am.

Again, I can't help but weigh the pros and cons of our band reuniting. If I had a Magic 8 Ball right now like the one I had as a kid, I already know what its answer would be if I asked it whether or not I could keep my shit together.

Outlook not so good.

I square my shoulders and watch Gavin search the cabinets until he produces a small white, plastic container.

He tears open a small square packet containing what looks like a wet wipe. "This will help a little. But, seriously, no telling what you ran into in that chop shop. Promise me you'll go to the doctor."

"Chop shop?"

Gavin doesn't respond to my inquiry and I don't press it because the wet wipe on my hip both tickles and stings, igniting a tingling sensation that extends far deeper into the flesh. When he's done, he blows gently on my skin and my knees threaten to given out. I grip the marble counter behind me for support.

"You good?"

"Just fine," I tell him through gritted teeth.

He rubs some cream on my wound and blows some more before

standing and that's it. I can't take it anymore. His mouth is so close, *he's* so close. He seems taller or something, and even though I know the likelihood of that is ridiculous, I don't remember ever feeling so very aware of his presence. Or maybe I just blocked it all out. But here, now, in the room with him, everything is coming back.

All of it.

Every single second we spent connected on a physical level. His mouth on me, his lips, his tongue, his body inside of mine.

"You're good at this," I say, barely able to get my voice to go above a whisper.

"I've had a lot of practice."

I don't know if he means with first aid, which is likely since he's had to perform CPR on his mom more times than I can count, or seduction, which I also happen to know he's well versed in. Either way, I am in danger of losing my grip on my ability to remain upright.

It's as if my brain has been doing me a favor for the past few months, allowing me to focus on being pissed at him instead of . . . this. But clearly my brain has left the building and I am completely on my own. This is dangerous.

I am weak.

I want him.

I need him.

Screw it.

"There," he says gently, lowering my dress back down over my thighs. "That might help a little but you should still—"

My mouth captures his midsentence. His lips are slightly moist and even fuller than I remembered. I tense and a dull ache hits hard as my heart drops a few inches in preparation of being rejected.

Much to my surprise, Gavin doesn't stop me. He doesn't reject me. He doesn't spew some bull about my brother or our friendship or seeing anyone else or anything.

He only makes one sound—a soft, pained groan. His hands grip the skin just beneath my ass and he lifts me onto the counter. The dress is tight but I manage to part my thighs far enough to accommodate his broad figure between them.

My fingers press into his back, urging him closer even though it's not exactly possible. I try to catch his tongue but he's sweeping it deeply inside, then pulling back to suck on my lips. A muffled moan escapes my mouth and slides into his.

"You taste like whiskey, Bluebird." He chuckles lightly, then cuts off any chance I had of verbalizing a response by slipping his fingers between my legs and into the waistband of my panties.

"I've come a long way since strawberry ice cream."

A wounded sound like an animal might make tears from his chest and I feel his erection press into the tiny scrap of fabric between my thighs. "If I don't stop right now I won't be able to."

"Please don't stop." I don't even recognize my own voice—it's raspy and deep and filled with desperate need. Desperate wasn't quite what I was going for, but there it is.

Apparently desperate works for Gavin, though, because my plea fuels his enthusiasm and my panties are a mere memory in a matter of seconds.

His fingers explore my newly exposed skin before sinking into my pulsing wet heat.

"Fuck, you're wet," he bites out when I thrust myself harder against his hand. "So fucking wet."

"Seems you have that effect on me." I want him so badly and wanting this much can't be a good thing. He'll break me, burn me to ash. Again.

His mouth against mine blanks my memory. I want to forget the many reasons why this isn't a good idea—because it doesn't matter how much it will hurt in the end. All that matters is now.

I'm drunk, but not from the Jack Daniel's in Jag's flask. I'm lust drunk on the cocktail of emotions Gavin Garrison always sends swirling around inside me.

I can feel the smile on his lips when they meet mine again. But then he groans and pulls back, and I want to scream.

"We shouldn't do this. Not like this. Not here."

I whimper in protest, biting his bottom lip, then nipping his top one hard enough to let him know I'm not playing around. Either he's in or out. Literally. But the mind games are a thing of the past and I won't be that person again. He either wants me or he doesn't, plain and simple.

I open my eyes and stare directly into the fire flashing in his. "I won't beg. Not this time."

His gaze deepens and darkens simultaneously. "Bluebird . . ."

"Either fuck me or don't, Gavin. But I won't play this game again."

And I won't join the band if this is how it's going to be. Hot and cold. On and off. Yes and no. Soaring hopes and dashed dreams.

My heart does not belong on a yo-yo string and I won't allow it to be treated like one, no matter how much I love him.

His luscious mouth drops open slightly. I've caught him off guard. I raise an eyebrow while I wait for him to decide.

"You know I want you. I want this. I want us. But there's so much I should—"

A harsh loud knock on the door interrupts whatever he was about to say.

"Band's taking five and this is the only bathroom we're are allowed to use. Dying out here!" Levi, Dallas's friend and the leader of the band that's playing the reception, calls out.

"Just a minute!" Gavin calls back.

When he returns his attention to me sitting there propped spread eagle on the counter in all my undignified glory, I can't help but shake my head. I can literally feel my self-esteem being dashed to hell in a handbasket. I don't know how I became putty in Gavin's skilled and very capable hands, but between that and the pent-up sexual frustration, I'm about to explode.

Some things just aren't meant to be, I guess, no matter how badly we want them.

Maybe Leaving Amarillo is one of them. Maybe Gavin and I are, too.

"Have a good night, Gav. And for the record, I was going to keep my heart out of it this time." With that I hop off the counter and readjust my dress before throwing open the door to reveal a startled and relieved Levi Eaton.

"Oh shit," he mutters under his breath. "My bad, guys. I didn't realize—"

"It's fine, Levi. Take care of business. Someone should." I pat him on the shoulder and saunter away from what was either about to be the best or the worst thing that ever happened to me.

6 | Gavin

SHE'S EVERYTHING I EVER WANTED AND THE ONE THING I WAS never supposed to have. Now she's all I can think about. The scent of her, the taste of her, the feel of her.

Watching her storm off, away from me, which is probably the safest direction for her, I can't help but replay the past few minutes. Partially because my dick is still hard and there's a steady ache in the center of my chest as if she just left and took my heart with her.

She was going to keep her heart out of it? What the hell was that supposed to mean?

She doesn't dance with McKinley anymore, for which I am extremely grateful. Pummeling the absolute shit out of him at Robyn's dream wedding would piss Dallas off immensely. Dixie didn't seem at all concerned about him and Cassidy, which was also a relief.

Sure as hell could use my kit about now, though. Between trying to conceal my raging hard-on and the testosterone that surges every time I see another man so much as glance in her beautiful fucking direction, I'm pretty amped up.

I pull out my phone and text Cal to ask if I can use the kit at the bar after hours. My boss is kind of an asshole, but I'm the best employee he's got so he bends the rules for me a bit.

My bartending job at the Tavern is a condition of my probation, and since the court didn't specify *where* I could work, just that I had to, I of course took the most incongruous job possible for someone facing hard time for driving under the influence and reckless endangerment.

Mama always said do what you know. I know bars. I know addicts and alcoholics. Like it or not, a lifetime with one taught me how to handle them. They're my kind of people. I don't know what that says about me and I try not to think about it much.

The truth is, I'm a user just like the rest of them.

Maybe not of crack or meth or heroin, but I use what I need to get high and I'm as addicted as any of them. Or I was. Now I'm sort of in remission, I guess, self-imposed and somewhat court-ordered remission.

An attractive blonde in a tux much more revealing than mine offers me a tray full of champagne glasses. I shake my head and ignore the come-hither look she's attempting to drill into my skull.

You don't want to board this crazy train, sweetheart. You can't hold a candle to the competition. Move along.

It takes a full minute, but she gets the message and moves on to the next group of people standing near the open bar.

Champagne wouldn't even begin to take the edge off this kind of pain.

Dixie Lark was like my exact brand of heroin, the perfect combination of everything forbidden. She cured me and destroyed me with one taste. The worst part? All those years, I think I knew she would be. When Dallas laid down the "do not touch my sister or I will end you" law, I didn't even argue. She was beautiful and full of life and light where I was shrouded in darkness. People like her shine from within; they don't need the spotlight. People like me will wither and die without it, without attention and glaring lights forcing their demons to run and hide.

Touching her would've tainted her and I never wanted that. I could've admired her, loved her, worshipped her from afar for the rest of my life and just been happy for the brief moments of being in her presence.

And then she had to go and push it, push me, want me the way I'd always wanted her.

Now I live in a constant state of purgatory.

I need her.

She haunts my dreams and most of my waking moments.

Her whimpers, her breathy moans, her sweet, soft laughter.

She tamed the demons inside me, bringing them to heel with a gentleness I never expected them to submit to.

I fucking crave her like a desperate addict dying for his final fix.

I don't deserve her.

I will only hurt her.

As if my every thought is written all over my face, Jaggerd McKinley meets my hard stare and gives me a look that says he feels my pain but tough shit because I brought it on myself. Dixie has once again confiscated his flask and he's guiding her out of the party with a carefully placed hand on the small of her lower back.

One centimeter lower and he is a dead fucking man.

A powerful wave of adrenaline, testosterone, and primal territorial instinct hits me so hard I nearly stagger.

Only the image of breaking his hand slowly, bone by bone, brings me any sense of relief.

"Garrison? You good, man?"

Levi stands behind me looking both concerned and apologetic.

I clear my throat and nod. "I'm straight." Glancing around, I realize the crowd has thinned considerably.

"Hey, for real, sorry about the bathroom. We just had that one quick break and I didn't know—"

"Y'all done for the night?"

Fuck. How long have I been staring at Dixie? Apparently long enough for the band to call it a night and a middle-aged DJ to take over.

"Yeah, we are. Dallas was kind enough to give us the last hour to scope out the single girls. You know how chicks are at weddings."

"Huh." I regard him closely, contemplating this.

Is that what happened? Dixie was lonely because her brother was getting married and I just happened to be in the right place at the right time?

This is the problem with being a user. You know your own motivations and you project them onto others, assuming everyone else is like you.

But I know her. Don't I? I did, anyway. Hooking up for the sake of hooking up isn't really her style. Or it didn't used to be.

Damn it. In my quest to get my shit together, I've all but shut her out of my life completely. It seemed like the best idea for everyone involved, but now I'm wondering if I've made a colossal mistake. Because watching her now, half-dancing with Jag on her way to congratulate the happy couple or say goodbye or whatever the hell, I realize that my little Bluebird is all grown up—and maybe, for the first time since we were kids, I don't know who she's become.

"Obviously that doesn't include his sister. We all got the warning. And even if we hadn't, we've all watched you plot McKinley's murder for the last hour and a half, so you're good, man. No one wants to die tonight."

"What?" I tear my eyes from Dixie and return them to Levi. I forgot he was even still standing there, much less still speaking.

Damn attention deficit bullshit.

Levi looks at me like I'm high. I wish.

"Later, Garrison. Have a good night, man."

"You, too," I say absently as he walks away and I realize I've lost Dixie. She was right beside Dallas and Robyn and now she's gone.

"Hey, you. I get off in half an hour."

The voice is female and inviting. It belongs to an edgy-looking redhead in a server uniform. My hands are in my pockets and I realize I probably look nonthreatening for the most part, but I'm still loner guy at a wedding full of mostly happy couples. I guess that screams "dude looking to get laid."

Which I usually am. Or I used to be.

"Good to know," is all I say, because interested or not, there's no sense in being hurtful.

And who am I kidding? I might be in remission but I'm not cured. The attention still tempts me, still begs me to do what I've always done. Compliment, flirt, tease, pull away, and make them come to me. On their knees.

My fists clench at my sides because I've worked too damn hard not to be this guy to let one woman and a stunted sexual encounter with the girl I love fuck it up.

"Want me to get *you* off in half an hour?"

Feisty, this one. She looks me directly in the eyes while she waits for my answer. A challenge in her sea-green stare tells me she's a good-time girl up for anything and everything.

My cock twitches at her bold invitation and it's like . . .

It's like you've spent your entire life existing on sugar and empty carbs, cake and cookies, just because it was there and you had no restraint, and now another cupcake has rolled onto the floor in your direction and part of you thinks, *Fuck it—what's one more?* But deep down you know you won't be satisfied. There will be guilt. Shame and remorse. It's wasteful, really. You've had a taste of the real thing. Been sated by gourmet steak and potatoes and indulged in perfection so everything else seems . . . slightly nauseating.

"Thanks for the offer. And please don't be insulted—you're gorgeous. Obviously. But I'm going to call it a night." I nod toward where Levi is standing with his guitar player. "Lead singer is a decent guy. You should introduce yourself."

Red is very confused by this. I am, too—a little. The old me would've told her to meet me out back or in the kitchen or wherever my mind could conjure up on the spot. Technically I should be cock-blocking the hell out of Eaton for his previous fuckup, but he was genuinely sorry and he's the reason Leaving Amarillo got into Austin MusicFest to begin with, so in a weird way I kind of owe him. Guess this is the new me. Apparently I repay favors and shit. My addiction counselor would be so proud.

"Oh-kay," she says slowly, with a noncommittal shrug. "Maybe I'll do that. Your loss."

"You're absolutely right. Have a good night." I nod curtly, dismissing her because I'm ready to be alone so I can figure out where the hell Dixie got off to. McKinley is dancing with the bride and Dallas is shooting the shit with his buddy the sound guy.

"Where did you go, Bluebird?" I mutter mostly to myself.

"Dance with me, drummer boy," a voice calls out as I pass.

Well, shit. This time the woman making the demand is Robyn Breeland-Lark.

I may not be an expert on weddings, but I know you sure as hell don't turn down the bride.

"Your wish is my command." I smile and try not to bare my teeth at McKinley as he hands Robyn over to me.

She feels tiny and fragile in my arms and I'm almost afraid for her. She's pregnant, something only a few people here know, which is nuts because Texas is Texas and shit gets around. Being privy to that delicate knowledge makes me feel like she's made of glass, and I handle her accordingly.

"She's outside decorating Dallas's truck with lingerie and shaving cream and balloons and tin cans and all that silly, traditional stuff."

"What?"

Robyn scoffs at me. "Come on, Gav. It may be my wedding day, so I'm a little distracted, but I know who you're looking for. Who you're *always* looking for."

I smile in spite of the awkwardness of being busted. "Yeah? That obvious, huh?"

Robyn smiles and I realize she actually is glowing. I thought that was some sort of myth or a trick of lighting, but her skin seems to have a light of its own and it's strangely comforting.

"Pretty obvious. You know what's not obvious?"

"What's that?" I spin Robyn in a circle and catch Dallas's eye. He's watching closely. I don't know why this hurts my feelings, maybe because I just recently discovered that I have them, but it does. Dallas Lark knows all my shit and is on a first-name basis with my addictions and issues, but surely he knows me better than that. This is his *wife*, for fuck's sakes, and if anyone knows how deeply in love I am with his sister, it's him. But I see it, the wolflike glint in his eye warning me to behave myself.

"Why you don't just tell her the truth?"

My heart stutters in my chest. This is Dallas's wife *and* Dixie's best friend I'm talking to. She knows all my secrets and is close with the one person I never want to know them.

"Meaning?" I choke out over the significant stone of fear rising in my chest.

"Meaning you have been in love with Dixie Lark since we were kids, Gavin. And you and I both know how she feels about you. Even Dallas knows and has known, though he would rather not think about it, I'm sure. But this game you are playing, you and Dixie," she clarifies. "It won't end well if you aren't honest with each other. Every second you spend in the dark about your feelings for each other is dangerous. People do stupid things when they're hurt or sad or confused. Stop torturing each other and lay it out there. Or . . ."

"Or?"

"Or let her go, Gav," she says softly. "Man up if you can't be what she needs and deserves and let her go already. I can't stand to see her hurting and closing herself off to everyone and everything while she waits for you to decide if she's worth it or not. Life is too short to spend it pining for someone who will never come around, wishing for something you will never have, and holding on to something or someone that doesn't want to be held."

"Pregnancy has made you wise. And blunt." I wink, and Robyn punches me playfully me in the chest.

"I was always honest. You know that. That's why Dallas loves me, because I tell it like it is."

"I love you for lots of reasons, babe." Dallas reaches out to cut in and I step back and allow him to take my place.

"Good thing, because you went and knocked me up. Now you're stuck with me." Robyn winks, and I laugh, but in Dallas's face I see pure love and adoration. If anything, she's stuck with him because when Dallas Lark looks at any woman like that she is undeniably his for life.

"For the record, I was behaving myself," I say quietly to Dallas. "That's your wife, man. Congratulations. I'm happy for you."

Dallas looks confused and I know the offense I took at his warning look and cutting in is probably misplaced.

"I know you were, Garrison. Far as I know, you want to see your next birthday, right?"

I shrug.

Honestly?

I could give a shit.

"Hey," Dallas says, placing a hand on my chest. "I didn't come over here to protect Robyn from you, man. I came over to protect you from her when I saw her punch you. She may be my wife but she's also my sister's best friend, so you are currently on the asshole list where Dixie is concerned. I didn't want her getting her blood pressure up and decking you for real. Then I would've had to deck you for hurting her hand on your thick skull."

He smiles and I force the best grimace I can on a deep breath. The tension in my chest lightens. It's somewhat of a relief that he wasn't worried.

I may have done some lowdown shit and Dallas knows all about it, but I would never mess with another man's wife—my best friend's or otherwise. Period. I did once, not knowing she was married, and that did not end well. Lesson learned.

"In that case, thanks for cutting in before she took a swing."

Dallas hardly acknowledges my comment. Robyn murmurs something that sounds like "Did you talk to him yet?"

"I haven't told him yet, no." His ice-blue eyes are cold and hard when he returns his attention to where I'm standing, doing one hell of an impression of an unnecessary third wheel.

"Told me what? Is it twins?"

Dallas shakes his head. "Funny. That's the same thing my sister said."

The mention of her sends another pang of guilt or maybe regret through me. Whatever it is, it hurts like hell.

"Yeah? Great minds, I guess."

"One baby," Robyn hiss-whispers at me. "There is only one in there and I'll thank y'all to quit putting the idea of multiples out into the universe. I'm freaking out enough as it is."

I grin at her because she's ridiculous. If she can handle Dallas, she can handle anything.

"So do I just keep guessing or what?"

"Or what," Dallas says, before kissing Robyn quickly and allowing her Elvis impersonator uncle to cut in. "Come with me. We need to talk."

The tension in his voice is freaking me the fuck out. "Dude. Whatever is going on, just tell me already. You know I don't do well with beating around the bush."

I half-expect him to make a manwhore joke about the bushes I've beaten but ever since I walked away from touring to get my life right, he hasn't made a single crack. I don't know if it's Robyn's influence on him or what, but I appreciate it. Nothing makes moving on from your mistakes harder than having them tossed into your face on a regular basis—whether it's people kidding around or otherwise.

Once we've stepped away from the crowd, Dallas jerks his chin to a giant willow tree and we step behind it.

"So the battle of the bands at the Tavern," he begins. "I talked to Dixie about it again after the rehearsal dinner."

Could've been worse, I guess. I nod. "And?"

"And she's still not sure. She's taking the Over the Rainbow business—giving underpriviledged kids music lessons—very seriously and it takes up a lot of her time."

Jesus. Of course she does. And yes I do know how she is. Because she couldn't just be beautiful or talented or amazingly gorgeous. She has to be perfect. All of that light shouldn't be tainted by my darkness.

But something is creeping up on the edge of my consciousness. It takes a few seconds but then it's staring me full-on in the face.

"Wait. Only underprivileged kids?"

Dallas swallows so hard I see his Adam's apple move behind his undone shirt collar.

"Yeah. Children of single parents, terminally ill parents or guardians, deceased parents, low-income families, and, um . . . drug addicts."

I can't verbalize how I feel right now, but I have a dangerous desire to hit something. It doesn't make sense. She's doing a good thing. Because she's a good person, period. But it feels . . . personal.

Dixie the Fixer. Just grab a fiddle and fix everything right up. Kiss it all better—or in my case, fuck it all better.

"Gav. Breathe. She's not doing it to hurt anyone or to get attention. She takes ridiculous stuff as payment, like one single dad mows the grass at the house and a young unwed mother makes her dinner once a week. Stuff like that. It's not meant to upset anyone."

"I know," I choke out. "She would never hurt anyone on purpose."

"Right. And like it or not, man, what you went through growing up, everything with your mom, we kind of went through it, too, once we moved to Amarillo. It affected me and Dixie both and sometimes it influences our decisions."

"Doing favors for junkies is a bad idea, Dallas. Period. You know that. She should know that. It's her getting hurt that I worry about."

Dallas shakes his head. "Back up a step, man. I can see you making this about something else. She's not doing favors for junkies. She's sharing her gift with kids. Kids, man. Stop and let that sink in. Kids don't deserve to be punished for their parents' decisions. *You* should know *that.*"

Don't they? I sure as hell got punished plenty for my mom's choices. Still do from time to time. But none of that should ever come near my Bluebird.

"They come to the house? While she's there alone?"

Dallas sighs. "Yeah. I guess. Sometimes." He runs a hand hard through his hair. "They bring their kids, Gavin. Drop them off for forty-five minutes and then pick them up. End of story. Dixie's a big girl. If she didn't feel safe, she'd—"

"She'd what, Dallas? You know her. She gives everyone the benefit of the doubt. And you're shacked up with Robyn so the last thing she's going to do is tell you to leave your pregnant girlfriend or wife or whatever and come home because she's worried about the meth head coming by later."

"Gavin. Chill."

I huff out some of my exasperation with how clueless the Lark siblings are. "No, I will not fucking chill. You live in this shiny fucking world where people are mostly good. And that's great. I'm glad that you and Dixie both get to live there. But I know about the other side, the wretched, repulsive underbelly where the guy who changes your oil runs a chop shop out of his garage, and the knock-knock-joke-telling cook at Rio's Diner hands out crack to kids not old enough to drive yet. I know that world because that's where *I* fucking live. I've worked my ass off to keep her away from that and you're telling me she's inviting it over for fucking dinner. So no, I will not fucking chill."

Dallas stares evenly at me. He knows by now it's best to just let me get it all out, otherwise my best friend and I will come to blows on his wedding day and he will go on the fancy honeymoon *OK!* magazine paid for in order to get *Dallas Walker's* exclusive wedding photos, with a shiner or a busted mouth.

There's a reason you don't ever see two alpha males in a pack. It's really nothing short of mind-blowing that he and I have yet to actually lay each other out.

"How many?"

Dallas raises his eyebrows instead of speaking.

"How many drug addicts are coming by there? How many of them are using her for free child care while they go out and get high and then come back wasted if they come back at all? How many local junkies know where she lives?"

He shrugs and glances over to where, speak of the angel, Dixie is making her way over to us with shaving cream on her hands. "A couple. Two that I know of for sure. McKinley keeps an eye out. I know you don't like him but he's good people. He cares about her."

Kick me while I'm down, why don't you.

"McKinley's pop is crooked as they come, Dallas. I don't know what Jaggerd knows or doesn't know, but they're not exactly salt of the earth. Trust me."

"Not everyone is out to hurt her, man. And in fact, if we want to get technical, the only person I know that has really hurt her so far is . . ."

"Thanks for the reminder."

"You're welcome." Dallas tilts his head to the side as she gets closer. "For the record, I should kick your ass. But I'm going to tell myself that you're both adults and you can work this out on your own. That's what I brought you out here for. To tell you that you're the only one that can find out the truth about whether or not she really wants to give Leaving Amarillo one more shot and if the contest at the bar is worth entering. I think this could be our last chance and we'll regret it for the rest of our lives if we don't take it. And hearing her sing like that tonight, I wish I'd known she was interested in singing more, and I would've added in that layer with our band. But I won't push her if she isn't ready. Pretty sure the only thing holding her back is, well . . . you."

"Great. No pressure then."

Dallas nods. "So there's that. And also, Afton Tate should be here any second now. Robyn's a big fan so he's coming straight here after a concert in Oklahoma to sing us off onto our honeymoon."

"Fantastic. I can hardly wait."

Dallas smirks at my tone. "If you ask real nice he'll probably give you an autograph. Maybe sign your tits."

"Eat a dick, Dallas."

Between McKinley and Tate, if I don't end up drunk or high or screwing a random waitress tonight, it will literally be a miracle. My nerves are frayed as fuck and what I really want is to toss the woman coming my way over my shoulder and tell everyone else to back the hell off.

"Come on, boys. Robyn's changing into her leaving dress!" Dixie flicks remnants of shaving cream off her fingers in our direction.

She's lucky it's not whipped cream or I would be following through on my desire to carry her ass out of here.

"Come see me off, man. Throw some rice or blow some bubbles

or whatever Robyn picked out. Relax for a change." Dallas shoulder-checks me as we walk. "I'll be back in one week. I'll expect an answer when I return about the battle. Whatever she decides, whatever she wants, we respect that, okay?"

"Always," I answer honestly.

My mind whirs back to what feels like a lifetime ago, when I had her in my arms so wet and warm and willing in the bathroom.

I meant what I said. I will always respect what she wants. Even when she wants all the wrong things.

7 | Dixie

"YOU HAVE A GOOD TIME TONIGHT?"

I shrug off Jag's question because what can I say? I had an awful time until Gavin almost screwed me on the bathroom counter. Then we got interrupted and I bailed because I couldn't face him after humiliating myself like that.

Seems like TMI for the moment.

"It was nice. I'm just tired is all," I tell him. "You?"

Jaggerd is usually pretty even-keeled so I can't help but notice he gets a little twitchy and squirmy in his seat when I volley his own question back to him.

"Yeah. Pretty good."

"Thanks for coming tonight." I turn on the leather bench of his Mustang and notice that his eyes look like they might bulge out of his head. "Jag . . . something you want to talk about?"

"You're welcome." He continues staring out the windshield as if driving requires every ounce of his attention. "And nah. I'm good."

"You sure? 'Cause you seem a little . . . off." I vaguely recall Gavin saying something about Jag and Cassidy but I was slightly distracted during that conversation.

He clears his throat, probably to buy himself some time. I wait patiently, deciding to start the long, arduous process of removing bobby pins from my wedding hairdo.

"I'll just sit quietly over here untangling my tangled rat's nest while you decide if you want to tell me why you seem so bajigity."

"Not even a word, Lark."

"Don't care, McKinley."

Houses blur and I don't even bother trying to count them. I'm not actually able to focus very well at the moment. He's adjusting himself in his seat, so whatever he's stressing about obviously is having an effect on his man parts. If he tells me he wants to get back together I might punch him in the throat. He knows a little about my Gavin drama and that the last thing I need right now is him wanting to be more than friends.

"So . . . your friend Cassidy . . . she's single?"

Oh, thank God. I breathe an audible sigh of relief. "Yeah, as far as I know. Why? You got a crush?"

"Something like that," he answers low, but the corners of his mouth quirk up.

"She's a sweet girl. Got a raw deal in Nashville and had to come home to deal with stuff. Her parents moved away years ago, though. Basically said that if she moved to Nashville instead of going to the Ivy League college she was accepted to, she was dead to them. She crashed with Robyn at one point and now . . . huh. Now I don't actually know where she's staying." I make a mental note to ask her the next time I talk to her.

"Wow. Ivy League. Smart girl."

I nod, becoming increasingly curious about Jag's new love interest. It's nice to have someone else's complicated situation to focus on. I can always analyze the relationships of others so much better than my own. Go figure.

"She is smart. She's also super-impulsive and kind of overly trusting. Or at least she used to be. Life has a way of sucking the hope and trust and free spirit out of some of us."

"Including you?"

I don't answer right away because he already knows from our talks in the garage. Seeing Gavin in the bar that night, realizing he'd been here the whole time and hadn't bothered to so much as shoot me a text to let me know, it changed me. Not that I'm ruined or anything but it hurt and I know I've become more careful and withdrawn. Jag and my brother have both pointed it out and Robyn is pretty much constantly on my case about it. *"Talk to him,"* she says. *"Tell him how you feel. Demand answers."*

Right. If only it were that easy. I talked to him for five minutes tonight and look how well that turned out.

"Especially me," I say quietly into the darkened car interior without checking to see if Jag heard me.

In my head, it's black-and-white.

Gavin and I had a fling. One I pushed him into. He got me out of his system and moved on with his life without any further thoughts of me. Sadly, I'm not quite that detached and I was hurt and, well . . . heartbroken. But I'm a big girl. I'm no stranger to pain. Just wish I understood the purpose behind it sometimes.

In my heart, though, it's one big Technicolor mess.

I love him with everything that I am and there isn't much I wouldn't give to make him love me back. *In that way.* The reason I don't push him for answers is that I know what he'd say. Or something close to it.

I care about you, Dixie. You're like family to me.

Basically, "I love you, too, but not in that way."

My Nana used to say for everything there was a season. My season with Gavin wasn't a season at all but more like a sunny spring day that appears too early, promising sunshine and warmth, only to tease you before an avalanche falls on your head and buries you in the cold, unforgiving snow for the foreseeable future.

"So, um, who was that guy? The singer that showed up and sang and then monopolized all of your friend's attention?"

It takes me a second to catch up. My friend meaning Cassidy.

"Afton Tate. He's a nice guy. I met him in Austin, and Dallas toured with him for a bit. Robyn's a big fan."

Jag's mouth twists into a sneer. "I gathered that when she nearly fell over. Nice of him to come all this way."

"Mmhm."

The silence feels heavy and suffocating. I've kept quiet about so much for so long and I feel like I've outgrown the need to be a weed in the breeze. I want to sway and move of my own accord. I want to grow. So here goes.

"Jag?"

"Yeah?"

"True or false, you have a thing for Cassidy?"

Wide hazel eyes regard me as if I am a foreign species in his vehicle. "Um . . . true. I guess. Sort of."

"No. Man up and grow a pair. It's simple. I'm super tired of half-ass answers and folks hemming and hawing around. You're either interested in her or you aren't. Which is it?"

"I am," he answers, like a soldier on command.

"So. What are you going to do about it?"

He scratches the light scruff on his jaw. "Um, ask her out sometime?"

"Are you asking me?"

He chuckles low and the sound reverberates like the car engine. "No. I'm going to ask her out. I should, right?"

"Stop asking me and decide. For the love of God, man." We laugh and I mimic ringing his neck. "Guys kill me. You're all tough as nails and manly men but then when confronted with a woman, particularly one who is openly interested in you, suddenly you're mute and confused."

"She's probably too good for me. I mean, Ivy League? And then that Tate guy makes a beeline to chat her up. If Robyn nearly fainting dead away was any indication, dude is a big damn deal. I can't compete with that."

I roll my eyes. "Who says it's a competition? Ask her out. If she's into you she'll say yes. If she's not, she'll say thanks, but no thanks. What's so complicated?"

"Rejection is complicated, Dix. It messes with your head and confidence and self-esteem and all that shit. I feel like she got what she wanted tonight, then she moved on to the next guy. Seems to be a pattern with me."

"Whoa there, cowboy. Do not hang your wussing out on me." I jab a finger in his direction.

"It's not just you. I've dated other girls, you know. I didn't just sit around and pine for you, Lark."

"Good. Life's too short to pine. Believe me."

Jag nods as we pull into my driveway. "Seems someone else got tired of it also."

Standing under the golden glow of the porch light is Gavin Garrison in all of his half-removed-tuxedo-clad glory.

"He must've hauled ass to beat us here," Jag remarks under his breath, and I know he's wondering about the size of Gavin's engine compared to his. Boys.

"Wonder what's wrong." I don't make a move to get out of the car. I can't. I'm not ready to face him unexpectedly. He missed the rehearsal dinner because he had to work and I was braced to deal with him at the wedding, but this, this beat-down yet still beautiful and sure of himself version currently lowering himself onto my weathered wooden porch swing, I'm not ready for him.

"If you're waiting for a good-night kiss, I'm going to have to take a rain check. You're a great girl and you know I'm always here for almost anything you need, but I've grown pretty attached to my teeth. All of them. So . . ."

"Shut it, McKinley. I'm thinking."

"About?"

Getting him to admit he was interested in Cassidy was like pulling teeth. When it's my business he's chatty all of the sudden.

"About what he's doing here. What he wants and why it couldn't wait. About what I should say to him and how I should approach this particular—"

"You're overthinking it."

I make a noise of agreement in my throat. "I do that."

"Get out of my car, Lark. Man up and grow a pair, as you said."

I shake my head. "That advice doesn't work on women." I stare at Gavin as he leisurely begins to swing back and forth, swaying slightly. A man on the outside, still kind of a little boy on the inside.

I love them both. All of him.

Probably not going to lead with that, though.

"All right. I'm going."

"Later, babe. Good luck with . . . that."

"Good night, Jag. Good luck with Cass. Oh! She likes that Greek place, the one with the awesome hummus."

He laughs gently. "Thanks. I'll make a note of it."

Maybe my tip earned me some gentlemanly behavior or maybe he's delaying calling Cassidy, but Jaggerd gets out of the car before I can and walks around and opens my door.

"Wow. Now it's like a real date."

His cheeks pink just a little. "Nah. Like I said. Old habits."

I smile as he nods curtly to Gavin, who nods slowly back while stretching his arms across the back of the swing. How Gavin Garrison manages to exude such constant calm, I will never know. Even in the bathroom tonight, he totally had his shit together while I was coming apart at the seams.

Wait. No. *Seams.*

He did tear my panties completely off, so maybe he didn't have it as together as I thought.

Walking with carefully measured steps up my front walk toward him, my body heats at the memory.

Is he here to finish what he started?

Do I want him to be here for that?

"Hey," I say in greeting when I step onto the porch and remove my heels, holding the pair in one hand.

"Hey." He rolls his lower lip between his teeth and every memory I have of his mouth comes flooding to the forefront of my mind.

I wonder what his lips taste like right now. Do they taste like me? Like wedding cake? Like liquor?

My attention has dropped noticeably to his mouth and when I recover my sanity his eyes gleam as he takes notice of my slip.

He stands, rattling the porch and causing my entire body to vibrate with need. My cheeks flare with the same heat that spreads across the rest of my flesh from the inside out.

The glow of the dim porch light catches the glint in his eye. The darkness surrounding him makes him look even more like a threat to my sanity. I finally see what other people see now, people who don't know him or don't know what he's lived through.

Gavin Garrison is dangerous. Seductive and complicated and made entirely of muscles and ink and testosterone. Or at least it seems that way at the moment. Because he exudes maleness the way some women leave traces of their perfume everywhere they go.

"Can we talk?" Even his voice is a low rumble laced with the promise of dark pleasure.

I nod dumbly. "We can try."

"Want to stay out here or can I come in?"

My thighs want to clench and give me away. I want him to come inside. Deep, deep inside. I want the dark pleasure and the pain only he can give me. I want it badly.

"Um." I swallow and attempt to moisten my mouth as all of my bodily fluids seemed to have fled to a locale farther south. "It's up to you. You're the one who came by to talk, so you can decide."

He glances at the door with a wistful expression on his face. "I should stay out here. For now."

Disappointment weighs on my chest. "Okay."

"Come," he says evenly, making his demand sound more like a request for a favor while stepping backward in retreat toward the swing. "Sit with me?"

I comply, lowering myself onto the creaky old swing and groaning a little myself because it's been a long day.

"You were right here. Right here where you are now the first time I saw you."

I watch him remembering. His eyes glaze a little and the hint of a sad smile plays at his mouth.

"You and Dallas looked so . . . I don't know. Clean. Perfect. Like kids from one of those black-and-white photos in the picture frames at the drugstore."

My mind travels back in time along with his. The day of my parents' funeral. People came, a lot of people, in and out carrying covered dishes and desserts and remarking just a little too loudly on what a shame it was our grandparents had to spend their golden years raising children who weren't even theirs.

"It was a tough day. My aunt Sheila dressed us. She nearly tore all of my hair out trying to brush it." Straight-haired people so do not understand the plight of those of us born with naturally curly locks. The struggle is real, people.

"You looked beautiful. And I was not the kind of kid who thought of girls as beautiful."

"Did you think they were icky and had cooties?" I tease.

Gavin doesn't smile back. He shakes his head. "No. I'd seen things. Seen men and women doing things. In my house. On my couch. My mom was too high to really care or pay attention. I knew how it worked, and frankly, it seemed gross and kind of terrifying and I planned to steer clear of females forever."

A gripping sense of dread overtakes me and I forget to be upset with him or nervous around him. Gavin doesn't talk about his childhood much and when he does, my heart aches to make it better.

"I'm sorry," I whisper, unable to imagine what that must have been like, to witness those kinds of things at such a young age.

"Don't be. I'm not telling you to make you feel sorry for me. You know I don't do pity or charity."

"I know."

"The reason I was telling you was because that day, things changed for me. For the first time in as long as I could remember, I saw a girl that didn't terrify me, didn't make me feel strange or confused, or slightly sick to my stomach."

"What did that girl make you feel?" Chills break out across my skin as I wait for his answer.

"Hope." There is so much emotion behind his answer I'm almost overcome with the need to kiss him, climb him, cover and smother him with love and kisses and whatever else I have to give. Somehow I remain still, and he continues. "I saw you and I felt hopeful. You were like no one I'd ever seen before. Wild and still all at once. Kind and selfless and beautiful. It's a rarer combination than you realize."

"You were hungry. Looking for food. Maybe your eyes were playing tricks on you."

It might be the wrong thing to say or too sensitive an issue to bring up, but I have to lighten the mood or I'm going to combust. Or completely humiliate myself with a profession of undying love.

"They weren't." He's smiling, and God, I love that smile. His dimples, his lips, the way his eyes crinkle at the corners. "And it wasn't just my eyes, Bluebird. I *felt* different. When you ran inside, I thought maybe you were running away from me because I was a mess and I'd scared you or something. But you came back out with food and I knew it was for me, but you didn't make me ask for it or even act like it was a big deal. You didn't treat me like a stray dog or a charity case. You and Dallas treated me like a person when no one else did. That meant something to me." After a beat of silence, he goes on. "It still means something to me. Which is why—"

"Which is why you and I can never be anything more than friends that are like family. Right. I got it. You made that perfectly clear a long time ago and I should've listened."

He's opening up to me and as good as that feels, this "here's why we can never be together" speech is breaking me apart on the inside.

"That's what you think? What you really believe?"

I almost say, "That's what I know."

Months. He was here and didn't tell me. I was on the road alone and then going to bed alone night after night and he was *right here*. No phone call. No text. Not a single smoke signal to be seen. There has to be a reason for that. The words hang out on the tip of my tongue and new me is bolder and mouthier and says how she feels, but this feels like a lie.

The truth is I don't know. So I tell him that.

"I don't know what I think or believe, to be honest."

"I think you do, Bluebird. But I understand why you would fight it. I haven't done much to make myself clear, have I?"

"Not exactly," I whisper, afraid of breaking this magical trance where he opens up. I stare at him, unsure whether he's testing me or not. His eyes are dark, but his lips are slightly upturned. I could stare at him every second of every minute of every hour for the rest of my life and still not get my fill of him.

My head knows he just wants to keep me in the friend zone where he feels I belong, but my heart is leaping for joy as if he's made some huge declaration my head hasn't processed yet. There's always been something about him, about us. Something magnetic. Something enticing. An unrelenting force pulling us toward one another.

Something more powerful than either of us as individuals.

He remains still, watching me as if waiting for me to catch a clue, but I can't seem to put it all together. I can tell he's trying, but his eyes are always so guarded. He's difficult to read and when you add that to how little he actually verbalizes, it's like trying to put together a puzzle while someone holds the picture of what it's supposed to look like behind their back.

With a deep sigh, Gavin stands, leaving me rocking a little harder backward on the swing.

"I should go. Being here, with you, after tonight . . ."

"I'm not going to beg you for one more night, if that's what you're worried about."

Whoa. That just shot right out of my mouth. Apparently I have some repressed anger still hanging around.

Gavin frowns at me. "I'm not worried about that. Not in the least."

Ouch. Thanks for that. "Oh. Okay. Well, I just wanted to be clear. I got it, that it was just the one night and then the second time I was all upset over my grandpa and—"

"That was the fourth time, sweetheart. For the record."

Now I'm flustered. I don't know what his game is, but he's better at it than I am. I flush all the way from my head to my toes and it's a deep burn. Gavin always was the flame and I always was the bluebird flying too close.

"Right. Anyway, I just wanted to say that I'm not going to be that girl anymore."

He shoves his hands in his pockets and gazes at me as if I've said something amusing. "What girl would that be?"

I stand because I don't like the positioning of him looking down at me. "The one who had some silly notion that one night would change anything. The one that pushed you into something you obviously didn't really want to get involved in."

"Ah. That girl." He nods a little too emphatically. "I see. The one who took what she wanted, consequences be damned?"

"Um."

"The one who was honest about her feelings and bared her heart and soul to an undeserving asshole? The girl who stood her ground and demanded I stop being a fucking coward and give her what we both wanted and needed?"

"Yeah?" Now I'm confused.

"Oh good. That girl is nothing but trouble. Glad I won't be seeing her anymore." There's an undeniable gleam of mischief in his eye and I can't help it—seeing him playful and teasing makes me smile.

"You're twisting the situation," I bite out at him.

"Am I? Because if memory serves, that girl was pretty honest about what she wanted. It's this new one that seems to keep her true feelings on lockdown. But that's why I came by."

"To unlock my feelings?"

He grins at my dubious tone. Pretty sure this is the most I've ever seen him smile. Like, ever.

"To tell you that I understand why you're being careful. Why you're guarded. I deserve that."

And we're back to square one. My gaze narrows on him. "I'll consider myself warned."

"For now," Gavin says easily while making his way down the porch steps. "I want you to be careful around me. But one day, one day I will get my shit together, I will have something real to offer you, and hand to God, I will be someone you can trust again."

"Gavin Garrison, if you tell me to wait for you right now, I'll—"

"I'm not telling you to do anything. I'm just letting you know that once upon a time a devil fell in love with an angel," his hypnotic voice tells me. "And now that devil is working on becoming the kind of man worthy of an angel's love. That's why I didn't call you when I came home. I have a few issues I need to work through and straighten out."

"Do these issues involve the blonde from the bar?"

He flinches. Noticeably. Did he think I forgot about her?

"Sort of," he answers. "At the moment, yes. It's complicated. But it won't always be, if that makes sense."

"It doesn't."

"I'm sorry." In his defense, he does appear genuinely apologetic.

"Me too," I say, because it's all that comes to mind.

"Good night, Bluebird."

"Night, Gav."

I watch him walk down my driveway toward wherever he parked on the street and disappear into the night. I don't even know how I feel, just that I feel so many things all at once. Too many to divide and decipher.

My panties—what was left of them—were in his pocket. I saw the corner of them. I was going to tell him but the opportunity didn't exactly present itself.

If I'm being truthful? I'm just catty enough to hope the blonde finds them.

8 | Gavin

THREE DAYS GO BY AND NOTHING.

I thought I'd see her, run into her, something. I even took my mom's barely running Oldsmobile to the McKinleys' to get an oil change in case she was hanging around.

Dallas is going to be pissed that I haven't discussed the battle of the bands with her. I want to. I do. I just don't want to appear like someone trying to talk her into something. The last thing I would want would be for her to think the whole spiel about getting my shit together is to bully her into participating in the battle.

I care about that, too, but nowhere near as much as I care about her. She can say fuck the band for all I care, as long as she allows me to be in her life.

I have a plan, one that does not involve the band at all. Basically I have to finish paying the penance for what I did the year she was in Houston. Then, once that's all squared away here in a few weeks, I'll tell her about it and how I've successfully completed all required conditions of my probation, and once it's over, I just want to take her on a date. A real date. Dinner, a movie, a long walk where I grovel and beg for forgiveness for any and all pain I've caused. But first, I want to be her friend again.

I wouldn't trade my memories from Austin for all the money in the world. But if I said I didn't have regrets, I'd be lying.

Dixie deserves better than a hot fuck in a Days Inn. Granted, it was the hottest night of my life, but still. She deserves dinner, and candlelight, and romance. Most of all, she deserves honesty. I have so much I have to come clean about but with the battle and Ashley and my mom disappearing for days at a time, telling her now would ruin everything. I need time, time for her to see me as her friend again and not just the guy that screwed her and then screwed her over. Then and only then can I tell her everything, and if the pieces all fall apart, I'll be there, as her friend, to put them back together. My hope is that once she knows everything, processes it, and, okay, *maybe* hates me with the fire of five Hells, she'll eventually understand why I did what I did and forgive me. Then maybe we can be . . . more. I hope. God, I fucking hope. This girl makes me hope like a madman.

So far this all seems feasible. For the most part. With a few exceptions.

Jaggerd is a jagged fucking thorn in my side. He may have nailed Cassidy at Dallas's wedding, but his entire demeanor changed at the sight of me and there is definitely still some love for Dixie Lark left in his system.

I recognize the gestures. Squared shoulders, tense jaw, refusal to break eye contact even after it's appropriate to do so.

Territorial. Protective. Possessive.

He's like a stand-in for Dallas but in Jaggerd's case his connection to her is physical, not biological. Which in turn makes me a raging meathead tempted to pound the shit out of him just for good measure.

Cavemen had it so much easier. Dude encroached on your territory? You straight-up killed his ass. Or beat him so bad he hoped like hell never to cross paths with you again.

I should've been born in the prehistoric era.

As it is, McKinley and I sort of circle each other. He comes in the bar sometimes, sits as far from me as possible. We both politely refuse to acknowledge the other's existence with anything other than grunts and short nods. Both of us pretend not to hate the other, as if we don't feel intimidated or threatened in any way. This is the socially acceptable version of caveman behavior, I guess.

When I go in to get my oil changed, I check my phone a few more times than necessary and he stares under the hood like he's examining a labyrinth.

"Saw the flyer at the bar."

I glance up from my phone as if I forgot he was even there. "Oh yeah? Which one?"

"The one about the battle of the bands."

"Yeah. That's coming up soon."

McKinley wipes his hands on a cloth and slams the hood closed. "You and Dallas going to enter?"

I tuck my phone into my back pocket. "The *band* is considering entering."

"The band as in Dixie?" He says this as if he knows something I don't.

"The band as in the three of us. Why? You gonna come out and show your support?"

He huffs out a laugh. "Tried that once. Didn't end so well."

No shit. More like he showed his ass. Dude got six sheets to the wind and showed up and made a scene. Dallas had to escort him out to keep me from knocking his ass out. He said some very unflattering things about Dixie, and she was his girlfriend at the time. My blood pressure spikes just thinking about it.

"Yeah. I remember."

He snorts. "I bet you do."

"You got a problem with me, McKinley? 'Cause if I'm honest, I'm not your biggest fan. But I'm not really losing any sleep over whether or not you plan to start me up a fan club, either. In some way, I think that makes us even."

He regards me warily for a full minute before responding. "You hurt her. You're still hurting her. And I have a feeling the little detour you took on your way home after the wedding has more to do with you wanting her to play in the battle than trying to patch things up."

This guy is something else. "Let's be real for a second, man. You don't know me. You don't know jack shit about me other than local rumors, and let's face it, if we all believed those, I'd be able to get this chop shop shut down with one phone call." His eyes widen and he keeps his mouth shut. *Enjoy being speechless, asshole.* "Yeah, so, I don't know. Maybe don't waste your precious time worrying about my intentions with Dixie. And I won't worry about your dad's intentions when he does thousands of dollars' worth of work for cash only."

Just when I think I've won, dude laughs. Straight-up laughs out loud like I am damn comedian.

I arch a brow and cross my arms over my chest. "Something funny?"

He takes longer than necessary to compose himself. "Yeah. You. You're hilarious."

"Which part exactly did you find humorous? Just so we're clear." I narrow my eyes, hoping he gets the message about just how close to an ass beating he is.

I can hear Ashley telling me to keep my nose clean if I want to get off probation anytime soon, but the rage is already beginning to rise to the surface. I need my damn drum kit. Now.

Once he's got a hold on his giggling, McKinley stares me straight in the face. "Just so we're clear, I was particularly amused by the part where the local drug dealer, you know, the one that takes sexual favors as payment from anything with a pussy, threatened to rat out my dad."

The shock on my face must show. I didn't know that was common knowledge, but there it is.

Dixie doesn't know how far I fell the year she was in Houston, but Jaggerd McKinley obviously does. What I can't work out is why he wouldn't have told her already and gotten me out of his way.

"No wait, wait," he says mockingly, as if trying to stave off another fit of laughter. "It might've been the part where the strung-out cokehead told me I didn't know jack shit about him when I'm the one who rebuilt Dallas's truck last year after you nearly killed him in it. News flash: the Amarillo PD don't go out of their way to protect low-life scum like drug users and distributors so I got a nice, long look at the details on the paperwork when it passed through here for insurance purposes. So, who knows, man. I guess it's a toss-up on which part of your bullshit speech I found the most entertaining."

There is no trace of humor in his voice. He's good and pissed now and so am I.

If ever there was someone I didn't want to know my business, particularly business I have successfully managed to keep from Dixie for this long, it's her jealous ex-boyfriend.

When I speak, my voice comes out low and lethal. "You and I live on the same side of this town and I bet you've got a few secrets you'd rather not be made public. Daddy's side business is probably just one of them." When he doesn't argue, I finish speaking my piece. "You can judge me all you want and I couldn't give two shits what you think. But I can tell you this: if any of that information makes its way to Dixie through any channels other than me directly telling her—which, believe it or not, I do intend to do—you will wish you'd kept your mouth shut."

It's low, the empty threat. Well, mostly empty. But I'm panicking. If McKinley knows that much, then it's likely there are people who know more and might be less inclined to keep that knowledge to themselves.

I thought I had more time.

I had a plan.

My plan is shot to hell.

9 | Dixie

DID GAVIN TALK TO YOU YET?

I wake up Wednesday morning to my alarm blaring out a song called "Better Than You Left Me," and an hour-old text from my brother.

I wipe the sleep from my eyes and squint while texting him back.

Sort of. Why?

Dallas doesn't respond right away and he's on his honeymoon, so I don't really want to think about what he might be doing or risk calling and interrupting.

I take my time showering and eating breakfast. My first lesson isn't coming until 1 P.M. so there's no rush.

After I've tamed my hair into a manageable low ponytail and dressed in well-worn jeans and a black tank top with red letters that say KEEP CALM AND HUG A DRUMMER—what can I say, I have a thing for drummers—I pick up around the house and unload and reload the dishwasher. How jealous people would be if they could see my glamorous life.

It's not until the doorbell chimes that I realize it's time for Maisey's piano lesson. I don't realize how empty the house seems until I have company.

"Hey, ladies," I say to six-year-old Maisey and her mom, Leandra.

Leandra was a sixteen-year-old rape victim who used pain pills and narcotics to try to ignore her resulting pregnancy until she couldn't anymore. They've have a rough go of it and Maisey is tiny for her age, something I know Leandra still feels an immense amount of guilt over, but she's actually one of my best students. Maybe the best.

"Hi, Miss Dixie," Maisey says. "I practiced on my princess keyboard all week!"

"Yeah!" I give her an enthusiastic high-five. "Go you!"

Leandra grins at us and shoots me a thankful look. "She really did. She's getting so good. I'm going to grab some groceries and I'll be back, probably before you're done."

"Sounds good." I close the door behind Leandra and usher Maisey over to the piano bench. "Show me which piece you've been working on."

For the next half hour I work with Maisey. Her mom arrives a few minutes before her lesson is over and we play a mini-concert complete with a curtsy.

In the hour before my next lesson, I sit and I wait.

He'll be here. He always is.

He won't ring the bell or knock. He'll just wander almost aimlessly up to the porch and stand there until I let him inside.

It took him two weeks to come inside and a third week before he told me his name.

Liam.

I don't know what his story is, or why he shows up here, but I always make sure to have a snack and a beginner piano lesson ready.

Today is the same as before. I listen for him, opening the door once I hear him on the front porch.

The sight of him breaks my heart and yet again, I don't see a car in sight that could've dropped him off. His clothes are stained and threadbare and his hair is oily as if he could use a good bath. I want to offer him more than cookies or a sandwich or a piano lesson but I can't find the words that would make this appropriate. So I just stick to our routine. For now.

"Good afternoon, Liam." I'm careful to keep my voice low. He's got the demeanor of a cornered animal that might flee the room at any time.

"Hi," he says just as quietly.

"Come sit," I say, pulling out the piano bench. "I picked out 'Twinkle, Twinkle Little Star' today. It's a good one."

His eyes narrow like they always do, as if he's waiting for this to be a lie or a trick. Liam is a dark-haired little boy with matching eyes that darken when he gets frustrated, which happens often. He reminds me of another broody musician I know. I contemplate asking Gavin to give him drum lessons because piano, violin, and even guitar pretty much just piss him off. I want to love and hug Liam the same way I want to smother Gavin with love to help guide him out of the darkness, but that would likely piss him off, too.

Liam keeps a shield up, an impenetrable one I'm almost envious of.

He stumbles through the song with my encouragement two full times before telling me he's done.

"Okay, that was good. Did you want to try any other instruments today?"

He shakes his head and stares at the floor.

"Whew, playing piano is tiring work. You want a sandwich and some pretzels or something? Tea? A soda?"

Liam's eyes lift and lighten for a few seconds before he shrugs. "That'd be okay I guess."

Once I've retrieved the peanut butter and jelly sandwich and pretzels, I set them down on the table along with a sandwich for myself. I grab both a grape soda and a glass of iced tea, not sure which he'll prefer. He reaches for the soda and downs almost all of it in two drinks.

Watching him eat makes me lightheaded and heartbroken. He eats like he hasn't eaten in months.

I slide my plate in his direction. "You know what? I messed up. I put grape jelly on my sandwich and I only like strawberry. Think you could eat mine, too, so it doesn't go to waste?"

He barely takes a breath before nodding and inhaling the second sandwich.

Every week I tell myself I'm going to find out what this kid's deal is, who's neglecting him this way. Every week I get scared that if I push him he'll disappear. Asking about his parents has been a major failure each time. His mom is dead, he says, and his dad doesn't like "no one in their business."

I decide to take a different approach.

"Liam? Can you tell me about your house? What it's close to?"

He wipes his mouth with his sleeve and takes a long drink of soda. "Where the big trucks are. It's by where the big trucks get gas."

I rack my brain for a few seconds. There's a truck stop beside the highway . . . but the only houses out there are run-down and mostly condemned. I tell myself he can't possibly be crossing the highway alone to get here.

Can he?

"Can you tell me what your house looks like? Does it look like this one?"

His chair scrapes the floor as he backs up quickly to stand. "I gotta go. I'll get in trouble if I don't get home soon."

I stand as well. "Can I drive you home? You could show me the way. That way I'll know—"

"No," he says, coming the closest to shouting as I've ever seen him. "My daddy doesn't like people on his property. Says it's trespassin'."

"Okay." I nod and walk slowly with him to the door. "You come back anytime, Liam. Okay? Tonight, tomorrow, whenever you want."

"Yes, ma'am," he answers as I open the door for him.

After he leaves and I've composed myself a bit, I remember to check my phone and am surprised to see two messages from Dallas. One says to call when I can and the other asks what I think. What I think about what?

Jag texted and asked me if we could have dinner to talk. I assume he's planning to ask Cassidy out and I find it mildly amusing that he's asking me, queen of disastrous and impossible relationships, for advice.

I text Jag back and tell him to let me know when and where and then I dial Dallas, praying he doesn't answer out of breath and totally gross me out and ruin my lunch break.

"Hey, Dix," Robyn answers cheerfully. "Dallas just got out of the shower but I know he wants to talk to you. Hang tight."

"'Kay." My lungs finally take in air, something they've struggled to fully do since my brother went missing. "How's the vacay?"

"It's good. Amazing, actually. But, um, Dix, I'm going to say this fast because he doesn't want you to know because he doesn't want it to affect your decision but—"

"That Dixie?" I hear my brother call out in the background.

"Yeah," Robyn calls back to him. "We're gonna have a little girl chat. Go ahead and get dressed."

"Thanks for that mental image of my naked brother. Lovely," I say while making another sandwich.

"You're welcome." Robyn laughs lightly but there is still tension in her voice, "Listen, you did not hear this from me, okay?"

"It's twins, right? I knew it!"

"Seriously I am going to cut you if you keep saying that."

I take a bite of my PB&J. "If I say it enough it will eventually happen. Then you can name one after me."

"You're crazy." I can hear the eye roll in Robyn's tone.

"You love me. So what's the top-secret news?"

Her voice lowers to an actual whisper I have to strain to hear. "The label released Dallas today. Officially. He's reaching out to some other contacts in hopes that he can still cut his record one way or another, but it's pretty up in the air right now, so he's stressed. Even more than usual."

My heart sinks even though I know he suspected this would happen. "Oh no. That sucks."

"Yeah it does. Here he is with a pregnant wife and no job. He's trying to play it cool and not worry me but I see it, the strain it's put on him since we found out this morning. Anyway, I just wanted to give you a heads-up in case he's moody or assholish in the near future."

I can't help but laugh because she totally gets him. "Got it. Thanks for the warning."

"And just know that we love you," Robyn says. "Whatever you decide is fine. If you're not feeling the battle right now, we totally understand."

"I'm guessing you're referring to the battle of the bands competition?"

"Yeah. Wait, here he is, hon," she says before explaining herself any further.

"Hey," Dallas says, his deep voice booming through the phone much more powerfully than his wife's.

"Hey yourself, Mr. Breeland."

He chuckles at my comment. "Pretty much sums it up. So how's it going back home?"

"Not quite as tropical and exotic as Costa Rica, but we make do."

"It is beautiful here. Though not as beautiful as the girl I get to wake up to every day."

Sheesh. "Who are you and what have you done with my brother?"

His chuckle warms my insides. Dallas and I may never have had the easiest life but we've known love and happiness. It makes my entire life to hear him so deeply overjoyed in love. It also makes me a teensy bit jealous but that's my own hang-up.

"I'm still here. As much as I hate to do this, Dix, we're running out of time. We have to confirm this practice gig for next week like two days ago and I don't know what Gavin told you but I think this might be the perfect opportunity for us. One last shot, you know? It's like . . . fate or something."

I move my tongue back and forth to remove the peanut butter from the roof of my mouth and then take a big swallow of sweat tea.

"I'm thinking about it. I am. I swear."

"Did you and Gavin talk about it?"

"Um, negative. Gavin didn't say a word about any of that."

My brother huffs out a loud breath of annoyance. "Of course he didn't. Because that would've been doing something I asked. Ask Gavin to turn right and he'll go left every damn time." Now he sounds more like the overbearing bandleader I know.

"So . . . the competition?"

"We don't have much time to rehearse, and Robyn and I have to get the nursery ready, but it's two songs in round one, one song in round two, and an original if we make it to the final round."

"And you really want to do this? What if you get a better offer as Dallas Walker?"

"Dallas Walker was a joke, Dix. You know me. I belong with the band . . . and honestly, so do you. But there's more I need to tell you about the competition. Details I'd hoped Gavin would discuss with you," Dallas adds. "And I don't want you to feel pressured, but I've seen a few of the other bands performing and I think we have a decent shot."

"Spit it out, D."

"The contest is sponsored by Rock the Republic Records. First prize is a recording contract and a significant amount of cash."

My chest aches at the idea of ruining this for him. This is why Robyn wanted me to know he might be a little nuts and why she mentioned that his label released him. The tabloids have had a field day with the *Country Music Crooner Dallas Walker Walks Away from It All for Love* headline and they've already sold the exclusive rights to the baby announcement and first photos, but like everything else in this life, that money will run out eventually.

Turns out babies are expensive.

I've told him repeatedly that even after the renovations to the house and the money I spent on equipment and licensing needed for starting Over the Rainbow, I still have royalties leftover from what Capitol paid for *Better to Burn*. But we are Larks and Larks are stubborn.

I want to be ready for this. I want to stand up there with my band and own it like I should've done in Nashville instead of letting a bitchy manager get in my head. But so much is still uncertain. This life, in this house, my meager existence, it's safe. Safer than the road, than hotel rooms with Gavin and nights of watching groupies fall all over him. And truth be told, I like giving music lessons. I look forward to it and it makes me happy.

"It sounds like a huge opportunity, Dallas. I'm interested, but you know I have a lot going on with Over the Rainbow and—"

"Dixie, if we win this thing, you can have half the money to incorporate OTR and hire more instructors. If we tour, you could visit inner-city schools during downtime and give group lessons. I have thought about this and I don't want to take anything away from you. I swear. I don't even care about the money at this point. We'll survive. What I want is our band back. I never should've walked away from it, never should've left you when you were hurting. I should've been there for you."

Tears well in my eyes because I can hear them in his voice. "Well, shit, Dallas. Now you're making me cry. Stop that."

"Sorry. I'm not trying to upset you or manipulate you. I really will love you just the same if you say you're not into this at all. But I had to ask. Technically, Gavin was supposed to ask but I'm getting used to him chickening out when it comes to you."

Maybe he's right. Or maybe Gavin was going to play another hand—the "I know you want me" hand. Was he going to screw with me like that? Pretend he wanted to be with me, eventually, when he's done with the blonde, to get me to go along with this?

My emotions twist into an intricate knot in the pit of my stomach.

"I need some time to think about it. Either way, we can still do the warm-up gig. Go ahead and confirm."

My brother barely suppresses a yelp of joy. Gavin says we don't have poker faces. He's right. We don't. But he sure as hell does.

"Awesome. I'm so glad you're on board," he tells me on a huge sigh that sounds like relief. "I'll text you all the details and the competi-tion info with my thoughts on the songs we should play as soon as we hang up."

" 'Kay. Love you, big brother."

"Love you, too, Dixie Leigh." My usually closed-off brother is overflowing with the emotions. I like it. It's different, but I like it.

After we hang up, my phone buzzes in my hand and texts from Dallas come in one after another.

My vision blurs trying to read it all.

Dallas has really put a lot of thought into this. I agree with all but one of his song choices and I text him back to tell him so. I'm a little surprised when I notice the excitement and anticipation welling up inside me.

I want this. I want to do this.

Moreover, I want to win.

At the edge of my awareness, there is still that same nagging con-cern that is always there. The thought of playing music with Gavin feels like facing a giant mountainous incline the world expects me to climb. One with terrain I have no clue how to navigate and haven't had time to train adequately for.

I shake my head and stand. This isn't about Gavin Garrison. This is about my band—a band I am just now acknowledging is as much mine as Dallas's or Gavin's.

I can do this. I have loved. And lost. I have grown. I am stronger.

I've learned a few vital lessons over these past few months. It's not knowledge and experience that helps us to grow and mature.

It's pain. It's damage. It's recovering from it. Surviving it.

I am stronger because I had to be. I've been hurt so many times. By life, by death, by love, and by loss. I am happier because I've known profound sadness, wiser because I've made epic mistakes and learned from them. But I am still standing.

Damn straight I am.

Oz sits faceup on the kitchen table and I run my fingers over his strings. "You ready for this? Want one more run at this thing? Think we're ready?"

The buzz of electricity hums through my fingertips like an answer and it ignites every cell in my body. I am grinning like a maniac as I use my ancient laptop to research the competition.

I'm still smiling when my next student rings the doorbell. I have survived everything in my life so far—this won't kill me.

At least I hope it won't.

10 | Gavin

"GARRISON! HOW MANY TIMES DO I HAVE TO TELL YOU? NO PERsonal calls at work."

My boss looks sunburned 365 days a year. He's turning a deep shade of crimson nearing on blood violet while he goes off on me.

"I mean, you're the bartender. Get it? The name says it all. *Bar* and *tender*. As in tender of the bar, as in the asshole that holds up the line because he's on the phone instead of pouring drinks. When you don't pour the drinks, I don't make the money. I don't make the money, I can't write you a paycheck. Got that?"

"Cal? Not to be a smartass, but my phone call probably won't last half as long as that speech just did."

"Two minutes," he says, shoving the phone at me. "I mean it."

"I'll keep it to one," I say, just to aggravate him because he makes it so easy. Once he shakes his head and moves out of earshot, I lift the phone to my ear.

"I told you not to call me at work. We had an agreement. I can't keep doing this with you—"

"Garrison?

Fuck me.

"Dallas Lark. Holy shit. How goes the honeymoon? Y'all make a sex tape yet? 'Cause I can probably find a buyer."

"I'm guessing you didn't know it was me," he practically growls through the phone.

"Yeah, no. My bad. Thought you were someone else calling."

"I gathered that. Something going on?"

"Nah." Not anymore, anyway. "What's up? Other than you being married and all?"

"The sky. Sorry about calling you at work but I tried your cell and it was off."

Yeah. There's a reason for that. One I have no desire to discuss with him. "It's fine. Just make it quick and I'll call you when I get off."

Dallas chuckles. "All right. Well, here goes."

I shove my palm against my free ear to close it off from the commotion in the bar.

"I checked in with Dixie about the competition. Funny, she said you hadn't mentioned it, you freaking pansy."

The bottom drops right the fuck out of my gut. Between him and McKinley, everyone is going to ruin my chances with Dixie Lark before I've even begun to have one. "Sorry. The opportunity to discuss it just didn't quite present itself."

"Well, I just talked to her and I have to tell you that she sounded kind of stoked about it. She doesn't know I got released from my label and I don't want to dump that on her while she's trying to decide. Nothing's for sure, but she was definitely interested."

"Shit. They dropped you? As in do not call us we won't call you?"

"Yeah," Dallas says slowly. "I'm not all that surprised but I don't want it to influence her decision. I want her to do this because she wants to, for her, you know? So could you and her maybe rehearse one day this week? Get a feel for if you can handle your romantic drama and get a handle on it so after I get home and get the nursery set up we can get to rehearsing?"

My eyes close involuntarily and my throat constricts. If McKinley tells Dixie what he knows about me, she will have no interest in ever seeing me again. Which I will fully deserve. "Definitely. I'll see what we can work out."

"Awesome. And, Garrison?"

"Yeah?"

"You know I love you like a brother from another mother, but seriously, I will end your young life if you hurt her again. I won't tell you to stay away because Robyn has convinced me that it would be unrealistic and futile for me to try and enforce that. But I will tell you that life has a way of catching up with you when you least expect it and if you don't tell Dixie everything soon, it might get out of hand before you get a chance, and if that happens in the midst of this competition, I will be ridiculously pissed for multiple reasons."

Says the dude not telling her he got dropped from Capitol. But he's right. "Roger that. I know, man. Believe me, I know. I gotta get back to work but send me a list of songs you're thinking about."

"On it. Talk later. I have to go make sweet love to my wife."

"Poor Robyn. It's bad enough you knocked her up—now she has to see you naked for the rest of her life."

Dallas chuckles, or he's choking to death. I can hardly tell over the noise in the bar.

Before we hang up I need to ask him one more thing. "Hey, quick question."

"What's that?"

"How'd you know Robyn wouldn't shut you down? I mean—you left the tour. Walked away from everything. Got dropped from your label. That's fucking huge. What if she'd told you to go straight to Hell?"

Dallas is quiet for so long I think we got disconnected, until I hear him clear his throat.

"For years I told myself she was better off without me. I couldn't give her the perfect life, the picket fence and all that. But it was the damnedest thing. Robyn didn't want the perfect life or the picket fence. She just wanted me. Once I figured that out, it was either risk it all and tell her how I felt or live the rest of my life wallowing in regret. Thank God she said yes."

"You got lucky," I say, not in a sarcastic way but in an honest-to-God happy for him way. "Still . . . that's a huge-ass risk, man. I'm glad it worked out how you wanted it to. Good thing Breeland kept her standards low all these years."

I'm screwing with him. I am also jealous as hell.

"No shit," he says on a laugh. "You know, it's funny. I thought music was my first love. All I'd ever dreamed of was making it big. Then I did and I realized that without her, it didn't even matter. None of it. You know?"

Yeah, I knew. Or I could imagine a pretty close scenario at least.

"I need to get back to work."

"Hey," Dallas begins, sounding like he has one more urgent detail to share. "My sister is going to be pissed at first, but you know her. She loves you and when she loves someone, that's that. She'll come around eventually."

I huff my disbelief into the phone because he has no idea. Dallas knows mostly everything but not every single detail, not the details that will crush my sweet Bluebird if I don't explain them first. I wish I had some actual dirt on McKinley, but for now all I can do is hope and pray he continues keeping what he knows to himself.

After we disconnect our call I take my place behind the bar. Cal heads my way as soon as he sees me and I brace myself for the ass-chewing.

Instead he slams a stack of bright yellow flyers with black block print on them in front of me.

"Hang these up on your break. Matter of fact, plan to work right through all your breaks for the rest of the week."

"Got it."

I fill a few orders before I even look at what's on the flyers. But when I do, I almost drop the shot glass I'm towel-drying.

Dixie Lark is playing the Tavern this weekend. Like, playing *playing*. As in solo, as in all by herself. The flyer has a black-and-white photo of her with her head down and Oz on her shoulder. She looks beautiful—angelic. My inner demons roar to life.

They want to dirty her up, fuck her deep and hard without giving a single thought to telling her the truth or protecting her from the darkness within me.

Among the hissed whispers and dark desires, a sliver of hope, like a light slicing into a dark room through a door left ajar, carves a path inside my chest.

Maybe she is ready. Maybe she misses performing and the band really will get a second chance.

Maybe I will, too.

11 | Dixie

"No you did not do this." I gape at the yellow flyer in my hands. "Are you outside of your mind? This is insane. I can't do this!"

Leandra shakes off my massive freak-out. "You already did, babe. Remember? I was there. I saw how amazing you were. The entire place was captivated."

I shake my head, wishing I could crumple the paper into a ball and make it disappear. "Lee, I know you mean well. But I can't . . . seriously. I just . . . I don't perform solo ever and—"

"You do, Dixie. And you told me yourself you miss it. Anyone who looks at you can see how badly you need to play." I didn't realize she was paying such close attention. "You do so much for us. Let us do something for you. Everyone is coming. We're going to be your cheering section."

"You doing something nice for me somehow turns into me having to perform alone in front of a live audience. You could've just bought me a box of chocolates or a cookie bouquet."

She laughs as if I'm kidding. "Girl, you are the most talented thing in Amarillo. You have a true gift—the kind most people would give their eyeteeth for. And here you are, holed up and giving free lessons to kids because you love to play. You *need* to play."

"I love these kids."

"You love everyone, Dixie, and I love you for that. But sweetheart, you're young, you're free, and you should be out there. Go on a date. Play a show. Have some drinks. Dance with a stranger. Kiss someone full on the mouth just because you can."

I give her a pouty frown. "You're not that much older than me."

"Yes, but I'm a mom. It adds like five years to my actual age. Trust me."

I laugh and nudge her hard enough to nearly knock her skinny butt off the piano bench. "You're gorgeous. You could have any guy you wanted."

I regret my words immediately.

She's told me her story over the past few months. When she showed up at my door asking about Over the Rainbow, I was obtuse enough to ask what happened to Maisey's dad. I had no idea it would be such a painful story to hear and tell.

She's a beautiful blond girl with a swimsuit model figure and magazine cover face. When she was sixteen, she was madly in love with the varsity quarterback at my rival high school. Then she had too many drinks at a party, got assaulted by some disgusting pig who never should've been there, and got pregnant. Golden boy couldn't deal and ran away to college, leaving her in the dust. I don't think she's ever recovered from the heartbreak.

Her smile is there but it's small and doesn't reach her eyes. "I'm not looking for a man. I just want to focus on Maisey and being the best mom that I can be. But I'm happy with that. I don't think you're happy, Dixie. I think you're settling for safety's sake."

She's always been honest with me, even when the truths haven't been easy to tell, so I'm honest with her. "I do miss it. Performing. Being onstage. The band." I sigh loudly. "But it's a big dream. Sometimes a terrifying one. One that takes a lot to chase and has no guarantee of coming true. I'm okay with my life as it is."

Not to mention the fact that Gavin is so tightly entwined into my dream that I can't figure out how I feel about it from one moment to the next.

"Okay? You're *okay* with your life? Lame. We're talking about your *dream*," she practically moans. "They're supposed to be scary. If they aren't, you aren't doing it right. And it's within reach. Do you know how rare that is for most people?"

I nod, because I do.

"Friday night. We're all going to be there. Cheering you on."

I close my eyes. "Even if I'm terrible?"

"Even if you shatter glass and make the local dogs howl like banshees."

"**G**arrison, one of your girls is asking for you," a red-faced heavyset man calls out.

Of course that would be the first thing I hear when I step into the Tavern Friday night. I came early in an attempt to shake off the preperformance jitters.

So much for that.

After entirely too much deliberation, I pulled out a black leather top and a short, black lace skirt. The McQueen ankle boots I got at an estate sale years ago had been collecting dust in my closet pretty much since the showcase in Nashville. Slipping them on, I began to feel like *me* again. Who knew shoes had so much power. I didn't. Until now.

I put on some eyeliner and mascara and a quick coat of my one splurge in life, Marc Jacobs lip gloss in a bold shade of red, tossed my hair up and down a few times, and called it good.

It wasn't until I was just about walk out the door that I caught a glimpse of myself in the mirror in the living room.

Eyes wide and shining, lips full and glistening, and my skin creamy and just flushed enough to make me look alive. I was holding Oz's case and for a moment I was transported back in time. Austin. Music. Performing live and setting my soul free.

Somehow I'd lost sight of what that meant to me, of what it did for me, for my heart and soul and general well-being. Now I remember. I need music like I need oxygen. But I'd been depriving myself for so long because . . . because it seemed indulgent. Selfish, even, after Papa died. Joy in the midst of grief felt so wrong . . . and yet, now I could see that it was so very necessary. I read somewhere that when you're happy you enjoy the music but when you're sad you understand it. Music was my salvation, it always had been. But when Dallas was leaving to follow the dream we'd shared for so long, I felt like I was abandoning the memory of my grandfather.

Give yourself permission to dream, little one, my Nana used to say. *Dream big and wide and run full speed with arms stretched out wide to catch those elusive dreams.*

Did I forget that? Did I forget her?

No. I forgot *me*.

It's as if I've awakened from the dead. I place my hand over my mouth to keep the sound of surprise from escaping.

There I am.

More important, *Where have I been?*

Hiding behind messy topknots and sweatpants mostly.

Maybe Leandra was right. She smiles and waves at me from across the room as she plops down at a table near the piano where Cassidy and Jaggerd are already sitting. I wave and they wave back but Jag looks strangely unsettled.

I sang at Dallas's wedding but it's not something I typically do unless it's backup vocals. That night I saw Gavin for the first time in months, I was just messing around because the girls talked me into it. This was not what I pictured for my life, but I can finally see how Dallas did find some joy in performing solo. It's like doing a trapeze act with no net.

Somehow my life has taken an abrupt left turn as of late.

I'm not sure how I feel about it.

Excited.

Scared.

Anxious as hell, really.

My eyes scan the room without my permission. I pretend I don't know what I'm looking for, but I know exactly who I'm hoping to see.

He's probably busy working, Dixie, I tell myself. He may be getting off soon but he might not be leaving alone. His complicated blonde could be here.

I feel sick.

Nothing I try to console myself with is really helping matters much. I feel like all of my nerves have been stretched to their absolute breaking point and I'm on the verge of a complete mental breakdown.

A few minutes after I've stepped into the small backstage area, which apparently also doubles as storage for stacked cardboard boxes, someone closes in behind me.

"Hey there, Bluebird. Or should I call you Songbird now?" His breath tickles the back of my neck and the delicious heat shimmies down my spine.

"Gavin," I say, turning to face him. "Heard there was a girl looking for you."

His gaze doesn't even waver. "Oh yeah? Too bad for her. I already found the girl I'm looking for."

My nose scrunches, my unfailing tell that I am confused. "What's with you these days, Mr. Smooth Pants? You sure are laying on the charm lately."

"And here I thought I was just being nice."

There's something about the way he says the word that lulls me into a false sense of security. I feel like I'm being hypnotized by the seductive lilt to his voice, the liquid warmth in his eyes. It's disorienting and mesmerizing.

"*Nice* isn't really the word I'd use to describe you, Garrison."

"And what word would you use?"

Being put on the spot so suddenly flusters me. I'm unprepared for this pop quiz. "I, um, I'm not—"

"I don't want to distract you tonight. I'm looking forward to seeing you play, but if my being in the crowd will throw you off or something, I can—"

"*Arrogant,* Gav. That's the word I'd use." I smirk at him. "And don't worry, I can perform just fine with you front and center."

He appears to take my defiance as a challenge. He leans forward to whisper in my ear and it's everything I can do not to melt into a puddle. "You sure? Be honest, Bluebird."

Heat creeps up my neck and spread across my face. His voice lowers as he leans in closer.

"Tell me you don't want me here and I'll walk out the door right now. No questions asked."

"I want you. Here," I say, hearing the waver in my voice.

"Good. Because I want you, too." He rests his forehead on mine. "Here," he says, gently kissing me on the temple. "Here," he breathes while brushing his lips down my jawline. "And a few other places not appropriate to place my mouth on in public. Unless you're into that."

My blood has turned to gasoline and Gavin Garrison has tossed a match on me.

"Gav," I whisper, turning away shyly because we're visible to the folks sitting at the front tables. "People can see us."

One person specifically appears particularly disconcerted about our exchange. Jag's normally handsome face is twisted into a mask of unadulterated disgust.

I shoot him a questioning "what the hell is your problem" glance and he looks away as if he can no longer stand the sight of me.

Surely he's not jealous. He's here on a date and anyone with eyes can see he's enamored with Cassidy.

Men confound me and I've realized it's because deep down, they're mostly little boys in oversize bodies.

"Five minutes," a guy calls out as he walks by. "Then you're on."

"That's Cal, my boss," Gavin says, nodding at the man's retreating figure. "He's kind of a dick but running a bar this size can be stressful. His bedside manner isn't the greatest."

"I bet. Maybe that's what he's got you for."

"The only person seeing my bedside manner is you, baby."

I roll my eyes to cover the effect his words have on me and I glance at the piano sitting in the corner. Taunting me. Daring me. Beckoning me. Musical instruments call to me in some strange way—as if they beg me to tame them. Gavin's soul calls to me in a similar fashion—only his is a siren song promising unimaginable ecstasy at the price of utter and complete obliteration. "Guess I should get out there."

I take a step forward and Gavin pulls me into the shadows. "Knock 'em dead, Bluebird. I'd say good luck but you don't need it. You have so much more than luck when it comes to music."

I lift my eyes to his penetrating gaze. "I want to believe that."

"You will. One day. Promise."

"Hope so."

He nods like he was expecting this answer even though I can see the pain that flashes behind his eyes. "I'll spend every day reminding you if you'll let me."

"That would mean spending every day with me, Gav. Which clearly you have no intention of doing anytime soon."

"I'm trying, babe," he says with sincerity. He winks at me and I try not to melt into a puddle in the floor. "A few weeks and I'll be off probation and if the battle goes well, maybe we'll be back on the road together soon. If you want that, that is."

"Of course I want that. It's just—"

A booming voice announces me onstage and there is a surprising amount of cheering from the audience. I start to turn my head in that direction but Gavin catches my jaw with a firm but gentle grip. "Have a great show, Bluebird."

Without asking for permission, he lowers his mouth to mine and gives me a tender kiss full of unspoken promises.

"Don't tease me, Garrison."

"Never." He kisses me gently again, then once on my nose and once on my forehead before squeezing me into a hug. "Not a tease, sweetness. A promise."

I give myself a few seconds to enjoy the warmth of him, to indulge in the clean, male scent of him.

Reluctantly, I pull out of his arms and make my way to the stage.

Never in my life have I been so grateful for glaring, blinding stage lights. I can't actually make out any faces in the crowd, which is probably for the best.

I introduce myself and am greeted with a surprising second

round of cheers. Sitting down at the piano, I shake my head, because truthfully, I am not a solo act and I've never wanted to be one. Yet, here I am.

"Here goes nothing," I mumble under my breath to myself.

My fingertips familiarize themselves with the keys, caressing them once before I launch into my first song.

And then . . .

Then I am lost.

And found.

Then I am free.

12 | Gavin

"WHERE IS HE? WHERE'S MY BABY?"

The first word that comes immediately to mind is *No*.

"Baby? Are you here?" A loud rapping sound comes from the bar and it's almost loud enough to be heard over Dixie playing onstage. "Gavin Michael! Gavy-poo! Where are yooouu?"

I nearly knock over Jake the barback in an attempt to get around the bar and silence the woman calling for me in the singsong voice.

Cal steps in front of me before I get to her. "I don't care who she is, just get her the hell out of here. Now."

"On it. Um, I might have to leave to get her to—"

"Do whatever you need to. I can dock your pay for the rest of the night if needed. Cara and Jake can handle this crowd."

Cara is an extremely capable bartender and her girlfriend Missy works security here so I know she's got this. Jake has also proven himself lately and has even learned to make a few drinks and use the taps. Which is good, because I have a feeling I am not coming back to the Tavern this evening.

"There he is. Isn't he handsome?" She practically knocks over the drink of the lady sitting next to her. "Hey, baby. I saw the flyer about your little friend playing tonight and thought maybe me and my date here could get a few drinks. You know, on the house, since I'm related to the bartender. They have a family discount, right?"

She giggles at her own joke. She's slurring her words, barely standing upright, and her eyes are so glazed over it's a wonder she can see me. The man with her gives me a once-over, then leers at a young girl on the other side of him. I recognize him. He's been over a few times—one of the local dealers and I'm pretty sure a bruise my mom was sporting on her neck a few days ago came courtesy of him. He practically runs out the door every time I walk in, which has been the one intelligent decision he's made in his life.

I have a strong suspicion I might be going to jail this evening.

So much for light at the end of the probation tunnel.

I glance longingly at the stage, wishing I could stay to watch my Bluebird finish her set.

She's amazing. She's captivating and strong and her voice is this haunting mix of sweet and sultry I never knew she was capable of. She is capable of so many things, so much more than being held back by a bartender with a record and a junkie for a mom.

I sigh and walk around the bar, apologizing to the woman whose drink my mom just knocked all over the place. I signal to Jake to replace it on the house and he's Johnny on the spot, handling it quickly and apologizing profusely as he cleans up.

He shouldn't have to apologize. This is my fuckup. My mess. My problem.

"Let's go home, Mom," I say, taking her elbow sharply.

"Easy, kid," her "date" warns. "She'll leave when she's good and ready." He knocks over the drink of the man behind him and I can see the impending bar brawl behind my eyes. If I don't stop this it will ruin Dixie's show. If I do stop it, I'll miss her show.

The verdict is in. I'd rather give her the moment even if I can't be a part of it.

My mom's friend is a few inches taller than me but older and clearly out of shape. He's broad, with a beer belly and yellowing teeth and already bruised knuckles that tell me this isn't even his first fight this week.

"Care to discuss this outside?" I tilt my head toward the door and he smiles, a predatory scowl with a hint of anticipation. This is what he really came for.

Violence.

I don't know why, but it has always seemed to surround me. To find me. Like it seeks me out for some unidentifiable reason.

As I practically drag my mom outside, leaving Dixie's angelic voice inside, the heavy weight of dread settles on my chest.

This is my life. There's no escaping it. No cutting ties or starting over or a future. It's bleak and it's bullshit but it's true.

Dixie deserves so much better than this.

She will have better than this.

Even if it kills me to let her go.

Several bruised ribs and a possible concussion later, I tuck my mom into her bed. She's out cold and snoring and her "friend" is probably still unconscious in his beat-up blue Ford pickup where I left him. His face will likely take a while to heal and his pride might, too. When it does, I know he'll be back for round two.

I'll be waiting.

For a few long minutes, I watch her sleep. She looks so tiny and fragile.

Part of me wants to be angry with her, for doing this to herself, to me. For all of it. But I know why. I get it.

My mom was abused in the worst way from the time she was old enough to form memories. When I was younger, she'd get sober for a while and come clean about why she did what she did.

She'd been molested, beaten, tortured, and eventually put into foster homes, where she'd been locked in closets for days, urinated on, and starved nearly to death.

She's still completely terrified of enclosed spaces and her pain is still my pain.

I know why she does what she does. She gets high to forget, to get numb, to get some type of relief from the trauma and the pain and the horrific nightmares that have plagued her ever since. Only they aren't just nightmares. They're memories.

Sporadically over the years she would get on these healthy living kicks, swearing over and over that she was done for good with the meth or the crack or whatever she'd binged on that time. She'd clean the trailer from top to bottom, replacing all the empty boxes of off-brand Pop-Tarts and week-old pizza lying around with actual groceries when the state put money on our food assistance card.

"We're going to be okay, baby," she'd say. "You'll see."

I saw all right.

Each and every time, I would be stupid enough to hope. That this time would be different. That this time her sobriety would stick.

It never did.

It never will.

Deep down I know this. There was always a boyfriend who'd hit her and trigger the memories, or a packet she'd find in a pair of dirty jeans. There was always something. A few times it would be me. I'd snap at her, say something hurtful, and send her spiraling. I will carry the guilt for this forever. Maybe that's why I can't leave her, why I can't just walk away and stop trying to protect her from the evils she brings on herself.

She and I are the definition of hopeless.

Just like when I was a kid, I make the same, stupid wish I always do. That she'll stop this and get better, *be* better. But I'm not a naïve kid anymore and I know this is unlikely.

The sun is coming up and I need sleep, but I decide it's not just time for me to get my shit together, but way past time for her too. I pull out my phone with the intentions of searching local state-funded rehab centers and see several messages that nearly cause me to drop it.

> **Dixie:** Where did you go? I looked for you after . . .
> **Dixie:** Your boss said you left with a woman. So . . .
> **Dixie:** I hope you had a good night, Gav. I'm worried about you but maybe don't call me or stop by for a while, okay? I need some time.

Fuck. Me.

And just because the shit cake of life always has additional hidden layers, there are more.

> **Dallas:** Robyn and I came home early to see Dixie's show. Where were you? Did you know she could sing like that?
> **Dallas:** Call me, man. 911.

And one more.

> **Unknown Number:** You're an asshole, Garrison. Plain and simple. Tonight was the final straw. I'm done watching you pull this shit on her.

I know that the last text is from Jaggerd McKinley, just like I know the sky after a night of rain is the same shade of stormy blue as Dixie's eyes.

I will deal with him later. In person.

Right now I need to call Dallas, so I do.

It rings and rings until his voice mail answers.

When the beep comes, my mind blanks and I'm at a complete loss for words.

"Hey, man. It's me. I . . . it just, shit got crazy last night so I had to leave early. Hate that I missed you. Call me later."

My voice sounds like I had gravel for breakfast but I'm too tired to care. Dallas might think the worst, which sucks. Thanks to McKinley, Dixie will probably think the worst now, too, which sucks far more than Dallas possibly being pissed at me.

I lower my battered and exhausted body into a kitchen chair and place my elbows on the sticky table. Propping my head in my hands I decide the only thing I can do is just wait for Dallas to call me back. Maybe he can figure out a way to get Dixie to talk to me. Maybe he can tell me what I should say, help me figure out how to tell her that I love her more than anything in this world but that I love her enough to know that I am not what's best for her.

She was beyond amazing, the epitome of an incredible performer last night, and she needs to follow her dream, not stay here in this nothing town waiting on some local piece of shit who will never get his act together. But I know her. I know exactly how deep she is capable of loving and forgiving. She would wait. For me. Forever if needed.

When we were kids, my stuff tended to break on a regular basis. My bike, my shoelaces, my book bag. You name it, mine was crap. It wasn't secondhand, it was fourth or fifth or sixth hand, usually donated from the local Junior Leaguers, Goodwill, or a counselor digging through our school's lost-and-found box.

Dallas is one of those people who are constantly in motion and typically he slows down for no one—though I suspect that is changing these days. But Dixie always waited for me without fail. She never once left me behind.

I'd tell them to go on without me while I dealt with my mess and time and time again, I'd look up to see her bending down to help me.

Acidic pain stings my eyes at the montage of memories playing in my sleep-deprived head. Dixie at nine years old handing me food from her parents' funeral reception. Thinking of me, a stranger, in literally her darkest hour. Dixie at eleven, giving me half her sandwich at lunch when she found me smoking to cure the edge of hunger behind a rotting oak tree. Dixie at thirteen helping me fix the chain on my bike when it broke and Dallas sped off without me. Dixie at fourteen, leaving a party with her friends to come hang out with me while I cried and raged on like a lunatic when my mom nearly OD'd for the second time. Her face, her beautiful heartbroken face a few months ago when she realized I was home and hadn't called her.

It dawns on me that that night was the last time she played music live until now. And I ruined this show, too, by bailing on her when she needed me. She's always been there for me and I've done nothing but cause her pain. I've used her like the other women in my life, just in a different way.

I drag her down.

I drag the band down.

The only two people in the entire world who try to pull me up, and all I do is yank them into the pathetic pit of Hell that is my world.

I saw the love shining in her eyes at the bar, the excitement glowing on her face, and the joy beaming out of her eyes. She loves to play music. She loves to perform.

Worst of all, she loves me.

She's the only reason I even know what love is.

And I have to break her into a million pieces.

Sitting there at the dirty kitchen table, I know it as sure as I know my own name. It will be the only way to make her let me go. To make both of them finally let me go so I can slink back into the gutter, where I belong.

I'll have to use her one last time.

13 | Dixie

"SO YOU THINK IT WAS THE BLONDE? THE SAME ONE YOU SAW HIM with a few months ago?" Robyn sits on my bed hugging a pillow to her chest and waiting for me to answer.

"That's what the barback said. His boss said he left with a woman; the barback piped up and said a belligerent blonde he knew was making a scene and asking for him."

"That's fucked-up, Dix."

I pick at the fringes on the edge of my favorite pillow. "I know."

"Especially since he made such a scene right before with the kissing and all that. It's like he wants to stake his claim on you for the world to see, keep every other guy away, but then he can't deal with the rest of what comes with that."

"I know."

She tosses her hands up and the pillow tumbles down her lap. "I mean, seriously! What the fuck is his damn deal?"

"Your kid's first word is going to be a swear word if you're not careful."

Robyn glares at me. "Do not change the subject, Dixie Leigh Lark."

"Sorry."

She rests her back against my wooden headboard and sighs. "I'm sorry, too. He just frustrates the hell out of me."

"Ditto."

"I mean, the way he was watching you like a hawk at the wedding and the reception, the way he has *always* watched you as if you are his and only his and he is protecting you from all the world's evil—it's beyond infatuation. It's like, I don't know . . . borderline obsession. Then he just straight-up bails without so much as a word—with another woman! That plus the not calling you when he was back in town, this pregnant lady's patience is running slap out."

I smile because Robyn is so . . . Robyn. If she's your friend, she is one hundred percent committed. She is angry on my behalf and I don't know if it's the pregnancy hormones or what but I'm pretty sure she's angrier than I am.

I don't even know if I'm angry. I'm just sad. Hurt. Confused.

The show was beyond incredible. It was one of the best nights of my life and I felt so alive. All I wanted when it was over was to see him, to wrap my arms around him and celebrate my euphoria from performing. I wanted to tell him that I was ready for the band to get things going because I finally feel like *me* again.

But he was gone. Just . . . gone.

"This isn't okay, Dixie," she says, a warning edge to her tone as if she thinks I don't realize this. "I see you over there working up a million excuses, but it's time for him to grow up. He needs to understand that he can't just pick you up and set you down whenever he feels like it."

"I know," I mumble, closing my eyes and burrowing back down in my covers.

"Can I ask you something?"

"Sure."

I'm expecting it to be something about Gavin so I'm confused when it's not.

"Have you ever thought of moving into the master bedroom? I mean, all the upgrades to this house are beautiful and this room is nice and it'd make a great guest room. But it's your childhood bedroom, love. You're a big girl now and the big bedroom is just sitting empty."

I glance around my room. Faded lavender walls sparsely adorned by white weathered wooden shelves my grandmother refurbished to match my headboard. Old desk my grandfather gave me to do my homework on.

"Huh. I guess I never really thought about it."

"Can I tell you why I think that is?" Robyn looks nervous, like she's worried her answer might hurt my feelings.

"Shoot."

She takes a deep breath and I can see her mentally organizing her thoughts the way only she can. I suspect all information in her brain is color-coded and cross-referenced.

"Dix, please don't take this the wrong way, but I think you're kind of living in the past. Please know I say this with love, but honey, you've outgrown it and that's okay. You need to move into the current century and I think the reason you haven't done anything about that is because deep down, you know this is a temporary pit stop in your past. Eventually you are going to have to face the fact that you were born to perform. You need it. The world needs it. I know it's hard to let the past go—hello, I married my high school sweetheart. But sometimes it's necessary." She sighs and pats my hand gently before continuing. "Dallas and I had to grow up, we grew apart, and then we grew together. We are still growing, in friendship and in love and as people. In my case, literally." I smile when she pats her expanding belly. "I want that kind of love for everyone, especially for you. But I can't stand to see you hurting like this, stuck like this, bogged down by the past. Your face last night . . . you were so excited when you came offstage and my heart broke for you when I watched you realize he wasn't there. You just . . . you were crumbling. Piece by piece. I could see it. Dallas could see it. Everyone with eyes could see it. You kept the mask on for us, but I want you to know that you can break apart. You can fall down. We will be there to pick you back up. I promise."

I don't know what to say. Everything she's said is true so I just keep quiet, swallowing the lump of emotion currently clogging my airway.

"Girl, you rocked it last night. Hard-core. We were all blown away and I'll admit, I didn't know you had that in you. I don't know if you knew you had that in you."

"I didn't," I interrupt, my voice hitching on the last word.

"Right. Well, now you do. You're coming into your own now and everyone saw that. And now it's time to do something about it. But first, something has to give with Gavin and I don't know what it is, but he needs to either be there for you and make you a priority, or bow out gracefully. For your sake, for the band's sake, and for his sake because I suspect if he hurts you like that, Dallas might murder him. I really don't want the father of my child to spend his life in jail."

"I think he just . . ." I search for the right words, but how do you explain what's going on in your head when you can't even understand it yourself?

" . . . needs to make an actual choice. It's time, Dix. For what it's worth, I think he loves you as much as he is capable of loving another person, but he made his choice last night and for whatever reason, it wasn't you."

A thick knot of emotion keeps any more excuses from escaping.

"I'm sorry," Robyn says while patting my hand. "I don't mean to say that it will be easy, because I know it won't. But it's time to move forward. With or without him."

I nod because she's right. "I know."

Robyn stands to leave but then she stops abruptly. I have a mini panic attack that she's going into preterm labor or something but she gives me a sad smile.

"Remember Billy Gleason? From middle school?"

I nod. "Yeah, the freckle-faced asshole who heard the boys shortening my name and started calling me 'Dicks' and drawing penises all over my stuff."

Robyn laughs softly. "Yeah, him."

"Dallas heard him teasing me and beat the crap out of him. He was suspended for three days and Papa was superharsh on him those days, making him do slave labor at home from dawn till dark."

Robyn nods. "Yeah, about that. It wasn't Dallas who beat him up. Billy, I mean."

I feel my forehead wrinkle in confusion. "Yes, it was. Busted him up pretty bad, actually. He had to get stiches in his cheek and lip and eyebrow, if I remember correctly. Billy carried my books and my lunch every day for weeks and pretty much spent the remainder of sixth grade apologizing to me."

Robyn looks at me like I am clueless. "I know. I remember. But it wasn't Dallas that made that happen." She tilts her head to the side as if contemplating not telling me the rest. But then she finishes. "It was Gavin. Dallas took the fall because Gavin had already been in trouble one too many times that year."

I feel as if my entire life has been a lie.

"Seriously?"

She nods. "Seriously. And there have been . . . other things, other times when Dallas took the fall for him because he thought he was doing the right thing. But you and I both know that won't be possible forever."

"What are you say, exactly?"

"I'm saying that there is a darkness in Gavin, a side of him that is dangerous to people who care about him. To Dallas and to you. He hurt that kid, badly. For *teasing* you. And he let Dallas take the blame and deal with the consequences." Robyn continues before I can argue. "Gavin's always had it rougher than any of us, but you need to know, Dixie, that his salvation is not on your shoulders. The battle he's fighting this time is his and his alone—and hopefully he'll conquer his demons, but if he doesn't . . . you will be okay and we will be here for you. And him."

I glare at her steadily until she finishes her statement.

"Sometimes even things done with the best of intentions can wound and destroy. Sometimes the darkness wins. That's all I'm saying. I just worry is all." She shrugs almost imperceptibly and then adds, "We'll leave you be, but call us if you need us, okay?"

I nod and with that she leaves my room and closes the door behind her.

Now I'm the one left in darkness.

I wake to loud knocking on my front door. Sitting up in my bed, I glance over at my phone and see that it's after two in the morning.

Something's wrong.

I don't know how I know, but I know it even before I'm fully conscious. Stumbling to the door, I mutter inaudibly to my late-night visitor to hold the hell on. I've barely registered the figure standing in the door way before I open it.

His scorching hot mouth fastens to mine. It's a kiss and then a lick and then a hard pull of my flesh into his mouth. It's a familiar mouth, one that affects even more parts of my body than he's actually touching.

Before I can say a word or mutter in either protest or approval, his hands grip my ass and I am lifted onto him. My legs instinctually wrap his waist and the burning kiss continues as he carries me to my bedroom. It's dark in the house so he's making his way through by memory.

Heat sears my back—hot enough that I'm slightly concerned my mattress is on fire when he lowers me roughly onto it.

Is this a dream? Am I awake?

Using both hands, I reach for his face and drag his mouth to mine. Immediately I know that I am not dreaming. The Gavin in my dreams tastes only like Gavin, like mint and sometimes a faint hint of tobacco even though he quit smoking. This Gavin tastes different.

The liquor on his breath is so strong I'm instantly drunk at the first touch of our tongues.

It's an addicting flavor, Gavin and stout whiskey.

He tears his shirt off over his head and my brain tries to warn me, to remind me about something. I'm mad at him. Or I'm supposed to be mad. Or . . . something. But there is only heat and need and skin. So much skin.

I fell asleep in my threadbare Civil Wars T-shirt and he's wearing only jeans that scrape roughly against my exposed skin.

His strong hand assaults my bare breasts. One, then the other. Rubbing hard then tugging gently on each nipple until the ache in them rivals the one between my legs.

I want him to keep touching me, to taste me, to be as consumed with his need for me as I am by mine for him.

He growls low in my ear. "I need you so fucking bad. I shouldn't have you. I don't deserve you, but I need you. Can I have you?"

"Yes, Gavin. God, yes. You have me. I need you too. I—"

He cuts me off with a kiss that plunges into the depths of my mouth, leaving no inch unexplored. I moan loudly, thankful for once that the house is empty.

I feel his hard denim-covered length press between my legs and writhe beneath him.

"Gav. I need. I need . . ." I can't breathe. All I am is need.

"I know what you need, sweetness. I have every intention of giving it to you."

"Yes, please," I plead shamelessly.

Liquid heat pools where I need him most and I thrust myself harder against his jeans.

"Not yet, my impatient girl. I'm going to take my time with you." Without waiting for permission or a response, he moves swiftly down my body and delves his thick, wet tongue between my already slick folds. My body bows up off the bed and I cry out as pleasure tears through my body.

My legs spread farther apart, granting him access to every inch of me. His tongue wrecks me, circling slow then fast, then plunging inside. I'm begging for mercy, for release, for something. I can hear myself but I can't control anything coming out of my mouth.

"Fuck me, Gav," I beg. "Please. Pretty please."

"So fucking sweet. You're so fucking sweet, baby. You shouldn't be allowed to taste so sweet. I have issues with addiction, you know, and I. Am. Fucking. Addicted."

"Please," I cry out when I feel myself ascending to that place, to that pleasure-to-the-point-of-pain peak where only he can take me. "Now, please. *Please.*"

"You know me, sweetness. I'm going to fuck you all night. I'm going to take you there as many times as you want to go. I want you to come on my tongue, on my cock, and everywhere in between. Ready?"

I want his tongue back inside me. Or his dick inside me. Both. All at once. I want him to keep his mouth there until his dick can immediately replace it. I need the contact. I need it to never stop.

Tension strings me tight and I'm throbbing so hard I assume he can feel it.

Something unintelligible slips out of my mouth, a plea and a whimpered moan combined.

Gavin sucks my clit into his mouth at the exact instant that two of his thick fingers fill me completely.

"Oh my God." It's a good feeling but a full, stretched to maximum capacity feeling. I haven't had sex since . . . since after my grandpa died.

The last time I did was here. In this bed with Gavin.

Maybe that's the real reason I can't leave this room, this bed.

He alternates gentle thrusts with hard sucks and vice versa and I am coming.

And coming, and coming.

His name slips past my lips with a slew of other words of adulation.

He licks me down from my orgasm, easing his fingers out of me in a torturously slow motion.

"See how good you taste, baby? He runs his wet fingers across my lips, then kisses me hard. "I could live on this. On you and only you."

For all the havoc he's wreaked on my body, my heart pounds at his words, at the taste of myself on his mouth, and I feel my insides begin to clench rhythmically once again.

I didn't know pleasure like this even existed. He didn't fuck me like this in Austin or here. Austin was slow and we took our time. Last time we were here it was about comfort.

This is about primal need and hedonistic desire. It's all-consuming and mind-shattering.

"More, Gavin. Please. I need more."

"Your wish is my command, Blu—babe."

The fuck?

"Why didn't you call—"

His mouth covers mine aggressively while he yanks his jeans and underwear off. I hear them hit the floor and my hands reach down instinctively to stroke his length.

He's smooth and hard and perfect.

"Inside. I need you inside," I mumble against his mouth. His kiss has turned punishing and it's confusing but I'm tough. I can deal. I give as good as I get until teeth gnash together and I'm sure both of our mouths will be sore and bruised in the morning.

"It's not going to be sweet. Or soft or slow. I am going to fuck you. I need to fuck you. Hard. Can you handle that?"

"Yes, Gavin. I can handle it. I want it." I spread my legs as far as they will go and grip his bare ass with both hands.

"Fuck." He tries to rear back but I need him now.

"Condom?"

"I don't have one. I haven't been having sex. With anyone since . . ."

"Since?"

"Since you. Since last time I was with you."

I can't help but doubt him. We've spent a lot of time apart and I've never known him to deny himself.

"Swear?"

"I swear. On anything you want."

"Swear on me. Cross my heart."

He leans down and places warm, wet kisses across my chest in the shape of a cross, stopping centimeters shy of my nipples. I reach for them to ease the ache but he grips my wrists and pins my hands above me.

"We don't have to fuck. I can just get you off all night. I'm good with that." His head dips again and his tongue runs languid circles around my areola until I cry out and he sucks my nipples hard enough to hurt. It's a good pain, though; he walks that line between pleasure and pain perfectly.

"Come inside me, Gavin. I want you inside of me."

He groans as if I've stabbed him.

"Please. I want to feel you. Just you. Only you. I take my birth control regularly. Never miss a dose. Robyn texts me every day to remind me."

Any other argument I was going to make or any defense he planned to counter with is null and void the second the head of him breaches my folds. I'm so wet from his mouth that he slides in easily, like a hot knife into butter.

The moment he is fully inside, I lose myself. My body begins to buck against his but I can't get far because he's still holding my wrists.

Once again I hear myself begging him for more as our bodies create the delicious sweaty friction I crave. He gives it, thrusting everything he has into me again and again.

"Come. Fucking come, babe. I need it. Now."

His plea is so desperate, I clench around him until my body complies with his request.

"Fuck," Gavin bites out when he slams into me and comes explosively inside. "Fucking fuck."

He releases my wrists and collapses on me and all we do is breathe. Just breath and sweat and remnants of pleasure between us.

Just when I think he's dozed off, he jerks up quickly and grabs the tops of my legs.

"Turn over."

"What? You're not serious." I can barely move, much less turn over.

"Turn," he says slowly, like I'm mentally impaired. "The fuck," he punctuates by yanking me roughly toward him. "Over."

"Gavin." I don't know this version of him. "Look at me, please." I'm not prepared for it. I thought it was lie-around-in-post-orgasmic-bliss time.

He looks but his eyes are flat black in the darkness, as if he's figured out how to look without seeing. "Each second you make me wait, I will spank you. Hard. Do you want that, baby? My handprint branded on that sweet, perfect ass of yours?"

Um . . . maybe?

My vagina is on board even if I'm still swimming in confusion.

"Do you want to spank me, Gavin?"

"Fuck, yes, I do. I want to spank that tight little ass, to bite it and mark it, and when you let me fuck it, I plan to sign my name on it."

And just like that, I'm on board.

"Okay. Let's do this. Fucking spank me then. Show me how you like it." I turn over abruptly and try not to be self-conscious about presenting him with this view of my backside. Seems silly to be embarrassed now.

"Ready, baby? You get two for making me ask you twice to turn over."

"Do your worst, drummer boy." It hits me a second too late that Gavin is, in fact, a very strong, very powerful drummer.

I flinch involuntarily when his hand makes the first crack of contact.

"Oh. Okay. Ouch. That fucking hurt."

He rubs me gently until the stinging subsides. Then he trails his fingers down the middle of me and dips it briefly into my opening. I am amazingly still extremely wet. And turned the hell on.

"One more, sweetness. Can you take one more?"

"Um, yeah. Just maybe not as—"

His open palm makes contact again and it's just low enough to send a shock wave through to my clit.

I cry out and Gavin begins whispering soothing things as he moves. I start to ask where he's going but before I do I have my answer.

His mouth launches a thorough assault on the parts of me that are exposed to him in this position. All of the parts. Even the ones I didn't expect would feel good.

Soon I am adrift in the overwhelming sensations and I'm not even sure which are fingers and which is tongue until I'm coming again and mid-orgasm his cock slams inside to the hilt. And I am coming again. Or maybe it's more of the first one continued, stretching out long and thick like never-ending taffy. All I know is I can't stop it—this, whatever this is.

He wraps my hair around his hand and jerks hard enough to hurt but I'm coming so hard I can't bring myself to care.

"Gav. Gavin. *Fuuuck.*"

He's pounding me now, a steady slamming of his cock into my body until my bones are rattling.

"Where do you want my come, sweetness? Three choices," he grounds out through gritted teeth. "Pussy, throat, or inside that tight little ass of yours?"

I don't know. I can't think. I'm growing numb and disoriented from the brutality of how hard he's still fucking me.

"W-where do you want to come?" Even my teeth are rattling. He is literally fucking every part of me.

"Everywhere. Your mouth, down your throat, all over your sweet little clit, across those perfect fucking tits. I dream about fucking your ass, about making it impossible for you to sit down for a week."

I am speechless.

"Do you get it, now, baby?" He jerks my head backward by my hair until I'm upright and surprisingly his dick is still buried safely inside of me. "This is how I am. Fucked-up. Rough. Dangerous. This is how I fuck. That shit in Austin, and the pity fuck here a few months ago, that wasn't me. This is me."

Nothing hits me quite as hard as those two words.

Pity. Fuck.

I cannot have heard that right.

But I can smell his breath again from here and I know he's drunk. Actually, I'm pretty sure he's shitfaced because the Gavin I know would never handle me this way or speak to me like this. I'm not complaining, it's kind of hot. But not if he's angry and not if he's too drunk to use sense.

"Fucking come, Gavin. Get it over with and get the hell away from me before you say something else you're going to regret."

A strange manic sound escapes him. He thrusts in hard and deep and holds me there, tethered by my hair, impaled by his cock. "That's the worst part. I have no remorse, baby. Ever."

"Fuck you," I hiss out because I don't like this anymore. It's not fun and it feels malicious and hateful. And wrong. "Actually, I'm done fucking you right now. Thank you."

I slam my elbow backward, catching him in the rib cage and startling him enough that he lets go of me.

As soon as I'm free I run into the bathroom and shut the door hard behind me before sinking onto the cold, tile floor with my sore, bare ass. It actually helps a little.

I don't know what just happened, or why he behaved that way, but I know now that Robyn is right.

Gavin is fighting his own battle. He has darkness inside him and it is capable of destroying me.

It just did.

14 | Gavin

SHE'S IN THE BATHROOM. LOCKED ON THE OTHER SIDE OF A BAR-rier I'm more familiar with than most.

If there is anything lower than scum, like scum that grows on scum, that's me right now.

It wasn't supposed to go there, to get like that.

"Mommy? Please come out now. I'm hungry . . ."

Where the fuck did that come from?

"Dixie," I call out over the uninvited sound of my warped child-hood. "Baby, I'm sorry. Please . . . I can explain . . ."

Can't I? I don't even know anymore. All I know is I can't leave like this—having done what I did, hurting her that way.

I lean forward until my forehead touches the door.

"I'm so sorry, Bluebird. I lost myself but that's no excuse." And I'm hammered as hell but that's no excuse, either. The hall spins around me and I am grounded only by my forehead pressed to the wood.

"Please come out, Mommy. I'm scared. Someone is knocking on the door."

Memories I thought I'd effectively smothered years ago attempt to break through the surface. My mom had a habit of running to the bathroom—sick, high, or to elude the local dealers, she'd run in there and hide—leaving me locked out on the other side. Alone, helpless, starving. Scared for countless reasons. Some nights I slept outside the bathroom door. Many nights.

My own heartbeat throbs inside my skull.

"Dixie, please." I hear my voice crack and I let my fist bang lightly against the door. "Please don't shut me out, baby. I am so, so damn sorry. Please. At least let me see that you're okay and then I'll go. I promise."

I fucked her dirty and I was an absolute dick about it. It wasn't necessary. To take it that far. But I was blind drunk and I lost myself.

I remember seeing her there in the doorway, angelic and innocent with her hair flowing all around her, and me thinking *This is how it has to end. She's too good for me and I have to make her see that.*

That was the last rational thought I had. She was warm and soft and wet. The scent of her, the unique salty sweetness that flavors her skin and deepens intoxicatingly between her legs, it overtook me and I was so far gone I couldn't see my way out.

"Get dressed, Gavin," I hear her say quietly. "And I'll let you in on one condition."

I nod even though she can't see me. "Got it. Getting dressed right now."

The entire time I'm putting my clothes on I'm praying the second part of her condition isn't "get the hell out."

I don't know if she's scared or just royally pissed-off, but I need to know. I was aiming for the second one but I never meant to make her afraid or actually hurt her.

I pull my clothes on slowly and try to blank it out. I can't. I'll never be able to no matter how hard I try.

I told myself I'd just pretend she was one of the others, the ones I used to use as if they were disposable. I tried. I tried that but it was so . . . wrong. The girls I used to fuck liked it that way; they asked for it that way and there was a mutual understanding beforehand. Doing that to Dixie, to my Bluebird, to the girl I would cut my fucking eyeballs out not to hurt, will forever be the worst thing I've ever done and I've done some messed-up shit.

God have mercy on my black soul, I am a fucking disgusting human being. But there it is. I have mommy issues like a motherfucker. Well, wait. No. Gross.

Fuck.

But my mom never hugged me, never wrapped her arm around me or patted me or kissed me. She never showed me any physical affection because she was always high and in her own universe. I didn't even know I needed it until the eighth-grade field trip to an art museum downtown where Lindy Preston sucked me off in the boys' bathroom.

From then on, I was an addict, much like dear old Mom.

I think Lindy has a handful of kids now by a handful of different guys. But blow jobs were my gateway drug. Soon I needed more and even after having full-blown sex, I sought sex with multiple girls at once. Surprisingly, many of them were down with that.

It felt so fucking good, to be touched, to be pleasured that way, as if they existed only for that reason. To let go and just feel. I have a relatively large dick and word got around. By the beginning of tenth grade I had fucked every varsity cheerleader at my school and a few from others.

I used to feel proud of that. Now I feel . . . sick. Sick to my fucking soul, and who the hell knew I even had a soul?

Dixie did once, I guess. Even if she's still questioning it, she'll soon know I don't, or not one worth saving, anyway.

The year she was in Houston, I kept picturing her with some fancy college guy, or the maestro of the orchestra taking her to expensive dinners, wining, dining, and fucking her six ways to Sunday. It drove me insane.

In-fucking-sane.

I became obsessed. I was literally waiting for her wedding invitation to arrive in the mail. I'd missed my shot and I missed her. I missed her so much it caused me physical fucking pain.

Missing Dixie was hell. It was the deepest, darkest pit so when my mom left drugs out on the kitchen table or in the bathroom or in the laundry basket, I traded them for blow jobs in back alleys. They needed their fix and I needed mine. Seemed like an even trade-off.

I can tell you exactly where most downtown Amarillo bars' security cameras are and what they can and cannot see.

Dallas has caught me more than once. He once yanked me out of a very lively foursome while I was butt naked and swinging at him with both fists. He made me get tested and while everything was negative, I'm not going to pretend I didn't sweat it pretty hard while I waited for the results to come in.

Hence his hesitation about letting me date his sister.

But in a strange way, he seemed to understand. He called me out for self-medicating, said he'd done some similar stupid shit when Robyn dumped him. Though he thought I missed the band, not his sister specifically, and I never clarified.

We played a few gigs, just me and him, then we met up with Dixie for a few and it did help. Some. For a while.

But then the knowledge that I could never have her, could never hold her, and would eventually have to watch some other fuckhead marry her would get to be too much and I'd slip out to downtown and fuck the first girl who made eye contact.

I imagine Hell will be a lot like my life only hotter and more densely populated.

Once I'm dressed, I make the bed, as if cleaning up the scene of the crime will somehow help. I catch a glimpse of myself in the mirror above her dresser and I look like hammered shit on a stick. Or worse.

Thank fuck it was dark.

I stagger to the bathroom where she's barricaded herself from the monster in her house. I lean against the door and I don't know how but I can feel her. She's sitting against the other side. I open my mouth to say I'm sorry, or to tell her to just steer clear of me for the rest of her life, but no words come.

Being soulless would be easier. I think I was once, but the first time I kissed her some of her soul slipped into me.

Damning me for life.

And maybe a piece of her, too.

"I'm sorry, Bluebird," I say quietly, barely getting it out over the hard sob threatening to break free. I clear my throat so I can continue. "I'm a fucking asshole and I wanted you to . . . know, I guess. To see who I really am, what I'm capable of, so you would move on or whatever."

Christ almighty this is harder than I thought it would be.

"Gavin." The pain in her voice shoots straight through my chest.

"Dixie—"

"Tell me why, Gav. Tell me all of it." She's trying so hard not to cry. I can hear exactly how much effort it takes to get those words out.

I sigh against the door and just start talking. I begin somewhere around the beginning, around why this reminds me of my mom locking me out of the bathroom as a kid. My rambling takes us through my horrific childhood, into meeting her and Dallas, and I do my best to explain why they've always been and will always be the most important people in my life. I tell her about Lindy Preston and how that became an addiction—physical contact and why.

"You hurt me on purpose," she says after a few minutes of excruciating silence.

"I did." My voice is raspy and I'm not sure she heard me until she responds a moment later.

"Why?"

I breathe deeply and do my best to maintain my composure while the emotions flood through me.

"To help you see how awful I can be. How selfish and just . . . fucked-up, for lack of a better term." I take a deep breath. "Asking you to wait for me to get my life together when I don't even know if that's ever going to be possible is unfair to you. But I know you. You have the biggest heart of anyone I know and you'd wait, you'd love me through whatever. And I love you for that. I love you for a lot of reasons. I love you because I didn't know what love was before you." And I apparently have opened that gate of unlimited I-love-yous. "You've been my Bluebird for a long time. But I've kept you in captivity. I've tried to hold you in some tiny cage and when you flew free, to Houston, I lost all control of myself. I . . . there's so much."

A sudden turn of the knob startles me and I'm face-to-face with her. She's wrapped in a robe I assume was already in there and I'm grateful she wasn't cold.

"Hey," she says softly.

"Hey," I answer barely above a whisper. "Thanks for opening the door. I have issues with . . . being locked out."

Dixie's eyes widen and gaze into mine. "It wasn't locked, Gavin. I could never lock you out."

Something about this, maybe because of my mom or my child-hood, or whatever, it breaks whatever has been holding me together.

Dixie rushes into my arms and I hold her until I can't stand. I rock her gently on the floor and we whisper comforting words back and forth. This is what Dixie is for me—what she always has been. Loving her isn't trading one addiction for another—it's finding peace and reassurance in a world of chaos.

Once she's fallen completely asleep in my arms, I place her gently back in her bed, careful not to wake her.

My Bluebird deserves to fly and be free.

She deserves to belong to herself and not to me.

Now that she knows the truth, maybe she will.

"Gav, it's me. Dallas. I don't know what's going on with you and my sister at the moment, but I need to know something and we need to rehearse if we're going to do this thing."

Delete.

"Hey, man. It's me again. Look, neither one of you are returning calls or messages and I'm starting to get worried. If I worry, Robyn worries. Which puts our child's health at risk. And Robyn's health. Anything happens to either of them, I'm going to be pissed. Call me."

Delete.

"Garrison I don't know what in the ever-loving fuck has gotten into you or why you and my sister have gone off the grid, but if one of you doesn't call me in the next twenty-four hours, I'm driving down there and kicking some ass."

I have no doubt he will drive to Amarillo from Dallas to do just that.

Delete.

"Hey. Robyn talked to Dixie and I don't know what happened but she said it was bad and that she was upset. She won't talk about it. That means you're going to. Be there in a few hours."

Delete. And then I make sure my door is locked. I guess if he really wanted to get in he could, he's done it before. Fuck it.

Pretty sure my mom is spending her days blitzed out at a crack house up the street that belongs to her boyfriend.

"I'm here. I'm outside. I will break in if I have to but I'd rather not. Man up and open the damn door please."

Delete.

"I'm guessing whatever is going on is your fault since you're avoiding me. 'Preciate the timing. You can withdraw us from battle since you've decided to be a fucking toddler. If you ever show your face at work again, that is."

Delete.

"Hey, it's me."

My heart pounds because it isn't Dallas's voice on my voice mail this time.

It's Dixie.

"Um, so I talked to Dallas and I'd really like it if we could go ahead and compete at the battle this weekend. The three of us. If you're up for it."

She pauses and I'm a burning man during that pause. Dying to hear more of her sweet voice and knowing it will wreck and ruin me at the same time.

"Anyway, we're going to rehearse tonight at the same place downtown where we used to go."

Another pause.

"We reserved two hours from six to eight if you want to come. Bye, Gav. I hope you're okay."

Repeat.

I play her message so many times, I feel beat to hell and back by the time my phone battery dies.

I put it on the charger for a while and when it comes back on I see I have another missed call. From her.

I play the message and it guts what's left of me to gut.

"Hey. Sorry to be all stalkery with the multiple voice mails in one hour but I should've said something on the other message and I didn't. So here goes. I want you to come to rehearsal tonight. I want you to play with us next Friday night at the Phi Kap gig and in the battle on Saturday. But mostly, I want us to not hate each other or hurt each other anymore. At least not if we can help it. I love you, Gavin. Bigger than your mistakes and bigger than the pain you cause me sometimes. Maybe that makes you mad or makes me seem desperate or stupid but I love you as much as I love music, maybe even more because I've loved you longer. Anyway, I do think we owe it to ourselves to see if the band has what it takes. Whatever happens afterward, I figure we'll deal with when it comes."

Since my mom hasn't been around, there are no drugs that I know of in the house. Which means if I want any kind of fix, substance or sexual or otherwise, I have to go out. I suspect Dallas might be waiting to pounce on my ass or pound this shit out of me, depending on how much he knows.

I play her two messages a few more times and then I sit in silence until it nearly deafens me.

I can't be what she needs. I'm not built to be the kind of man that could truly make her happy. But the thought of letting my mopey shit or temptations take away her dream is unthinkable.

If she wants the band, she'll have the band. This much I can't possibly screw up. If she wants a drummer, a drummer she will get.

15 | Dixie

"ACCORDING TO THE OWNER OF THE TAVERN, THERE'S A DRUM-mer that sits in with the house band we might be able to hire for the battle," Dallas tells me when I arrive at the studio downtown where we rehearse. "He says the guy has shit for brains and not the greatest work ethic but is a fantastic drummer."

It wasn't that long ago that Gavin and I stood on the rooftop of this very building and I wished for our dreams to come true. Feels like a lifetime ago. That was a different girl.

Gavin was right, though; that girl was honest and now it's harder for me to open up about what I want. Though I did leave a perfectly good and thoroughly humiliating message on his voice mail. I can't help but wonder if he ever listened to it.

"It's Gavin," I say, absently while applying rosin to my bow.

"Yeah, I know," Dallas answers. "Ideally Gavin will show. But I'm saying if Gavin *doesn't* show we should hire the house band guy as a backup."

"No, I mean the guy that sits in with them. It's him. Gavin."

Dallas's eyebrows shoot up. "Seriously?"

"Yep. You got a plan B?"

"I can see if Levi's guy might want to play with us. They got that contract with Sony and they can't participate in any events sponsored by other labels as their band, but I don't know if that applies to them as individuals. I can ask."

"Couldn't hurt, I guess. Just feels . . ."

"Like cheating on him or something?"

I nod. "Kind of. How's the nursery coming?"

"It's nearly finished." Dallas derails my attempt at a subject change. "You ever going to tell me exactly what happened?" He stops tuning his guitar and waits for me to answer.

I shake my head. "Honestly, I think if the situation were reversed, I'd rather not know this sort of thing about you."

Dallas winces. "Got it."

"Don't make that face. It's not just about . . . that. It's . . . he's not . . . I can't . . ."

"Gavin has demons, little sister. He just does. He battles them every day and some days he doesn't win. I know you love him, and I love his fucked-up ass, too, but I am your brother and it's my natural instinct to protect you."

There's a hidden confession in there somewhere. "Dallas . . . did you say something to him?"

My brother doesn't answer so I start packing up Oz. Either he can be honest with me or I can be done here.

"Wait. Calm down." Dallas sets his guitar on a nearby stand. "I may have told him to stop stringing you along. I saw how hurt you were after your show the other night and that was bullshit. So I talked to him."

"And?"

Dallas shrugs like his every word isn't of vital importance. "And his mom showed up high off her ass and he had to deal with her.

He picked her like he always does and always will, Dix. He could've called the police or a cab or had the bar security guys deal with her. He didn't. He left. So I told him if he wasn't going to commit and make you a real priority right now, then he needed to stop leaving you in limbo until he was ready."

"Dallas, what the hell? It was his *mom*." I'm slightly disgusted with myself for feeling relieved about this.

"It is what it is, Dix. He's always sneaking back into the gutter with her instead of standing in the spotlight with us because it's easier for him to hide that way. Until he decides otherwise, and it has to be his decision. You can't force him into the light."

"I didn't realize you were so jaded. Jesus. So what? We just give up on him? You know I can't do that."

"We'll love him and be there for him because whether he likes it or not, we're his family, too. But we can't put our own lives on hold while he figures his out. That's just the reality. The band has a shot. You have so much more to offer than you've been giving and I think part of that is because you didn't want to shine, either. You want to hide in the shadows with him but that's not happening on my watch. So stand over there by the mic because, you, sister of mine, are going to be on vocals tonight as well."

"Dallas."

"Dixie."

"I love you."

"Love you, too. We doing this or what?"

A commotion at the back door distracts me before I can answer.

"Sorry I'm late. Traffic was heavy." The door opens, sending a burst of light in behind Gavin.

Dallas puts his guitar back down. "Hang on and I'll help you carry your kit in."

I set Oz gently in his case. "I'll help, too."

My heart takes off in triple speed. He came.

He's not here for that, Dixie Leigh. He's here to play. Give him space.

We carry his equipment in without speaking but Dallas grins while they set up. "Glad you made it. Not gonna lie, I was pissing my pants a little."

"Can't have that," Gavin says quietly.

He's different. Even more withdrawn. Like he thinks his very existence is going to cause me pain.

He might be on to something.

A song lyric begins in my head and I want to write it down before I lose it.

Loving something, no, loving someone. Being addicted to . . . someone bad for you . . . it's like a drug, like being hooked on love . . . the perfect poison you can't get enough of.

The words are just coming randomly and I can't sort them in my mixed-up head.

"Dallas, do you have a pen?"

"Yep. Always." He tosses a blue Bic over and I catch it and uncap it quickly. I don't have paper so I start writing on my left hand. Then up my arm. Then down my inner arm. I'm glad my tattoos don't cover my forearms like sleeves or I'd be screwed right now.

Once I've gotten the lyrics down, I pick up Oz and look up to see both guys looking at me like I've gone mental.

"Sorry. Needed a moment. I'm good now. Let's do this."

Gavin nods without meeting my eyes. "Okay, here we go. One, two, one, two, three, four!"

And away we go, to that magical place where we fly together and nothing can touch us because we are completely free.

16 | Gavin

I HAVE TO KNOW WHAT IS WRITTEN ON HER ARMS.

I have no right to ask. But it's killing me not knowing.

I've never seen her do anything like that. Dallas has been known to get struck by inspiration and act a fool in order to find something to write with and on, but even he's never written that much at once and not ever on his skin that I know of.

What inspired you, Bluebird?

I want so badly to ask her it distracts me from my cues. I was late on two solos already and Dallas is getting agitated.

I want to tell him that if we can just take a break so that I can get close enough to read what she wrote, I'll be able to get my head on straight and do my job.

Her brother is curious, too, but he knows she'll tell him later. I don't have that luxury anymore.

Focus, fuckhead. You have one job here. Play the damn drums.

Doing my best to keep her inked skin off my mind, I play for the rest of rehearsal without screwing up . . . much.

We don't take a break. Drill sergeant Dallas has returned with a vengeance.

It's comforting in a way, to know that here, even with everything that has happened, I still have a home. I still belong.

They really are my family, which is why I never wanted to cross the lines I can't uncross. As much as I want to believe that, though, that it'd be for the best if I'd never been inside Dixie's body, I don't regret it. I only regret the pain I caused, the way I handled, well, everything.

When rehearsal ends I feel bereft. Hearing Dixie sing was soothing balm to my jagged wounds and now that we're done, the rawness is returning.

I don't want to be away from them, don't want to go back to an empty trailer on the side of the highway, but Dixie has her shield up and I am fluent in reading her emotions. So I pack up quietly and head to the truck I borrowed from Mr. Kyung to get here.

"Hey, man," Dallas calls out. "Want to get some food?"

I do. I want to have a meal with the only two people in the world who've ever given a damn about me. I want to sit and talk and crack jokes and hear Dixie's laugh. I want it more than I want food or water or air. But the flash of pain on Dixie's face hits me like a slap. "Can't. I need to get back to the Tavern. Jake covered for me but I need to get going."

"All right. Holler at me if you need anything."

"Will do," I call out before climbing into the truck. I've only just shut my door when the one on the other side opens.

"Give a girl a ride? I feel like playing some more so I thought I'd drop by the Tavern, too. Work this new song out on that piano."

"I . . . you . . . uh," I answer, but it comes out jumbled and all run together so it sounds like a grunted battle cry of some sort.

Verbal skills have vacated the premises.

"Yes or no, Gav? If you don't want me to ride with you it's no big. Dallas can run me by there or I can just work on the song at home."

I have no idea how she can be so relaxed, so nonchalant after what I did, how I treated her.

I love you, Gavin. Bigger than your mistakes and bigger than the pain you cause me.

"No, it's cool. I mean, yeah. Yes, you can ride—I can give you a ride . . . I can . . ."

Fuck it all.

"So . . . that's a yes then?" She hangs on to the door as if waiting to figure out if she should climb in or slam it in my face.

I nod. Sentences are apparently outside my realm of capability at the moment.

Staring straight ahead, I force myself not to stare at her arms while she buckles in. Dallas doesn't look thrilled as we pull past him but Dixie's a big girl now. She makes her own decisions. Not necessarily great ones, but they're hers to make.

"I'm sorry. I'm so damn sorry that I hurt you, that I came there drunk, that your pain was some half-assed premeditated attempt on my part at setting you free from my bullshit. I saw today, though, that what Dallas keeps saying is true. I won't ever really be able to cut either of you off because you're my family and that won't ever change unless either of you want it to."

"We won't," she says abruptly. "Ever."

I nod. Neither of us says much for a few minutes. It's not uncomfortable silence, though, just intense and thick with emotions and words we aren't ready to say just yet.

I sneak a quick look at her left arm but all I can make out are the words *addicted* and *poison*.

"Shoot," Dixie says suddenly while looking at her cell phone in her hand. "I forgot. Crap. Can you just drop me at home?"

I turn the truck around and hop on a back road I know will be a shortcut. "Sure."

"I'm so sorry. I hope I don't make you late for work."

"It's fine. I don't think the place will burn down without me."

She laughs softly and the sound warms my chest. "I have this one kid . . . he doesn't seem to like playing piano much but he shows up without fail. Barely talks, just kind of wanders over to the house. Reminds me of someone else I used to know."

A warning bell goes off in my head but I'm not sure why.

"I checked around and his name is Liam Andrews but I don't know much about him. I think he lives near you and I'm hoping he's not crossing the interstate by himself. Can't seem to find out much about his family."

"Andrews, you say?" There is only one Andrews near me.

No, please, please do not let her be even remotely associated with Carl fucking Andrews.

"Yeah, why? You know him?"

My foot presses harder on the accelerator.

"Gavin!"

"Dixie," I begin slowly, working hard to keep my voice even. "I am trying not to get worked up and or lose my temper while operating a motor vehicle. But you absolutely cannot have anything to do with Carl Andrews or his kid. Ever."

"Um, well, I'm not sure Liam is *his* kid for certain. He's just constantly angry. I was going to talk to you about him because he kind of reminds me of you."

I'm mildy offended. "I'm not constantly angry." She gives me a look that says she's calling bullshit so I shrug. "Not *constantly.*"

"Okay, maybe I phrased that wrong." She frowns and I can see from side-eying her that she's thinking extremely hard and choosing her words carefully. "It's like he's struggling to . . . find . . . something. A reason to be afraid or upset or violent, or I don't know. He's just a really angry kid and he's only seven years old. What is there to be angry about at seven?"

My grip tightens on the steering wheel and I watch my knuckles turn white.

"If Carl Andrews is his dad, trust me, kid has plenty to be angry about."

Carl is the owner of the local crack house, the one my mom has been spending her time in lately. He was with her in the bar the other night and he and I are not on good terms at the moment. I know I am heading into something bad, I can feel it in my gut, but all I can think of is getting him away from Dixie and keeping him the hell away from her. And then the troubling thought tugging the edges of the blanket of rage currently covering my mind.

He got custody of that kid? How in the hell could anyone give that disgusting fucking animal a kid?

" . . . drum lessons?"

I only catch the last part of whatever she's saying because that's the thing about actual fits of rage, they sort of block out all your other senses.

"What?"

Dixie sighs and holds on to the dashboard as I take a curve a little faster than I should. "I was asking if you'd be willing to give Liam drum lessons. He has a lot of anger and it seems to help you, playing, so I thought it might help him."

"It does help me. But I'm not exactly kid friendly. You know this."

She scoffs at me. "How do you know? Have you ever hung out with any kids?"

I contemplate this, desperate to focus on something other than the thought of Carl alone with Dixie in her house. "No. I guess not."

"Then you don't know, do you? You could totally be kid friendly. But even if you aren't, this kid doesn't respond well to friendly anyways."

"No?"

She looks so sad for a moment I almost pull the truck over.

"No. And all my other kids like me—they hug me and call me 'Miss Dixie,' which is really sweet. But he just averts his eyes and keeps his gaze on everything but me."

Her mouth does the quirky turn-down thing it does when she's about to cry. Hearing her call them "my kids" helps me to appreciate how important giving lessons is to her. It's about more than filling her time. It's her way of sharing her gift even though she's not performing much right now.

"Maybe he just doesn't want the lessons but he isn't sure where else to go. Maybe you're the first smiling face he's ever seen." The sad truth is, that's pretty much how I ended up on her porch all those years ago. And why I kept coming back.

She appears only mildly comforted by my words. "I am pretty fun. We play games and I give out candy. I even made him cookies. Special ones, just for him. I even put his name on them in icing."

She's a persistent one, my Bluebird. She will make you love her one way or another if it's the last thing she does. Poor kid doesn't stand a chance.

"Cookies, huh? You never made me cookies with my name on them."

"Gav . . . I'm serious. I don't get it. He's like, I don't know, *afraid* of me . . . or something. I don't know why he keeps his shield up all the time but I can't reach him no matter what I do and it breaks my heart."

I break her heart, too. And I'm about to again because the very minute we pull up to her driveway I see the beat-up blue Ford pickup and beside the driver's door Carl Andrews is slapping the shit out of his kid. I see red and then blinding white.

Somehow, I throw the truck in park. Somehow I get out and get to Carl before he can land another blow to the back of his kid's head.

They always hit you in the back of the head because marking your face up will get social services called. It's like they have a special seminar for child abusers.

One minute I'm there, in the moment, and the next thing I know I'm transported back in time to when one of the dealers my mom used to let crash with us used me as a punching bag and Carl's face transforms into his.

Devlan was his name and I was sure he was the devil himself.

I can hear her screaming from somewhere behind me. Begging me to stop.

I know it's because of me, but I can't stop.

I just can't.

When the police pull me off Carl he isn't moving.

And I can't feel my hands.

17 | Dixie

"HE MADE BAIL. I HAD TO CALL A BONDSMAN," I TELL MY BROTHER over the phone. For the first time I'm grateful that Katrina Garrison got arrested during Austin MusicFest and I knew what to do because I'd gone with Gavin to bail her out.

"They're going to charge him with assault," Dallas says evenly. "He has an attorney from . . . previous stuff. I just talked to her."

"Previous stuff?" After seeing the side of Gavin I saw tonight and now this, I feel like maybe I don't know him at all. Maybe he's always kept a part of himself hidden from me and I'm starting to understand why.

"Long story. And one he should tell you."

I sigh. Bro code. Those two have always kept secrets from me for as long as we've known each other and, frankly, it's getting old.

"According to the arresting officer, Carl regained consciousness in the ambulance and said Gavin had assaulted him before. Do you know anything about that?"

Dallas sighs loudly and I know I'm not going to get an answer.

I huff out a breath right back. "Look, I know you have the nursery to finish, and Robyn probably needs you, but I . . . I can deal with getting him out I just . . ."

"I'll be there in under an hour. Promise."

"Thanks, Dallas."

"Hey, Dix?"

"Yeah?"

"Gavin's hands . . . are they majorly fucked-up?"

It takes me a second to realize why this is even an issue worth discussing at a time like this. Musicians have to be careful with their hands, especially if they use them to make a living. They can be as important as any instrument.

We have only one more week until the battle, but if Gavin's fingers or knuckles are broken, he won't be a part of it.

"There was a lot of blood, D," I whisper, closing my eyes and trying not to remember that terrifying look in his eyes as he pounded on Carl. I was able to get Liam out of the way but just barely. "I don't know if it was his or Carl's."

My voice wavers at the end because the last few hours have been a complete draining nightmare.

Watching Gavin brutally attack another human being like that, watching the cops cuff him and put him in the back of the car, getting Mrs. Lawson to keep Liam while his dad is in the hospital. It hits me all at once when the adrenaline rush wears off and I am emotionally and physically exhausted.

As much as I know in my heart what Gavin did was wrong, I saw Carl hit Liam, saw the way Liam cowered in fear, and honest to God, I wanted to pummel the son of a bitch myself. I was torn between pulling Liam away and cheering Gavin on. Not sure what that says about me.

"Okay. Don't worry about that right now. I'll take him to get an X-ray when they release him. See you soon."

I mumble goodbye to my brother and drop heavily into a metal folding chair. When we disconnect our call I see the time on my phone. It's nearly one in the morning. I've been here for over four hours and I have no idea when they're going to let him out.

"Here, sleepyhead," I hear my brother's voice say from beside me. "Drink this."

I blink myself out of the nightmare I was having about Gavin being arrested only to find it wasn't a nightmare at all. I'm still at the county jail but at least Dallas is here now. And he has coffee, good coffee from the all-night donut shop next door and not the crappy weak kind they have here.

He looks as tired as I feel and like he could use a shower and a shave.

"Sorry you had to come all this way," I tell him. My voice sounds like that of a transvestite phone sex operator. Not that I know what they would sound like but I imagine it would be close to how I sound right now. I make a mental note to add that to the list of backup careers.

"Don't be. I would've been super-pissed if you hadn't called me."

I give him a pointed look that he doesn't seem to understand. "I caught a glimpse of the arresting officer's computer screen while I was giving my statement. Gavin's record was pulled up. This isn't Gavin's first rodeo and guess whose name is always on the bailed-out-by line?"

Except once. One of the times Gavin's mom's name was typed in, which makes me wonder if he owed her last time and that's why he drove all the way here from Austin. I couldn't decipher the exact things he'd been arrested for because they were in number codes but considering I never knew he'd gotten arrested, it hurt to see that he was in the system at all, regardless of what each time was for.

"It's complicated, Dixie Leigh," Dallas says before taking a long drink from his own coffee cup. "You were in Houston for most of it."

I narrow my eyes at him. "The two of you are eventually going to tell me exactly what happened while I was gone."

Dallas averts his gaze from mine.

"Dallas Walker Lark, I am serious. If we are going to do the band thing, for real, like one hundred percent all in, this keeping stuff from me for my own good has got to stop. Period."

He nods and takes another drink. "So you're still good with that? Giving it another shot and going all in?"

I nod. "You know I am. But on two conditions."

Dallas's eyes lighten a shade. "Name 'em."

"One, you and Gavin have got to come clean about everything. Everything and anything I missed or that has been kept from me."

Dallas's eyes go dim. "Dix, I know you think that would help. Women typically do seem to assume they need every detail of every event ever, but trust me, there are things you are truly better off not knowing. Especially when it comes to Gavin."

I want to argue, but I can't unsee what I saw tonight. So maybe he has a point.

"But—"

"No buts. I'm sure he plans to tell you the bulk of it, but some details are just that, pointless details and mistakes that don't matter. You have to learn to accept what he's capable of giving and not tor-turing yourself over things that have nothing to do with you."

"If it has to do with him, it has to do with me," I say quietly.

My brother puts his arm around me and gives me a light squeeze. "I know it feels that way sometimes, but believe me, even if that's true, it would kill him for you to know some of the things he's done at his lowest points."

"It's killing me not knowing."

My brother takes a deep breath and rests his head on mine. "I know, little sister. I'm sorry."

The clack of heels rings out like gunfire on the tile floor. I glance around Dallas and see her, the owner of the heels and the purposeful walk.

Gavin's complicated blonde.

She looks entirely too put together for nearly two in the morning with her white silk shirt and black dress pants. I can't be sure because I can't see the bottoms, but I'm almost positive her heels are Louboutins. Robyn has a similar pair.

"What is she doing here?" Maybe it's exhaustion or sleep deprivation, but seeing her here now confuses me to no end.

"Her name is Ashley Weisman. She's his attorney."

She looks too young to be an attorney, but whatever. And the way she was behaving with Gavin the night I first saw him at the Tavern sure didn't look like an attorney-client relationship to me, unless there are extra attorney-client privileges I don't know about.

I can feel my anxiety amping up as we watch her confer with an officer at the front desk.

When she walks over toward us, my heart pounds harder with each noisy step she takes. "How in the world did he afford her?"

Dallas closes his eyes as if I have asked a question far too complicated for him to answer. "It's—"

"Do not say 'complicated.' I am serious," I warn him. "It's not a hard question. Lawyers cost money. She looks expensive. Gavin is not exactly rolling in cash." I slow my speech to an intentionally drawn-out speed. "How. Did. He. Pay. For. Her. Services?"

He tries to look away before I see it, but Gavin is right. My brother and I do not have any type of poker face to speak of. We wear everything we think and feel right there for the world to see.

What I just saw makes my stomach clench and my chest ache. I can already smell her expensive perfume from where I'm sitting and she's not even all the way to us yet.

"She hardly seems like his type," I grumble under my breath. But then maybe I don't know Gavin's type. Maybe she's exactly his type.

He said he loved me.

Over and over actually. I tried not to make a "thing" of it because he can be twitchy when it comes to emotions, but he said it.

The corners of Dallas's mouth quirk up slightly. "She isn't. Believe me."

Ashley the Expensive Lawyer who apparently accepts sexual favors as payment makes a beeline for Dallas.

"Mr. Lark," she says with alert green eyes. "I'm Ashley Weisman. We spoke on the phone earlier. Thank you so much for calling me."

"No, problem. Thank you for coming out so late."

I have a childlike urge to kick her in the shin.

"I'm Dixie," I say slightly louder than necessary while stepping between them and shoving my hand at her. The surprise is evident on her face. "And now that we're all acquainted, can you tell us how much longer it will be until they let him go?"

"Ah, yes. The piano player. From the bar," she says as if the words taste bad in her mouth. "I remember." It's clear she's sizing me up and I make a point to not shrink in her presence.

Dallas looks confused by her statement and I attempt to mimic his expression. "Glad I made an impression. I don't recall having met you."

A twinge of annoyance creases her delicate features but I just smile. Once upon a time I was intimidated by women like her. Polished. Professional. Sophisticated in ways I could and would never be. But after the Mandy Lantram Experience, I have realized that we are all just human beings and that each of us has our own kind of beauty and our own flaws.

"Yes, well, I don't think we ever officially met. Gavin doesn't typically do well with introductions."

She knows what he typically does or doesn't do well with?

"And how do you know him, exactly? Gavin, I mean."

Ashley glances at Dallas and I dare him with my eyes to so much as give a slight shake of his head to deter her from answering. He looks away as if suddenly captivated by an immensely intriguing vending machine in the corner.

"He's a friend. And a client when necessary," she informs me with a smug grin. "Which seems to be quite often here lately."

"Yes, well, as I said before, thanks for coming out so late," Dallas repeats. "And were you able to get them to let him go tonight?"

She returns her attention to my brother and tucks a thick piece of her hair behind her left ear. "Unfortunately, due to his probation and the violent nature of the crime, he is required to stay for twenty-four hours."

My heart sinks like a stone to the pit of my stomach at the thought of him sleeping in a cold, lonely jail cell tonight. "So they won't let him out until tomorrow around eight or nine P.M.?" The night has been such a blur, I'm not even sure what time he was booked.

"Correct. But sometimes with shift change they let folks out a little early. If you're coming to pick him up, I'd come around six or six thirty. Of course I'd be happy to—"

"We'll be picking him up," I announce. "No need for you to come all this way again."

Likely sensing my tone, Dallas pipes up with another question. "What about his hand? Is there a way to get him any medical attention for it tonight? Did you tell them he was a musician?"

"They allowed him to have a splint and an ice pack. I'm afraid that's about all that's available at this facility."

My brother nods. "That's better than nothing, I suppose."

She smiles warmly while handing Dallas a business card from her purse. "Here's this if you need anything, anything at all." Her eyes are slightly tighter when she turns to me. "You witnessed what happened, correct?"

I nod. "I did. Carl had clearly not known Liam had been coming to my place because he was out of the truck, slapping him and trying to shove him inside the cab before . . . before Gavin stopped him."

Her mouth purses and she appears contemplative for a few seconds. "Well, that's good—not that he was mistreating his son but that you saw the abuse. Although I wish there had been another eyewitness that would be willing to verify your statement. Clearly you have a bias in Gavin's favor so that might prejudice your statement a bit. The ADA might not care about the defendant's girlfriend's interpretation of events. I know how they think. I know several of them personally."

I feel my eyes narrow. I backed down with Mandy Lantram. Too bad for this chick I've grown up a lot since then. I am a reliable and credible witness, dammit. "I'm sure you do—"

"Need to get going home before it gets too late. Have a good evening, Ms. Weisman."

Dallas nods to dismiss her but she stays put. "Please, call me Ashley."

"Have a good evening, Ms. Weisman," I say evenly, meeting her eyes. "Thank you for your help."

"It's my job. You do the same."

"Will do," Dallas says.

Once she's out of earshot, I hold out my hand. "Give it."

"What?"

"Her card. Give it to me."

Dallas frowns. "Okay." He hands me the sleek black card with white and silver print. "So now, what do we do about Gavin?"

"First, you go home and get some sleep. You look dead on your feet."

"Gee, thanks."

"It's true. Go get some rest and I'll stay here and hassle them a little more about maybe checking on his hands. If he's injured badly we'll have to cancel the Phi Kap gig and save his strength for the battle. I'll come home soon and crash and we can come back tomorrow evening and pick him up."

We hug goodbye but when I pull EmmyLou into my driveway I sit for a few moments, reliving the fight I never saw coming.

I wish I'd asked Dallas the question I need the answer to the most.

After everything, after Gavin is out of jail, after I demand they come clean about the year I was in Houston and everything is out in the open . . . then what?

18 | Gavin

"SHE CANNOT SEE ME LIKE THIS, DALLAS. I MEAN IT." I'M GRIPPING the phone tightly and my right leg is bouncing so rapidly I look like I'm having withdrawal symptoms.

He nods on the other side of the glass. "I know. But listen, the situation with your attorney and Dixie facing off . . . It's like I said before, either you're going to come clean about the past or it's going to get out ahead of you. You need to talk to her. Soon."

I nod several times. "I will."

"She says she's not doing the battle or moving forward with the band until we come clean about everything. I don't think she's kidding."

"I don't think she is, either." I bite a loose piece of skin off the side of my thumb. "And I don't know if she's going to be able to go through with it if she knows everything. Especially after what she saw last night."

He doesn't say anything right away but his demeanor changes dramatically and I know he wants to cuss. "What she saw, Gavin, was a child abuser get what he deserved. Stop beating yourself up already. Speaking of beatings, how's the hand?"

My eyes drop to the swollen, bruised, and scabbed-over knuckles on my right hand.

"Still attached."

Dallas frowns. "I'm serious, man. Between worrying about whether or not Dixie's going to bail because of your bullshit or if your hand is going to be functioning by Friday night, I am stressed the fuck out."

All I can do is give him the "sorry I'm such a major fuckup" look that I have to give a lot of people that I disappoint.

The officer standing behind me gives the two-minute warning.

Dallas appears to be doing a sort of deep-breathing thing Robyn probably makes him do.

"You okay, man?"

"Yeah, just trying to get centered," he tells me.

"Centered, huh? How's that working out for you?"

He smirks. "Scale of one to ten, how centered do I seem?" He rakes his free hand through his hair and my honest answer is negative fifteen.

"Five. Give or take a few."

Dallas shakes his head. "Sometimes I think I should just call Robyn's uncle and see if he needs me to play backup guitar for his Elvis act."

I open my mouth to make a joke, but then I remember something important—something that kept me awake all night other than the sweat- and urine-scented mattress I had to try to sleep on in a six-by-eight cell.

"Wait," I say when the officer taps me on the shoulder, meaning I have thirty seconds left. "I need you to do something for me," I say to Dallas.

"I know, man. We'll be back in a few short hours to pick you up. Your attorney said it could be as early as six or as late as eight thirty."

I want to laugh at Dallas because, God love him, I'm not scheduling a fucking manscaping appointment. I'm in jail. They can let me out—or not—whenever they feel like it.

"Right. No rush because paperwork and all that takes a while. But that's not what I need. I need you to tell Dixie to call Sheila Montgomery at Child Protective Services. Sheila can make sure Liam doesn't have to go back to his abusive father even once he's out of the hospital."

Dallas whips out his pen and the small notebook he keeps in his back pocket for song lyrics. "Shee-La Mont-gum-er-ee," he says as he writes each syllable. "Got it. Anything else? Need one of those prepaid cards for food or money for vending machines or—"

"Time's up," the officer behind me announces and there's a click. I shake my head to his last question. I can't hear the rest of what he's saying but he shows me the notebook where he wrote the social worker's name and I feel a few ounces of relief.

At least maybe that kid can get the kind of help I never could. Maybe someone will stand a chance of being better than what I've become.

"Garrison, you're up," a booming voice calls, sending my name ricocheting off the cell walls.

I fell asleep sitting up on the bed because I couldn't bring myself to lie on it.

Having grown up with a junkie for a mother, I can handle going without food. I didn't touch anything that was served through the slot in the cell door because I know a few guys who work at this particular establishment and they've told me some disgusting shit that has been done to food. But I cannot handle the feel of filth. I grew up in it and I hate it. I need a shower more than I need air right now. I also want to shave my face before I see Dixie but I know she's going to be out there as well as I know my own name.

I shuffle in line with the other guys heading to where we pick up the meager personal belongings we came with. I give my name and Social Security number to an African-American female officer who looks tired as she practically tosses a large Ziploc bag at me. Next is the paperwork part and I have to sign that, yes, I will appear in court on the determined date that will be sent to me by mail, and yes, I understand the conditions of my release.

Next is the bathroom, where I toss this ugly orange jumpsuit into the designated bin and put back on clothes that are partially covered in dried blood. Most of which isn't mine.

Great.

Filthy and blood-covered. Nothing says working on reformation and redemption like that particular combination. Naturally it would be my "Drummers Hit It Harder" T-shirt that I happened to be wearing when I nearly beat a man to death.

Basically I am karma's bitch right now.

Once I've changed, I wash my hands, splash some water on my face, and tuck my wallet into the back pocket of my jeans along with my folded-up pink and yellow release papers and dead-as-hell cell phone.

I exit the bathroom and show my ID at the final desk.

Walking out in the dingy gray waiting area would be a relief if she weren't standing there looking so delectable as she argues with the officer at the front desk.

"It's after ten. His attorney said eight thirty at the—"

Dixie stops midsentence when she sees me.

"Hey. There he is," Dallas calls out. He stands and strides over to me looking as worn down as I feel.

"Barely," I answer honestly.

Dixie hangs back but I can see every emotion she feels playing on a steady loop in her eyes.

Happiness. Concern. Longing. Confusion. Doubt. And the worst one of all.

Fear.

I don't know if she's afraid for me or afraid of me.

I can't stand the thought of it being that second one.

As the three of us walk to the exit, I give her the most comforting smile I can manage and meet her eyes when I say, "Hey, Bluebird. I meant to write while I was locked up but they wouldn't give me a pen."

The hint of a smile pulls at the right side of her beautiful mouth. "Got you some dinner. It might be cold, but it's got to be better than whatever they had." She produces a Jimmy Johns bag that I know will contain my favorite, a Vito sub, no onions, extra cheese, and heavy on the dressing. I can see a couple of bags of chips inside, too, and I want to wrap my arms around her or kiss her to say thank you but I know it wouldn't be an okay thing to do right now.

It's just a sandwich and yet knowing that she cared about me like that, that she took time out of her life to get my favorite one, and that she's paid attention over the years to how I like it . . . it does something to me. They say a way to a man's heart is through his stomach and they might be on to something. Whoever the hell "they" are.

"You need anything?"

"Just this sandwich and a shower and I'll be a new man." Or closer to being one, anyway.

We reach Dallas's truck and I open the door for Dixie. She climbs in and my eyes drop to her ass. Blood shoots to my dick, waking him as I remember taking her from behind. I want to kick my own ass right now. Here she is being so kind and sweet to me after everything I've done and I'm acting like a man who just did a yearlong stint in the state pen, not an overnight at county.

Swallowing hard and trying to think of fluffy bunnies and other non-erection-inducing images, I get into Dallas's truck and face forward for the entire drive.

"You should probably eat something, man. You look pale as fuck and like someone backed over you with their car."

Leave it to Dallas to give it to me straight.

"Well, I didn't win the cell block modeling competition, so you're probably right." I reach into the bag and pull out the chips. Once I've opened the bag, I offer it to Dixie and she shakes her head.

"I already ate. Thanks, though."

Her voice sounds strange. Strained somehow.

"You okay?" Despite my self-imposed ban on checking her out, I turn and examine her for signs of distress.

She avoids my eyes and a heavy weight settles onto my chest.

Maybe I've finally done it. Maybe seeing what she saw has finally shown her who I really am, and I didn't even intend for it to happen.

"I'm fine," she says quietly. "Tired."

I call bullshit. Dixie Lark is not a good liar. *Fine* is typically not a word you want to hear in the female vocabulary. Ever.

Dallas glances over at our exchange and I decide to save it for when we're alone—though I'm not sure when that will be. I have a lot of explaining to do, a good bit of begging, and probably some down-on-my-knees apologizing.

Tension and anxiety twist my insides into a complicated knot and I decide it's best to hold off on the sandwich while riding down a bumpy road in a pickup truck.

Dallas puts on his left blinker to head toward the highway and Dixie puts her hand on his arm.

"He's going to the house. With me."

Huh.

I don't know that I've ever seen her tell Dallas what to do. And technically she's telling me what to do, I suppose, but I do not feel at all inclined to argue. Except . . .

"I kind of need a shower. And clean clothes."

"You can borrow some of mine," Dallas says evenly as he drives on past the left turn.

"Okay. Thanks, man."

Dallas kind of grunts out his version of "you're welcome" and we continue to their house in silence.

When we pull into the driveway, I expect all three of us to get out and go inside but Dallas leaves the truck running.

"You're not staying?" Dixie asks him as she climbs out.

I watch their exchange, feeling a little like a voyeuristic third wheel and a lot like something is being discussed silently between them.

Dallas shakes his head. "I'm not. I've been away from Robyn for long enough."

"That's a five-hour drive, Dallas," Dixie reminds him, sounding unhappy about his leaving us alone.

He grins and nods. "I'm aware of this. I'm good. I'll text you when I get home."

"I don't have to stay if Dallas isn't," I tell Dixie quietly. The last time we were here alone, I was a monster of epic proportions. I can understand why she wouldn't be too thrilled for a sleepover.

Her eyes are tense when she looks up at me. There is so much there.

Dixie Lark in the daylight is beautiful. The sun seems to seek her out specifically and beams of light shoot off her skin and hair as if she were an ethereal creature come to life just to stand in sunshine. But at night?

At night her eyes gleam and moonlight turns her skin into a color that I have never seen on anyone else. Her ink paints a beautiful portrait on her delicate skin and it makes me wish I could draw or that I had a decent camera so I could capture the way she looks against the stark darkness of night.

"I want you to stay," she says, barely loud enough for me to hear over the rumble of Dallas's truck engine. "Please."

I have to close my eyes for a second because watching her right now will send my dick the wrong message entirely.

"Listen, I hate to be a dick," Dallas breaks in, "but we only have a few days until the Phi Kap gig, then the battle, and your hand looks like hell, Garrison."

Both Dixie and I snap to attention at his interruption of our moment. He's facing us, leaning forward on his steering wheel and looking like he's barely resisting the urge to throttle us both.

"More importantly, you two obviously have some major shit to work out and I can tell you both from personal experience, if you can't find some sort of common ground before the show, there's no point in even bothering. Either one or both of you will be distracted and we'll ruin any shot the band has at winning." He glares for a minute but then his gaze softens. "I love you both and I won't try and tell you how to live your lives or what I think is the best solution for everyone. But I will tell you that while I understand that nothing can be resolved in one night, I do think it would be a good idea to tell each other some hard truths." He hits me hard with a pointed stare. Then his tone softens slightly. "Better now than the night before the battle."

"Good night, Dallas," Dixie says evenly. "I'll call you tomorrow. Text and let me know you get home safe, please."

"Good night, you two," Dallas answers reluctantly. "Try not to kill each other."

Dixie rolls her eyes and slams his truck door. Hard.

This is the second time in a matter of minutes that I've seen Dixie let Dallas know how it's going to be. I don't think I've seen that happen ever in my eleven, almost twelve years of knowing them.

I'm still in shock as we head into the house.

Dixie switches the lights on and I stand in the entryway still holding my bag of food and unsure of what to do with myself.

"I'll get you something to drink," she says, adding "sit" and nodding toward the couch before she disappears into the kitchen.

I follow her orders like a zombie on autopilot.

Sitting down, I open my sandwich, unsurprised when I realize that she did, in fact, order it exactly as I do.

"Tea or Coke or water?" she calls from the other room.

"Coke is fine," I answer, knowing I need the caffeine, as this is probably going to end up being a longer night than either of us is prepared for.

Dallas is right. It's time to tell her the truth.

I just wish it didn't have to come on the heels of my beating a man in front of her and her picking me up at jail. So much for being the kind of man she deserves.

When she returns with a can of soda, I offer her half my sandwich. Or the whole thing. Or my heart and soul and whatever else she wants.

"You sure you're not hungry?"

She nods. "I ate earlier."

"You're sure?"

She nods again. "Positive. Promise."

It only takes a few bites until I've pretty much demolished the sandwich and another bag of chips. I drain the can of Coke while Dixie sips the one she carried in for herself.

"I left a message for Sheila Montgomery," she informs me. "But she hasn't called me back yet."

"Good. She will. When she does, give her Carl's name and address and any information you have on Liam."

Dixie watches me closely. "Okay. I will. And I called the hospital and Carl was moved out of intensive care into a regular room. He'll be out this time tomorrow or the next day."

"Where's the kid?"

Dixie blanches like I've hurt her somehow. "Liam. His name is Liam. He's staying right next door actually, with my neighbor, Mrs. Lawson. She's nice. A little eccentric and maybe kind of crazy about her cats, but she's a sweet lady. He's safe there. And her cookies are probably better than mine."

She smiles and the tension weighing on my chest lightens somewhat.

"Good. That's good."

"So . . . how long do you think Carl has been abusing him?"

I chew my food slowly in an attempt to put off answering.

Right here is the crux of everything that separates my world from hers. She looks at everyone and sees the light in them, the good, the potential. Whereas I see only darkness. The bad. The danger.

"Probably since he was born, Dix. Carl Andrews basically runs the local crack house."

Dixie pales. "Seriously?"

I nod. "Yeah, babe. Seriously. And by runs, I mean he lives there. It actually is *his* house."

Her brow wrinkles as I continue, explaining as gently as I know how to.

"*Crack den* is a more appropriate term because it isn't much like a house or a home at all. On the outside maybe. On the inside, these places are gutted. Sparse furniture, usually filthy, and crack pipes and strung-out junkies typically litter the floors and fill the corners." I stare at my hands while I finish because I can't bear to see how much pain this is causing her to hear. I'm tainting her worldview, casting my dark shadows on her light. "People come and go. Some looking for a fix, some looking for revenge if they feel they got sold something less than acceptable quality, some so high they don't even know what they're doing there, it's just become a beacon they end up at because they've been so many times."

When I finally look up, she's shaking her head. "No. No. His house can't be like that. He has a kid. Surely someone would . . ."

But here I sit, right in front of her. Living proof that someone might not.

Ever.

Dallas and Dixie's grandparents did the best they could to help me, to keep me fed and clean and safe once I was hanging out with their grandkids. But before that, there was no one. I lived eleven years in a filthy, foodless, Hell on Earth. I guess it says something that I survived it, but I'm not sure what it says.

"Seeing what we saw, seeing Carl hitting him like that . . . *hard*. It just . . . it triggered something in me. Kid barely flinched. He was used to it. Expecting it. It brought back . . . memories."

When I look up, it's Dixie sitting there with her eyes closed. Tears stream silently down her face and I return my gaze to my busted hand. "I know," she whispers. "It triggered something in me, too, Gav. If you hadn't stopped him, you would've had to pull me off of him."

"I just lost it. I didn't mean for it to go that far. I just wanted to stop him." The center of my chest aches. I wish she hadn't seen any of it, seen Carl hurting a child she cares about, seen me losing control the way I did. But there's not much I can do about any of that right now.

"I'm glad," she chokes out after a few seconds of quiet. "I saw the way Liam was cowering in terror. I've seen the way he is. Skittish. Afraid of everyone. Now I know why. I'm glad you did what you did."

Her approval catches me off guard. She's literally the most harmless person I know and here she is sounding bloodthirsty and honestly glad. "It's still not okay," I say. "We should've just called the cops. It's not the way I should've handled it in front of you or the kid."

"Gavin," she says evenly, suddenly moving closer to me and touching her fingers to the bottom of my chin until I look up at her. "His name is Liam. I want you to learn it. To know it. To know him. Say it."

I can't. I don't want to.

Because then he's real. Then he's an actual person, an actual child being abused and exposed to God knows what kind of shit right up the street from me.

He is me.

I shake my head, but she isn't having it. "Say it. Please."

"Liam."

It doesn't come out easy, but I manage, choking down the bile in my throat while the images of the many possible scenarios Liam has endured in his young life flash through my mind.

"Thank you."

Once the distraction of food and beverage is gone, I open my mouth to say something else but she beats me to it.

"Ready for that shower now?"

I pull in some much-needed air and nod. "Yeah."

She stands abruptly. "If you give me your, um, clothes, I'll go ahead and throw them in the washer."

"Throw them in the garbage if you want. I know you never liked this shirt anyway."

Dixie offers me a small smile and I accept the gift. "Nah, it's not so bad. Besides, it's true apparently."

Is she flirting with me? I'm not sure so I just sit stoically and wait for her to order me to the shower. I don't have to wait long.

"Go get naked, Gav. Toss the clothes out into the hall."

"Yes, ma'am."

Standing and collecting my sandwich wrapper and empty potato chip bag, I glance at her. She's biting her bottom lips as if she's nervous.

I want to ask if she's all right but I know I'm not ready for the answer just yet. After I've tossed my trash in the garbage, I head to the hallway bathroom.

The moment I see myself in the mirror, I completely forget the past few hours.

Jesus.

My left cheek has the beginnings of a faint bruise from where Carl Andrews was able to land a glancing blow before I took him down. My shirt looks like a canvas someone streaked with red and black paint in an attempt to imitate Jackson Pollock.

I've tried not to think about my right hand much. It aches like a bitch, deep down to the bones. The swelling has gone down a little, but I'm betting something in there is good and broken.

Part of me wants to go get my kit right now and give playing a shot just to see if I can. But the other part of me wants to put that off for as long as possible because I don't want to know if I can't.

I make a fist and open it a few times until the pain is too much.

Turning away from the monster in the mirror, I grab the hem of my blood-soaked shirt and yank it over my head. Then I unbutton my jeans and let them fall to the floor. I step out of them before pulling the waistband of my boxer briefs down and exposing my still half-hard-from-being-around-Dixie-Lark dick.

She's so close and the scent of her, wildflowers and vanilla and something unidentifiable that reminds me of moonlit nights by the lake, has me contemplating testing out the functionality of my hand in a way that doesn't involve the drums. It'd probably be a good idea anyway—take the edge off so I don't do anything stupid later.

As much as the counseling has helped, I'm still addicted to one thing.

It's not drugs, or alcohol, or even sexual gratification and physical intimacy.

It's her.

It's why I can't let go even when I know I should.

I take my now-throbbing cock into my left hand and use my right one to turn on the shower. I've just pulled the curtain back and prepared to step inside when the door swings open unexpectedly.

"Gav, you forgot to get a tow—"

Dixie halts the second she sees me standing there in all of my buck-naked glory. I drop my cock but he remains standing at attention.

She just stands there, dumbstruck and holding a folded white bath towel. Pink heat sweeps across her cheeks and I want to laugh at first at how shy she seems even though she's seen me naked before. Recently.

"Thanks, Bluebird," I say, reaching for the towel and setting it on the rack beside the wall.

"I thought you were in the shower already," she whispers. Dixie's eyes drop to my dick and then she averts her gaze quickly and stammers. "Um, okay then. I'll just grab these and, um . . ."

She leans down to get my clothes off the floor and my dick salutes her as she lowers her face to his level.

"Careful, Bluebird," I say when I see her lick her lips and then bite that delectable bottom one. "I'm going to behave myself this evening. He may not. He definitely won't if you keep looking at him like that."

She stands upright and her entire energy has shifted from nervous girl who accidentally walked in on her brother's best friend naked to confident, bold-as-hell woman who knows what she wants and is about to take it.

Retreat, soldier. I repeat, retreat now while you still can.

Fucking won't help us.

Well . . . it might temporarily alleviate some of the tension. But I know how this night is going to go. I'm going to tell her everything, even the shit Dallas said I should keep to myself. I would've waited until after the battle of the bands if Carl Andrews hadn't fucked up my whole world.

But when her eyes meet mine and I see it—the hunger and need blooming and swirling in her darkening eyes—I know it doesn't matter either way. She's strung as tightly as I am from all the recent insanity. She needs a release and she wants me to give it to her.

What my Bluebird wants, my Bluebird gets.

I just need to give her answers first.

19 | Dixie

Gavin and I have gotten pretty good at silent conversations over the years.

We're having one right now.

From the moment I saw him in the Tavern months ago, I have been in pain. A deep, wounding brand of pain that saturated my soul and seeped into the marrow of my bones.

I am in love with someone who is not good for me. Someone with darkness and addictions and more secrets than I can even imagine.

And I love him.

And love him.

And just when I think I can't, I love him some more.

Somewhere out there is a guy, an Afton Tate type who would make me laugh and come over and bring pizza and we'd have all-night jam sessions and really sweet and enjoyable sex and live happily ever after.

I have absolutely no interest whatsoever in meeting that guy. Ever.

I've probably met him a dozen times over already.

It's this beautiful, tortured man in front of me that I want more than I want air or water or food.

That I will always want.

My heart belongs to his heart. And whether he thinks he deserves me or not, his soul is forever connected to mine.

"I'm not good enough. I don't deserve you. I can't give you happily ever after," Gavin's eyes tell me.

"You can and you will," my eyes answer right back. Just in case he's not picking up the telepathic message, without a word I remove every stitch of clothing I have on.

His eyes widen and his exposed cock jerks suddenly. I take a step forward but he puts his hand out to stop me.

"Blue—"

I cut off what we both know will be a futile attempt at protest and take his hand in mine, guiding him into the now-steamy shower behind me.

There are questions in his gaze as he watches me beneath the spray of water. I move backward enough so that there is room for us both. I grab the bar of soap from the shelf built into the wall and lather it into my hands until they're covered with a thick, foamy layer of bubbles. Placing my hands on Gavin's chest, I begin to wash him and finally he closes his probing eyes.

We can have a question-and-answer session after.

I need this.

He needs this.

Sometimes that's all love is. Giving the other person what they need despite the price, despite the sacrifice or possibly painful outcome.

My hands glide across his chest, stroke up and down the thick bands of muscle on his arms, and linger across his chiseled abdomen.

"You're beautiful," I attempt to tell him with my appreciative stare.

He smiles and I know he knows.

I twirl my finger to let him know he needs to turn around and he complies. Leaning forward, he braces his arms on the wall while I scrub his back and legs.

His entire body twitches when I slip a soapy finger between the firm cheeks of his ass and I giggle.

"Easy," he says under his breath.

I smack his right ass cheek lightly.

"There. All clean." Next I step out of the line of the shower spray and watch while he rinses off.

I am wet in every way possible right now.

"My turn," Gavin says evenly, palming the bar of soap I just returned to the tray.

He gives me a much more thorough washing than I gave him, covering every inch of my skin with his strong, soapy hands.

I moan involuntarily when he digs his fingers into the flesh on my thighs and again when he massages my neck and shoulders. I'm practically panting when his fingers begin tracing the taut peaks of my breasts. He's behind me with his arms around me and I can feel his erection against my backside.

My body goes limp against him when he kneads my nipples between his thumb and forefinger.

"Gavin."

"Hmm?"

I smile because he's distracted—by me. By my body. Our connection is so powerful, I can hardly believe we denied it as long as we did.

I need him to make all the pain go away. What happened between us, the ways we've destroyed each other over the years, the lies, the images from the attack, the concerns about Liam. For right now, I need to be selfish and I need him to give me what I need.

"I need . . . I need the truth, please. And maybe this isn't the time or place and maybe there will never be a time and place that feels right but . . . I need it. The other night," I begin to tell him, feeling unexpectedly desperate for *him* to know the truth. "I didn't mind the . . . dirty stuff. I *liked* it."

His head snaps up and his eyes meet mine. "I took it too far. I—"

"I can handle it, Gav. If you need a hate fuck or a punishment fuck or a talk-dirty-to-me fuck, I can handle it. As long as it's not meant to teach me some type of bullshit lesson about how terrible you are."

I press my mouth to his, enjoying the sensation when he breaches the seam of my lips to sweep his tongue inside.

"I am so sorry, baby," he says while burying his face in my neck. "You know I didn't mean any of the—"

"I know, Gavin. I know you better than you think I do. I want all of you. The light and the dark and the broken parts."

"I am all broken parts," he says into my ear. "That's all I am."

"We are all broken. That's how the light gets in," I tell him, quoting something I read years ago in high school. Hemingway, I think it was. I remember reading it and thinking immediately of Gavin, but then I am always thinking of him in one way or another.

Gavin washes and rinses my hair and his own and shuts the water off. I'm vaguely aware when he wraps me in the towel I brought him.

I want to protest when he lifts me off the ground and carries me to my bed like a bride over the threshold but I can't make my mouth form words. The room blurs and disappears.

"Looks like you're sleeping in the buff tonight, Bluebird," he tells me as he tucks me into my bed.

"Stay," I mumble, growing sleepier by the minute as the last twenty-four hours crashes down on me hard. "Please."

"I am," he tells me. But I mean here, in my room, in my bed. I'm too exhausted to verbalize it so I just pull at him until he gets the message and crawls into my bed, naked and damp from the shower, beside me.

"Sleep, baby. I'll be here when you wake up."

Sweeter words were never spoken.

I'm hot. Burning up and sweating.

I try to kick the blankets off me but something is holding them down. The harder I fight, the tighter they seem to pull in around me.

Blinking myself awake, I see Gavin's body draped around mine. As gently as I can manage, I ease myself out from under his large frame. He makes a small noise of complaint but eventually rolls over so I can get out from under the covers. God, he's like a human furnace. There is literally heat radiating from his skin.

A gentle pulsating throb alerts me to my never-ending need for the man in my bed so I kiss him softly on the back of his right shoulder.

It's been such a rough few days, I know he needs his rest. We both do. And yet, he's here, exposed and, for the time being, all mine. Our time together always feels so rushed, so temporary and frantic. I want to take my time exploring and savoring.

Running my fingers across his back and down his arm, I feel my need for him becoming more and more pronounced. Any physical contact with him whatsoever awakens every cell that makes up my being. I can't help but wonder if it's like this for everyone.

I scoot closer to his back, allowing my bare breasts to absorb his warmth. My hand trails lightly to his well-defined hip bones, dipping into the V just before his pelvis. I feel a bit like a pervy creeper, taking advantage of the access I have to him at the moment, but I can't stop myself.

When I let my wandering hand venture to the patch of hair between his hips, he twitches and groans lightly. Stroking downward,
I feel him rousing to meet my hand and then I am encircling him.

He's already half-hard as it is, but a few slides of my hand and his
erection springs to full mast. Being gentle in my ministration of his
most important body part is obviously frustrating him, judging from
the small exhalations of breath he begins releasing.

"Looking for something, Bluebird?" His voice is groggy but
amused.

I duck my head against him when he rolls back slightly. "Nope.
Found it."

"Did you now?"

My mess of hair falls forward as I lean forward to kiss his mouth.

He captures my wrists in his hand and slides me gently to the side.
"We should talk first."

"Okay, then. Me first," I say quietly, overwhelmed by the sense of
vulnerability I'm feeling. "I love you, Gavin Garrison. I love the feel
of you, the taste of you, the scent of you. I love the way you touch me
and the way you make me feel."

His eyes are on fire when they lock with mine. "I love you, too,
Bluebird. More than should even be possible. More than I ever knew
I could be capable of." His hands grip my waist tightly, denting the
flesh and claiming me as his.

His fingertips drift lazily up the backs of my thighs, tracing the
lower curve of my backside, causing me to twitch in response.

"Can we stay like this while we talk?" I plead weakly.

With a low chuckle, he gives my ass a squeeze. "We could. But we
probably shouldn't. Wouldn't get much talking done."

"You couldn't just let me lie here and die happy?" I tease. Truthfully, despite how aroused my naked body is, my heart is hammering

into my skull with an urgency demanding I do whatever is necessary to find out what happened the year I was in Houston.

Gavin is a vault; he always has been. A beautiful, bruised vault hiding the world's darkest secrets. Secrets I am equally terrified of knowing and not knowing.

He's not Clark Kent or Captain America. I always knew that. Gavin is much more of a Bruce Wayne minus the money. He's a dark hero fighting to be good when we all know he could go either way.

"I mean . . . I *can,*" he answers, stroking my hair and then my back. "If that's really what you want."

I sigh in his arms, soaking up the last ounces of vulnerable intimacy while I can.

"I'll make some coffee," I announce as I peel my reluctant body from his. Something about our closeness without having had sex seems more . . . primal. Or intimate. Or . . . I don't know. It's just more. "Sun will be up soon."

20 | Gavin

I'VE BEEN IN A LOT OF TOUGH AND PRECARIOUS SITUATIONS IN MY
life. Hell, my life *is* one big, complicated situation. But none have
been daunting to the point of debilitating the way facing Dixie Lark
is about to be.

It's as if I'm about to face a firing squad and I'm the one supplying
the ammo.

Once I pull on a pair of Dallas's old gym shorts and a T-shirt featuring the name of our high school football team, I make my way to
the kitchen, where I can hear Dixie making coffee. My feet are lead
weights as I move, begging me to slow down and reconsider before
I ruin everything good in my life only moments after finally getting
it back.

For a moment, I just stand there, watching her making coffee.

What would life be like if I were normal? Would it be like this?
Waking up to her, morning coffee with her, holding her in my arms
every night—it sounds like Heaven on Earth and like a life I could
never begin to be worthy of.

"Hey. You want it black as usual?"

I blank out for a second staring at her full mouth.

"Gav? Coffee?"

I shake my head. "Black is fine. Like my soul."

She gives me a pointed look but doesn't comment on my mood. I take the mug she hands me and lower myself into one of the wooden chairs at the table.

"So what did you want to tell me?" she asks tentatively, eyeing me carefully while sitting in the seat adjacent to mine.

I take a long swallow of hot coffee and then a deep breath. "What do you want to know?"

Something flashes in her eyes. Intrigue? Worry? I can't tell for sure.

"Everything," she whispers softly. Then a little louder, "And nothing."

I force a half smile. "Oh, that's all? That I can do."

Neither of us speaks for a few minutes but then she sets her mug aside and clasps her hands together on top of the table. Her stare meets mine, an immeasurable number of emotions swirling in her eyes, and I know this is the calm before the storm.

Maybe we should take cover, have this conversation beneath the table or locked in a bunker somewhere that we can't escape, can't walk out of until our issues are resolved.

"Why didn't you tell me you were home? Even if you didn't want to see me, it would've been nice to know without finding out like . . . like I did."

Man up and tell her the truth, Garrison. Before someone else does.

I stare at my coffee mug, realizing it says WORLD'S GREATEST NANA on it. Dixie's has sheet music printed across it and the words DEAR MUSIC, THANKS FOR THE THERAPY.

I spin mine in my hands a few times before answering.

"I didn't call you when I first came home because I needed time. There were things—like the probation situation I told you about—

that I wanted to get handled and squared away before contacting you. There was some jail time involved and I didn't want you coming to that place, though eventually I guess you had to anyway." Or she chose to. Whichever.

"Okay," she answers slowly, tracing the rim of her cup with one finger. "So let's back up. How did you end up on probation to begin with?"

And here we go.

Deep into the year that I think of as my dark period, which, with my life, is saying something.

"The year you were gone wasn't a great one. I wasn't making very good choices. I was using . . . and then I was in an accident. One that was my fault."

I see the ripple of disappointed sadness that crosses her features. No matter what I do, I will always hurt her in one way or another. The knowledge settles onto my chest like a ton of bricks.

Dixie looks momentarily like she can't decide which part to question first. "Using what exactly?"

I rub my fingers over my eyelids. "Coke mostly. It was around all the time. Guy my mom was seeing wasn't shy about sharing. I'd drink a little, do a few lines, and go play my drums until I couldn't move my arms."

She frowns. "Were you addicted?"

I nod. "I don't know. Sort of. It was like . . . like I was trading one addiction for another. Losing you and filling the void with getting high."

"I see." But I know her tone. She doesn't see. How could she? Dixie doesn't understand living a life of crime to make ends meet because she's never had to and she probably never would. She's moral and good and pure. "So you got caught? How?"

I sigh because this is the beginning of the end and I don't know what I thought but I'd hoped I'd somehow figure out a way to avoid this part. I didn't.

"I got busted for possession in a back alley behind a bar a few towns over. Got a suspended sentence, days on the shelf basically, court-ordered addiction counseling and community service for it because Ash—uh, my attorney—was able to plead it down. But I'd no sooner finished the court-mandated program than I got into an accident. I was high and it showed in the tox screen. Since I already had one major strike against me plus a few minor arrests for assault for petty bar fights and other BS, the punishment was a little heavier that time."

She sits there processing for a while and I sit there hating myself for tainting her with my fucked-upness.

In a way, I'm glad that much is out there. I feel like I can breathe a little easier. But in my heart I know I've glossed over the most painful details of that year and my Bluebird isn't stupid. She'll catch on and demand the full story.

It doesn't take long.

"Were you alone in the back alley? When you got busted?"

I shake my head but don't answer.

"So . . . did the other person get arrested?"

I nod.

"Gavin, don't turn mime on me right now, please."

I swallow hard and choke out a quick "Sorry."

God, I am so fucking sorry.

"They got arrested for drugs, too?"

I shake my head, and she narrows her eyes at me. "For performing a lewd act in public, Dix. That's what she got arrested for. Is that what you want to know? That I found the only peace I could with other women?" She flinches and a white-hot blanket of shame covers me. "I'm sorry. I know it doesn't mean anything right now, but for what it's worth, I am sorry."

I'd say it a million times if I could. More if I thought it would help.

"That's why Dallas got so mad when he caught us behind the bar in Nashville. Because he thought maybe we were . . ."

"Yeah. Probably," I answer shortly. It still pisses me off that he thinks I would've been doing anything like that with Dixie, but I try not to dwell.

"Jesus." She's quiet again, contemplating her next question, I assume. I'd rather be questioned by the FBI, by people I don't give a flying fuck about, instead of by the woman I love more than life itself. But she deserves the truth and it's time she got it. "The accident . . ."

My chest constricts as if she's placing cinder blocks squarely on it. "Yeah. It was bad. Nearly totaled Dallas's truck and gave both of us concussions and severe whiplash."

Dixie's eyes are wide when they meet mine. "*Both* of you? As in, you drove high with my brother, with my only fucking living relative, in the truck?"

Her arm swings left and takes her coffee cup off the table and onto the floor. She barely glances down at where the handle now lies broken.

Technically Dallas wasn't her only living relative at the time, but this hardly seems like the moment to mention that. I clean up the mess quickly and efficiently setting the cup and its handle back on the table while she continues gaping at me and waiting for her pound of flesh.

"Yeah, Dix. I did. And I'm sorry. God, I am so fucking sorry that happened. He'd been drinking Robyn off his mind and called me for a ride. I didn't realize how messed up either of us was until it was too late."

Dixie buries the palms of her hands into her eyes and remains still for several minutes before talking to me again. "So you got charged with all kinds of stuff from the accident then. How'd you get out of it?"

One hard question after another. "Ashley. The attorney that you met." And wanted to murder, from the looks of it.

"The attorney . . . *Ashley*," she begins, and I can hear the venom and hurt in her voice. "How'd you afford her?"

There's no way to sugarcoat my answer so I give it to her as gently as I can manage.

"Pretty much the same way I've always afforded things I wanted and couldn't pay for."

"Wow. Okay. I guess I kind of knew that, but hearing it . . . from you . . . Just . . . Wow."

Her chair scrapes the floor as she moves it back. She shoots upright and takes the two pieces of her glass to the sink, but I know what she's really doing. She's disgusted and she needs space from me. I can't blame her. I'm jealous. I wish *I* could get away from myself.

I hang my head and wait for the interrogation to continue.

Dixie busies herself using some type of glue to repair her mug and I finish my now cold, bitter coffee. She takes my cup and washes it before returning to sit down. "So you got help because the court made you, but it didn't work?"

I nod. "Pretty much. *Mandatory* rehab is kind of a joke. It doesn't take until you're there because you want to be, because you want help and you want to change." She nods as if this makes sense so I continue. "That time I was just going through the motions, complying with whatever simply to stay out of jail. But after the accident, I hit rock bottom. I was the worst off I ever was and Dallas dragged me out of my house, beat the hell out of me, and brought me here to dry out. I did and then I started trying to get some real help. It has helped and I still see an addiction counselor."

"What were you addicted to?"

Now there's the million-dollar question. Most addicts have a drug of choice. Heroin. Meth. Coke. Narcotics. Alcohol. Not that some people won't just take whatever for the hell of it, but actual addicts tend to have a preference.

Mine was none of the above.

"I don't know that I was ever actually addicted to one particular substance. My addiction issues were more . . ."

"Let me guess. Complicated?"

I nod. "Yeah. Pretty much."

Dixie hates the generic use of that word and I don't blame her. It's vague as hell and basically a cop-out.

"That still doesn't answer my question. What exactly were you addicted to then, Gav?"

A dull throb begins at my temples and lands in the center of my forehead. She waits patiently for my answer.

"Oblivion, Bluebird," I finally answer. "I was addicted to anything and everything that helped me to check out, to escape my reality, to forget."

"Forget what?" Her eyes are wide and round and shining with the promise of tears. Answering will only cause them to fall. But I have to. She deserves to know the truth.

"You."

An hour has passed since I answered her final question and she went outside to get some air. She must've needed a lot of air.

I step out onto the front porch but she's nowhere to be seen. Walking around the side of the house, I'm reminded of playing hide-and-seek as kids, of me and her and Dallas running and laughing and daring each other to do ridiculous things like mix Pop Rocks into a bottle of Pepsi and drink it all at once.

This house has been my safe place since the day I met the Lark siblings on the worst day of their young lives.

I'm so lost in memories, I think I see a younger version of myself sitting on the cracked concrete garden bench in the backyard.

He's got dark hair like me, ill-fitting clothes like I did at that age, though at least his are clean, and I can see from a few steps away fingerprint bruises around the back of his neck. I sported those once or twice in my childhood as well.

I glance around but there is only me and him. The overcast day makes it seem like a dream or maybe a hallucination.

"Hey there," I call out to make sure I'm not crazy.

He flinches and when he turns I know why. The last time this kid saw me I was beating his dad half to death right in front of him.

"This bench taken?" I ask, pointing to the other half.

He doesn't answer, just returns his gaze to the empty field behind the house.

I take that as permission to sit.

Well . . . this is fucking awkward. Dixie was wrong, I'm not kid friendly at all.

A small flock of birds take off nearby as if we have offended them with our presence.

"Guess the birds didn't want to hang with us," I say, hoping to show him I'm not the monster I probably seem like.

He turns dark eyes briefly on me then goes back to staring. "They're blue finches."

"Yeah, I know." I remember a day when Dallas and I found one by a pond where we mowed grass for summer money. It was beautiful and delicate and despite seeming as if it was done for, it eventually chirped loudly at us and flew off. That day I understood something, something about myself and about Dixie.

As long as she had hope in me, I would have hope in myself.

I've called her Bluebird ever since.

I tell my unexpected company the story about the bird and when I'm finished he actually looks slightly interested.

"What do you think happened to it? After it flew away?"

I think on this for a long minute. "I think it explored the world for a while until it met another bird to explore the world with it."

"Or maybe it died. Everyone dies. My mom died."

Fuck. Me.

I suck at kids.

I have no words for this. Except, "I'm sorry to hear that, man. That was probably tough to handle."

He doesn't respond. Taking a closer look, I realize he can't be more than six or seven or so. I try to remember what that is. First grade maybe? Second?

"Hey, what grade are you in?"

"First," he says quietly. "But I don't really go to school much. They don't like me there."

I remember that. Being the addict's kid, being dirty, being made fun of. You learn how to use your fists instead of your words pretty quickly. "Well, I like you. And I know Miss Dixie likes you. Maybe we can just have school right here. I bet she could teach us some stuff."

He actually almost smiles. He wants to smile.

I know why.

It's her. If anyone could reach this kid, it's her.

She reached me, after all.

"Have you seen her out here recently?"

He nods. "She went for a walk. She asked me to go but Mrs. Lawson told me not to go past this point and I didn't want to get . . ."

"Punished?" I finish for him because I know exactly what he's afraid of. Thankfully I put what he's afraid of in the hospital.

He just nods and looks away again. My instinct is to nudge him lightly but I don't because I know better. It took me years before I was okay with unexpected physical contact.

I glance over my shoulder and see Mrs. Lawson standing at her back patio door talking on the phone. I wave and she lifts a hand in response.

"For the record, Mrs. Lawson's brand of punishment isn't so bad," I say instead. "She'd just make you let her cat tell you your future."

One corner of his mouth perks up. "She already did. He's over there."

The darker of the two cats belonging to Dixie's neighbor is hiding under a patio chair.

"I think my future was bad," the kid next to me says. "Mrs. Lawson wouldn't tell me what it said but she's been on the phone crying for a long time."

"*Liam,*" I hear Dixie say in my head. "*His name is Liam.*"

"Nah," I say with a shrug. "Mrs. Lawson gets emotional sometimes. I wouldn't worry about it, Liam."

He angles his neck to face me and his eyebrows are raised. "How did you know my name?" His eyes are guarded, like this must be some sort of trick. I can already see him retreating.

"Miss Dixie told me," I answer, hoping that calms him.

"She's nice to me," he says quietly.

"She's a nice lady."

"Is she yours?"

Huh. His question throws me and I'm left gaping stupidly for a few seconds.

Is Dixie Lark mine?

I scratch my chin, remembering I need to shave, and cross my ankles out in front of me.

"Miss Dixie is her own woman. She doesn't belong to anyone but herself. But I hope, one day, that she will be with me because she chooses to. People can't really belong to other people exactly."

"Kids belong to parents," he argues.

"Kind of," I agree. "But not like possessions. Not like your baseball cards belong to you or your dog belongs to you. More like . . . you get . . ." I don't know what word I'm looking for but I'm struggling to find it.

"Stuck with them?"

Christ this kid is beating what little unbattered fraction of a soul I have left to hell and back.

"No, Liam. Not stuck." I watch his face to make sure I'm not upsetting him. "If the universe or the powers that be see fit to give a person a kid, they should consider themselves lucky. They should be the best parent that they can. They shouldn't . . ."

Get high. Disappear. Let the kid starve half to death before bringing home three-day-old pizza and calling it dinner.

I close my eyes because now I'm upsetting my fucking self.

" . . . mistreat them," I finally bring myself to say.

"But sometimes they do," he says quietly, somehow reading my mind. Do kids read minds? God, I hope not.

"Liam," Mrs. Lawson calls from her porch. "Come back inside and eat something, please."

"I gotta go." He stands and his shirt rides up enough that I can see old scars down his spine. My rage flares and I regret for a moment that I didn't go ahead and kill Carl Andrews and do this kid and the world a favor.

"Okay. Nice talking to you."

He nods and then walks quickly and stiffly over to Mrs. Lawson.

I watch the blue finches come and go for a while, and wonder the entire time where my Bluebird went.

21 | Dixie

AFTER A WALK AROUND THE BLOCK, MY HEAD IS SLIGHTLY clearer. But so is my frustration.

Gavin is sitting out back on the bench when I return.

"So everything is my fault then? I went to college and all hell broke lose and it's entirely my fault?" I demand in place of a greeting. I cross my arms over my chest as I approach and wait for him to say something that makes any of this better.

Gavin stands and paces back and forth for a minute before turning to face me.

"No. It was my fault. Because I fucking loved you, I fucking missed you, and I didn't feel like it would do anyone any good for you to know that." He runs both hands through his hair, leaving it sticking up wildly all over the place.

"You should've told me, Gav. But I should've told you, too. We've kept so much from each other and now it's just—"

"Please do not say hopeless." His pleading eyes meet mine and he shakes his head. "I don't know what it is right now but I know it's not hopeless."

There is just so much. The drugs, the girls, the accident. And all of it concealed from me, hidden away as if it were possible for me to keep living in my safe little bubble.

I shake my head because it feels like a jumbled mess inside it. I can't think straight, can't organize my thoughts into a coherent stream that I'm capable of making sense of.

"I was sure you'd meet someone there, someone worthy of you. I looked at my life and saw how pathetic it was. I didn't think I'd ever be capable of giving you what you deserved so I just . . . gave up. Not just on you or us but on myself, too. I let the temptations pull me under and it took nearly killing my best friend to make me realize how bad off I actually was."

I can hear his words and I know that if I could let them in past the lies and the pain of being in the dark for so long, they would probably help somehow. But right now it's just too much, it's all too much.

Gavin isn't much of a talker and for the first time ever, I want him to return to the broody, silent version of himself so I can try to figure out how to make what has happened okay. How to make peace with the past so that I can figure out whether we have a future.

I'm one second from covering my ears like a child to keep his words out when he delivers the crushing blow to my soul.

"Ashley helped me, she represented me when no one else would. She accepted what I could give and it sort of turned into a . . . *thing*, I guess. But after Austin, I ended it. I swear to God, I have not touched her since. But she's still my attorney, she's a pretty damn good one, and she knows my case and is doing her best to get my probation ended early so that I can be a part of Leaving Amarillo—and not the anchor that weighs the band down and keeps us from playing out-of-state gigs." He swallows hard and stares at me with that look, that please-don't-hate-me-I'm-only-a-clueless-guy look. I frown, trying to sort my feelings in my head before I open my mouth and say something I can't take back. "Tell me what I can do, Bluebird. What I can say or do to make it better, to keep from hurting you. Please. Whatever you want or need, I will do. Name it."

A desperate Gavin. This is a switch. Typically it was me doing the begging and pleading and trying to push him into recognizing what we had. But now the tables have turned and I don't know what side either of us is really on.

"I don't know," I say softly. "I'm just . . . there's so much I didn't know and this other girl in your life that I can't compete with and honestly, I don't think I want to even—"

He cuts my sentence short by rushing forward and taking my hands in his. The contact assaults my exposed nerves. "I ended it with no room for doubt. I told her I would get the money I owed as soon as I could and I've been paying her weekly from my check. She still comes around every now and then, either because she's lonely or bored, or hell if I know, but I told her in no uncertain terms that I don't want that in my life anymore. I'm done with that kind of life— with temporary highs and empty relationships. With using sex as currency or as just a means to an end. I want this, what you and I have, what you and I could have if I stopped getting in my own way."

"Just . . ." I look down at our connected hands, then helplessly up at him, hating that I'm hurting him, hating that I can't just say it's okay. My instinct is to soothe him, to make it all better, to shine the light on the darkness within him. But this time I am lost in darkness, too, and I can't figure out how to get either of us out. "Maybe just give me some space, okay? I need to think and I can't think right now with everything so . . ."

The initial hurt of being asked to leave by the one person who has always wanted him to stay flickers fast across his features but he schools them quickly and nods, allowing his hands to slip from mine. The shutters he usually keeps between us slam shut in his eyes and I am on the outside once again—no longer privy to the inner workings of Gavin Garrison.

"Okay. I have to be at work tonight so I should go, anyway. But please know I would never do anything to intentionally hurt you or Dallas." A beat later, just before walking out of my yard and maybe out of my life, he adds, "You're all I've got."

If I ever wrote a book, I think I'd call it "A View from Rock Bottom," because that's where I am right now.

When a knock comes at my door I'm literally lying facedown on my living room floor.

I should probably sweep soon. It's apparently filthy at rock bottom. There's dust under the coffee table and what I think might be an old sock under the couch.

He opened up, told the truth, all of it, even the ugly parts I asked for, and I shut him out. I let him go.

As painful as our conversation was, I'd rather have it a hundred times over day after day than see that cold, empty look he gave me when he left.

Gavin is the one person I'd do anything not to hurt; he's also the one person I know would never cause me pain on purpose.

So why do we keep destroying each other?

I'm still contemplating this when I peel myself up off the floor and make my way toward the knocking.

"I'm coming, I'm coming!" I call out, assuming it's Robyn on the other side of the door. I texted her and Dallas both that I needed to talk ASAP right after Gavin left and upon checking my phone,

I realize it's been nearly enough time for the drive from Dallas to Amarillo. Jesus. That was a good chunk of the afternoon I spent on the floor.

I'm a bit surprised when I pull the door open to find Liam and Mrs. Lawson on my porch.

"Well, hey there, y'all," I say, forcing myself to sound less dead than I feel. "Come on in."

I step aside, pulling the door completely open. They do come inside but only just barely.

"Hi, sweetheart," Mrs. Lawson says, giving me a hug and enveloping me in her potent rose-scented perfume. I love the woman, but she's like a walking potpourri dish.

"Hi, Mrs. Lawson. Everything okay?" I glance down at Liam, who looks somber and maybe a little sleepy.

"Oh everything's fine," she tells me in her singsong voice. "It's just that I'm having my monthly bridge club dinner and Liam here has had just about enough of old ladies gossiping, I'm afraid." She smiles down at him before whisper conspiratorially to me. "You know that Mrs. Emerson from Atlanta, she moved into the old Johnson house on Lane Avenue? She's got the best stories," my neighbor continues without waiting for my answer. "She can't make a decent thumbprint jelly cookie to save her life but it's worth inviting her for the stories."

Her gray eyes twinkle with excitement and the promise of more gossip so I do Liam and me both a favor.

"Actually I was getting pretty hungry and thought I'd grab a late supper in town." I decide it's best to give Liam a choice instead of making him feel like he got dumped off on me. "I'd love some company, Liam, if you're interested."

His eyebrows lift and his eyes perk up a little. "Um, okay. That'd be okay, I guess."

"I can pick him up once the ladies clear out," Mrs. Lawson tells me, but I wave her off.

"He can spend the night here if he'd like. Dallas's room is empty and I have sleeping bags if he'd like to camp out here tonight."

It's like I said a magic word. Liam lights up like I just told him I had the Golden Ticket or a secret entrance to Hogwarts in my attic.

"What do you think, Liam?" Mrs. Lawson looks at him expectantly. "Want to camp out with Miss Dixie for the night?"

As if he realizes he's been too obvious with his excitement, he shoves his hands into his pockets the same way Gavin does when he's trying to pull himself inward. "Whatever." He stares at the floor and I check for an outline of my body in the dust.

Not seeing one, I escort Mrs. Lawson to the door and tell her I'll call her tomorrow. She thanks me and leaves, making her way much more agilely down my front porch than I would've suspected she could.

"So," I begin awkwardly, once she's gone. "Do you like waffles?"

Liam shrugs. "I don't know. Never had 'em."

I'm careful not to react to this even though it outrages me. I remember learning that Gavin had never had ice cream before when we were kids and feeling the same type of disgusted disappointment that any adult would allow such a travesty as denying the delicious joy that is ice cream.

"Well, they're kind of like pancakes but with little squares you can put syrup in. How about hash browns? Ever had those?"

He looks at me like I'm speaking a foreign language. I try a different approach.

"What do you usually eat for breakfast, Liam?"

"Pop-Tart thingies. Or cereal." He glances around slowly, his gaze lingering on the front window. "It's nighttime," he informs me gently as if concerned for my mental well-being.

I laugh softly and nod. "I know. I don't like early morning meals much, but I love breakfast for dinner. 'Brinner' is what me and my brother called it as kids when our Nana made it."

He stares blankly and I can't help but wonder if I'll ever get through to him.

"Come on," I say, grabbing my keys and then opening the front door. "There's a magical place that serves breakfast twenty-four hours a day for people like me. I'll take you. My treat."

He regards me warily for several minutes before finally walking out the door. I breathe a small sigh of relief. It's progress at least. I'll take my victories where I can get them.

22 | Gavin

"RENT'S USUALLY FIVE HUNDRED BUT IF YOU KEEP SITTING IN WITH the house band a few times a week, I guess I can knock it down to four."

I nod at Cal. "Thanks, man. I appreciate it."

"It's not a favor, kid. You don't pay the rent on time, I'll take it from your paycheck. Plain and simple."

I shake his hand. "Got it. And hey, this way I'll never be late for work."

My red-faced boss scowls at me. "Somehow I think you'll still manage."

Grinning, I nod. "Someone's gotta keep your heart rate up, Cal. Might as well be me."

He grumbles something rude under his breath on his way out, handing me the key to the studio apartment above the bar before slamming the door.

It's empty but it's mine. Exposed brick walls, a thin film of something on the windows, and heavily scuffed wooden floors don't exactly scream home sweet home, but it works for me.

Lord knows I've lived in worse.

After leaving Dixie's this morning, I found an eviction notice on the trailer when I got home. It wasn't the first and I knew it might not be the last, but looking around at that place, the dirty dishes, the stained furniture, and reminders of times I'd lost my temper and kicked in a door or had to remove one from its hinges to save my mom from overdosing on the bathroom floor, I realized there was no way in hell I was getting my fresh start in that shithole. Besides, my mom hadn't been home in weeks so I was pretty sure she knew she was getting evicted and her sense of self-preservation kicked in so she'd made other arrangements.

Luckily, Cal still had space above the bar available for rent. I make a note to check out some local garage sales for secondhand furniture and write my to-do list on a notepad from the bar. Once I've scrawled everything down, I appraise my list.

I've got to clean up a bit, get a few basic groceries including cleaning supplies, check in with my drug counselor, call the nearest rehab facility and see about getting my mom admitted, and I saved the best for last.

Make Bluebird fall in love with me. Again.

I got this.

Well . . . except maybe that last one. There is always that fear clawing at the edge of my awareness.

What if my darkness is too dark? What if the accident was the last straw and she can't forgive me? What if I really and truly just don't deserve her?

I've seen my life without her and it's bleak and empty and miserable.

I want her.

I need her.

I love her.

I know what love is because of her.

I glance out my smudged window. The glow of the Tavern's sign is bright from below. I sigh, wishing I could see stars the way Dixie and I used to watch them from her rooftop when we were kids.

Whether she wants to be or not, Dixie Lark is my happily ever after, and even a guy like me can't help but wish on stars—even if they are made of neon.

My phone buzzes and I retrieve it from my pocket.

Dallas wants one last rehearsal before the battle and he has sent me the time, date, and location. I text back that I'll be there.

I get to work on unpacking the few belongings I have: a futon, a toaster, a microwave, and more important, my clothes and drum kit. Best part about living above a bar is I don't have to worry about playing my drums too late or too loud.

Once I'm finished, I realize I'm almost late for work so I throw on a clean shirt, planning to head down to the Tavern. My phone rings in my back pocket. I slide it free, expecting it to be Dallas but seeing "Bluebird" on the screen instead.

I didn't expect to hear from her so soon, but I'm a liar if I say I'm not fucking thrilled she's calling me.

"Hey, everything okay?"

"Um, yeah. No. I don't know." The promise is clear in her voice. My adrenaline spikes and I try to remain calm.

"Can you tell me what's wrong? Are you safe? Where are you?"

I can hear the panic in my own voice and I realize I'm gripping the phone hard to enough to dent the damn thing. So much for remaining calm.

"I'm safe. It's not me." She sighs loudly. "I'm mean I'm not upset about anything to do with me. I'm at Waffle House with Liam and I just . . . he . . ." Her voice catches and a sob breaks through.

"I'll be right there."

"You got here fast," Dixie tells me when I walk into the Waffle House. When I glance around to see if she's alone, she explains where her date for the evening is. "He had to go to the bathroom."

"I was at the Tavern. I rented the loft above it. And I borrowed Cal's truck." Now that that's out of the way, I slide into the booth across from her. "So tell me what's going on. What's wrong with Liam?"

Dixie's eyes are still shining and I can see how hard her throat is working to keep control of the lump of emotion clogging it.

"He . . . He's got marks, Gav. Like all over. I saw his arms and his back when he was getting into EmmyLou and . . ." She squeezes her eyes shut for a brief moment. "I don't know if he's been starved or what but he didn't even recognize hash browns or scrambled eggs. How is that even possible?"

I sigh and keep my voice down since Liam is walking out of the bathroom and heading toward our booth.

"It's possible if the person raising you just feeds you enough to keep you alive. Scraps. Boxed and prepackaged stuff. Frozen meals full of unrecognizable substances. He said he doesn't go to school much."

The corners of her mouth turn down and my heart cracks open wide in my chest. "Is that how it was for you?" she asks. "Did your mom, did she not . . ."

"No, she didn't," I answer quickly. Turning to the side I slide out to let Liam in. I figure he'd prefer his own side of the booth. "Hey, Liam," I say in greeting. "It is cool with you if I join you for dinner?"

He moves slowly to the middle of the bench so I take the spot next to Dixie.

"It's breakfast," he says evenly. Then he looks at Dixie and says, "For dinner. Brinner."

I smile, remembering when Dallas and Dixie's grandma used to make bacon and pancakes and sausage gravy with biscuits and eggs however you wanted them for dinner. They called it brinner and I thought it was crazy but I didn't have any complaints about free food. And no one turned down Nana Lark's biscuits any time of day or night if they knew what was good for them.

"Awesome," I say while lifting a sticky laminated menu off the table. "Sounds good to me. What did y'all order?"

"Waffles and bacon and hash browns," Dixie says. "We were going to get eggs but Liam wasn't sure if he liked them or not."

I make a show of carefully considering my menu. "Hm . . . well, how about I get the cheese and eggs plate and you can try 'em out?"

He frowns while considering this and I study him while waiting for an answer. Was I this careful and introspective as a kid? I'm not sure, but Dixie says he reminds her of me and I do see some similarities. Mrs. Lawson has obviously been bathing him but his clothes are about a year too small and his hair is too long and falling in his eyes. His arms are small, wiry, and bruised and contain several sores and old scars.

"I guess that would be okay," he finally answers, and I have to think for a second to recall my question.

"Great." I set my menu behind the napkin holder and turn to the frizzy-haired, frazzled-looking middle-aged waitress bringing Liam and Dixie's OJs to the table. "Can I get a cheese and egg plate, white toast, with bacon and hash browns scattered, covered, smothered, and chunked?"

"Sure, handsome," the waitress tells me. "And to drink?"

I glance at my companions. "I'll have what they're having. Orange juice, straight up."

Dixie rolls her eyes but Liam looks mildly amused. Kid could use a little entertainment in his life. And I've been where he is. Having people feel sorry for you and giving you sad-puppy eyes, while I know they mean well, doesn't help. It just makes you more uncomfortable because now you've got the burden of their pity and pain and discomfort to deal with on top of everything else.

I understand something about Liam that Dixie may never grasp.

He doesn't know his situation hurts other people because they care about him. He only knows that his life is the way it is, and as far as he knows, everyone goes hungry, or has junkies all over their house, or gets shoved or hit or kicked or sometimes completely ignored like an unwanted pet. I was nearly in middle school before I completely understood that my life wasn't like everyone else's—that it wasn't that way for other kids. What I understood long before that, though, was the pity and sickening sympathy I got from teachers and social workers and ladies from the local Junior League. I didn't like it and I'm betting Liam won't, either, so I resolve to behave normally and to try to help Dixie ease up and mask her concerns—for now, at least. I remain cool and calm and laid-back on the surface, making jokes and small talk until our food arrives.

Under the table I am texting Sheila Montgomery like a madman telling her to call me as soon as humanly possible.

After taking a few bites of my food and scooping a few bites of eggs onto Liam's plate so he can try them out, I realize Dixie isn't eating. She's watching Liam. The way he's testing food to make sure it's edible—a habit that develops after you've desperately ingested soured fruit or chugged milk that has long since gone bad because you had no other option—and then shoveling it in like it's his last meal once he realizes it's okay.

I nudge her knee gently with mine. "Eat, Bluebird," I mumble under my breath.

She jerks a little as if in a trance and then picks up her fork.

Most of the time we eat in comfortable silence. Liam is out of breath when he finishes because he hardly took one while he filled his belly.

"After this," Dixie begins, turning to me as she continues, "we're going to have a campout at my house. Movies and a tent and sleeping bags. We're even going to make s'mores by roasting marshmallows on the stovetop like Nana and Papa used to. Would you like to join us, Gavin?"

The way she speaks my name, enunciating both syllables, I can tell it's an invitation of desperation. I know she'd really rather have space from me after everything I told her but she needs my help tonight, with Liam, in not letting her huge heart show.

"What do you say, man?" I dip my head to catch Liam's eye. "That okay with you? I'm pretty good at roasting stovetop marshmallows. Not to brag or anything . . ."

He shrugs but I can see the interest in his eyes. Not sure if it's for the camping or the marshmallows, but at least it's something.

When I glance over at Dixie, she has a certain gleam in her eye as well. Maybe she's not dreading spending time with me as much as I thought she was.

That's something, too.

I'll take what I can get. It's what I've done all my life.

23 | Dixie

I FEEL LIKE I CAN BREATHE AGAIN WHEN LIAM AND I ARRIVE HOME with Gavin following us in a green pickup.

Gavin seems to understand Liam in a way I can't. He relates to him, chats easily with him, and doesn't seem as nervous about screwing up as I am. When we were getting into the van earlier, I went to help Liam up and I saw some alarming scars on his back. One is dangerously similar to the shape of a belt buckle.

Each mark on him, each sign I missed all this time while giving him lessons, is affecting me in ways I can't understand. I do the best I can to hide how much I want to curl up and have a good cry. I don't deserve to get to cry. Liam is a tough kid and he deserves my strength, not my pity or my tears. Gavin has kept my pity party in check and I'm glad he's here.

But it's hard, too. Hard to look at him and not kiss him, hard to be so close and not touch him.

We walk toward the house, the three of us, and there is an odd peaceful feeling soothing me as if I am exactly where I need to be in this moment.

Gavin holds the door open and we step inside and get busy pulling out the old two-person tent he and my brother used to use and every pillow, blanket, and sleeping bag we can find. I put Liam in charge of organizing the snacks on a plate at the kitchen table and he remains very serious and intense about counting out and lining up marshmallows, graham crackers, and pieces of Hershey bar in methodical groups.

"Good job," I tell him once Gavin and I have the tent and pillow and blanket fort assembled in the living room. "Now let's get cracking on these s'mores."

Liam grins, proud of himself for his hard work, and it both warms and breaks my heart to see him smile. He's so small and vulnerable and my mind keeps drifting to how big his dad is and what kind of life this little boy has had so far.

Gavin catches me tearing up a little and steps in. "How about Liam and I handle the s'mores and you be on movie duty?"

I nod and my skin heats from the embarrassment at being caught breaking down again.

Buck up, buttercup, my subconscious scolds me. I take a deep breath and do that.

I'm tough. I lived on the road alone for nearly three months. I started a business by myself. I've got this.

Even though I do feel as if I can handle this, I also know that just as Gavin's pain is my pain, Liam's pain is also seeping into the broken places inside my heart and that I won't allow this child to receive another mark on his skin or miss another meal no matter what I have to do.

The ire burns in me, anger at the kind of people who allow children to be hurt or go hungry, rage at those who inflict pain on the innocent and helpless.

"Breathe, Bluebird," Gavin tells me quietly. "Go pick out a movie. One of those Disney ones you're always telling me I need to see."

I take a deep breath and turn to go into the living room, but not before hearing Liam ask, "Why do you call her Bluebird?"

I can't help myself, I need to hear the answer. Once I've stepped out of sight, I lean against the wall and do my best to eavesdrop.

"Well . . . that's kind of a long story, I guess," Gavin says, barely speaking loud enough for me to hear. He mentions something about a story he already told Liam outside this morning but I don't know what he's referring to.

When Liam doesn't respond, Gavin continues.

"When I was a kid, I didn't have a whole lot of hope. I didn't hope to see my friends, or hope to play with my toys, or hope to get anything for my birthday or Christmas. I had done that and been let down a lot. So I didn't have much hope or dare to think that my life would ever get much better."

I close my eyes and place a hand on my chest to keep my heart from breaking apart.

"Then I met Dixie. And her brother Dallas. And I don't know . . . I felt . . . alive. I felt hope."

Liam is still quiet and I wish I could see his face.

Does he have hope? Does he get birthday presents? Has he ever had a Christmas?

"Remember what I told you about today," Gavin continues. "When Dallas, my friend and Dixie's brother, was mowing grass by a pond and he saw a bird. One of the blue finches like you and me saw in the backyard. This one was small and lying down in some high grass but there wasn't a tree or a nest around. It was just . . . there. And it looked dead."

"But you said it wasn't. You said it flew away," Liam's voice is soft and yet heavy with the sound of betrayal.

"I told you the truth. It didn't die. We just thought it was dead.

But then Dixie showed up and Dallas picked it up and carried it home and the next thing we knew, it was chirping and flying away, right out of his hands."

"But . . . how?"

I have to strain to hear Gavin's answer. "I think, maybe, that our little bluebird was lying there, feeling bad and defeated and maybe thinking about giving up. But then we came along and lifted it up off the ground and took it somewhere safe. We gave it hope. And when it came to and we watched it fly away, it gave us hope right back."

I smile when the inevitable question slips from Liam's lips. "Okay. So you saved the bird but what does that have to do with Miss Dixie?"

Gavin chuckles lightly. "I call Miss Dixie Bluebird because she gives me hope. When I'm lying down feeling bad and thinking about giving up, it's her that makes me pick myself back up again and fly. Even when I think I can't, even when I don't want to. As long as she has hope, has faith in me, I'll still try to be the best that I can be."

And here I thought it was because I had blue eyes and my last name was Lark.

Fighting tears at this point just feels stupid so I let them out, wiping them gently and wondering why it took a child to get that story out of Gavin. Why he never told me how he felt.

The room falls quiet so I peek around the corner. Gavin turns on the burner and pulls up a chair for Liam to watch while he roasts the marshmallows.

Seeing them does strange things to my insides. I don't know what it is, but somehow they are right together. As if my only purpose in life was to unite these two wounded souls. As if somehow they belong to me and I belong to them.

"How goes the movie search?" Gavin calls out.

Even though his back is to me, I know he knows I haven't looked for movies.

I take a few steps back from the entryway and call back, "Oh, it's going. Disney really has the corner on the princess market, though. Not sure you boys would like any of these."

"How about *The Wizard of Oz*," Gavin calls back.

I smile because that's always been my favorite. Hence my fiddle being named Oz. "I think I can scrounge that one up. Bring me some s'mores! I'm starving in here!"

We play at the banter, mostly for Liam's sake, while we settle in with the movie and the s'mores.

"There's no color," Liam says when the black-and-white movie begins to play.

I smile, glancing over at Gavin and his tattoos and his hazel eyes and bright white smile.

"Don't worry," I tell him. "There will be."

Liam falls asleep somewhere around the time Dorothy meets the lion. Gavin looks pretty beat and I'm exhausted myself.

"Want me to turn it off?"

Gavin blinks sleepily and shakes his head. "Nah. Leave it on in case he wakes up."

He maneuvers onto all fours and tucks Liam in while I watch. There is something happening, something bigger than us that I can't explain, but I can feel deep down into my bones that this moment matters. That whatever is going on with our motley little group here is monumental.

Maybe it's just wishful thinking—not a promise of what's to come but the little girl in me still fantasizing about Gavin being my future.

Gavin crawls out of the tent and extends his hand to help me out.

The contact of our palms makes my entire body tingle. I stumble over the bottom lip of the tent entrance and nearly plow him down.

"Well that was graceful," I say quietly so as not to disturb Liam.

Gavin looks down into my eyes and I realize I am still in his arms. His full, masculine lips part and I don't know if he's going to say something or kiss me but he closes them and shakes his head.

"I'll sleep on the couch. Keep an eye on him and let him know where he is in case he wakes up scared."

"Okay," I say, gently extracting myself from his embrace. "Good night, Gavin."

"Good night, Bluebird," he says quietly. "Sweet dreams."

I watch him retrieve an extra pillow and blanket from the tent and toss them on the couch before I make my way to the bathroom. After I close the door behind me, I look at myself in the mirror. My hair is a mess, my mascara is smudged under my eyes, and I look like I haven't slept in a week. The s'mores were messy and there is chocolate smudged at the corner of my mouth. I would've never known by the way Gavin just looked at me. He gazed upon my face like I was the most beautiful creature he'd ever seen and I'd unexpectedly fallen from the heavens and landed in his arms. He released me as if holding me for just a moment was a privilege he didn't feel he had a right to. The reflection of myself in Gavin's eyes is a lot different from the one I see now in the mirror under unforgiving lights.

Leaning forward over the sink, I wash my face and brush my teeth. Drying off with a hand towel, I catch my own eye in the mirror and briefly remember seeing him behind me in a hotel in Austin.

Gavin is the color to my memories. He's the shadows that make my light shine brighter.

Our past, our mistakes, they seem so . . . small compared to what we have.

What he did the year I was in Houston was fake. It was empty and meaningless and I don't feel threatened by it—just sad that it happened. I was angry about the accident, livid, actually—but Dallas is a grown man and he wasn't completely innocent, either. It's the hiding it from me that still bothers me. The fact that he didn't trust me enough or think I was strong enough for the truth. Maybe I wasn't then. But I am now.

Tonight was real. I needed him and he was there. Despite what he may think, he is what I need, he's who I need, and he will forever be the one man I want to see across the table, beside me in bed, and behind me onstage.

Bracing my hands on the sink, I try to let my emotions wash through me the way the music does. I can handle Gavin. I can handle this situation with Liam. When the time comes, probably after the baby is born, but soon, I'm going to have a long talk with my brother about not telling me the truth about what was going on the year I was gone.

I'm going to let the guys know I want to play the new song I wrote and I'm going to play it my way.

I am stronger than I used to be. Better. Braver.

I can fight for what I love.

24 | Gavin

My body decides it has a pressing need to piss just before I fall asleep. I make my way carefully through the living room, careful not to disturb still-sleeping Liam as I go. I've already decided to teach him how to play the drums and I'm planning our lessons in my head.

Distracted by my thoughts, I don't think to knock on the bathroom door. When I swing it open, I'm surprised to see Dixie standing at the sink. She's in the same clothes she had on before.

"I thought you were in bed," I say. She doesn't move an inch. "You okay?"

When she finally turns to me, I see sorrow etched into her face and determination burning in her eyes.

She nods. "Sort of. I just . . ."

I take a step closer so I can hear her better.

"He's never going back to that man, Gavin. I swear to God. I don't care what I have to do."

"Hey," I say softly, reaching out to take her in my arms and pulling her to my chest when she doesn't resist. "Okay, baby. He's never going back to that man. Breathe."

She stiffens against my chest and then turns those wide blue eyes up to meet mine. "If I'd just—"

"Nope. Nothing you could've said, done, not said, not done, would've changed anything. You are not to blame. You are not someone who would assume any of those things and I would never want you to become that jaded a person, one who thought everyone in the world was out to do you or anyone else harm. You are full of light and you see the light in everyone else. It's one of the many things I love about you."

"Gav . . ."

It hits me hard, that she still trusts me after everything I've done, her vulnerability, the way I've taken her for granted, how majorly fucked my priorities have been for so long. Too long.

This is my whole world in my arms right now. All I want is to make her pain go away, the way she's always done for me.

"Shh," I say. "Look, I texted Sheila and she texted back. She's coming to talk with Liam in the morning. She's good at her job. She'll ask the right questions without upsetting him. She'll get Mrs. Lawson approved as his temporary guardian and she'll get an order of protection against his dad. It's all going to be okay. I promise."

Her body relaxes against mine and I notice our reflection in the mirror.

"We look good together," I whisper to the top of her head.

Desire blooms in her gaze at the memory and I smile.

"Behave yourself, drummer boy," she mutters as I kiss her forehead and squeeze her tight.

"Working on it."

"Speaking of that," she begins, pulling back a bit to look me in the face. "What's the word on the assault charges? Will Liam's statement to the social worker help any?"

I sigh because as usual, there's still always something to deal with, something I royally screwed up that needs to be handled before we can move forward.

"It's compli—"

"Gavin, so help me—"

"Okay, yeah. Sorry. It's just kind of up in the air because Carl is still in the hospital and technically they don't know the extent of his injuries. Ashley said I can plead no contest to the assault and agree to community service, anger management, and extended probation and agree to have no contact with him as long as Carl's injuries don't have lasting effects."

Dixie stiffens at the mention of Ashley, then slumps against me. "Jesus."

I stroke her hair, enjoying the feel of it against my fingers. Soft and rough. "I know. It doesn't help that I have prior convictions for the drugs and the accident. Or that my mom has been shacked up with Carl and I might've roughed him up at the bar one night not too long ago. Plus, Carl is milking this for all it's worth in an attempt to remain on a morphine drip."

"He's a child abuser," Dixie argues. "We saw him hitting Liam and you reacted after years of similar abuse. Can't she do something about that? Make them see why you did what you did?"

I hold her by the shoulders. "What I did isn't okay, babe. Besides, Ashley has no idea about my childhood. I know *you* understand because you care about me and you care about Liam, but that's not how the justice system works. Bottom line is I took matters into my own hands using excessive force. I committed a crime and there will be a punishment. I knew that. I deserve it." And I don't actually regret it, even though I know I should.

I don't discuss my childhood with anyone, so Ashley wouldn't know to even attempt to use that defense.

"This sucks, Gav. Seriously. Every mark I see on Liam makes me want to murder Carl myself with my bare hands."

I can't help but laugh at my sweet girl talking about murdering someone. "You save those hands for playing Oz, okay?"

"How's your hand?" She uses her delicate fingers to examine my still-battered knuckles. "Will you be ready by Friday, you think? Honestly?"

I cup her chin and kiss her on the nose. "I'll manage. I'm tough."

She frowns and I notice how exhausted she looks. "Yeah, but—"

"But nothing. It's late, Bluebird. Go to bed and get some rest so we can talk to Sheila in the morning."

She huffs out a breath and gives me one last hug before mumbling something about me being bossy like Dallas.

After she's gone, I take care of the reason I came to the bathroom in the first place.

When I go back to the couch, Liam is muttering softly in his sleep. I tense, fully expecting something that might trigger a flashback of my own, but all I can make out is "brinner" and "another marshmallow."

My life is still a mess, one I've mostly made myself, but I fall asleep smiling for the first time in a long time.

The knocking seems to be in perfect rhythm with the ringing of my cell phone. I almost reach for my drumsticks to tap it out. Rubbing the hazy blur out of my eyes, I remember I'm in Dixie's living room. Sitting up quickly, I glance over and see Liam still sleeping in the tent beside me. The knocking grows more persistent and I have a voice mail.

Sheila Montgomery.

I jump up and trip my way across the room to open the door.

Dark eyes narrow at me. "Did I wake you?"

"Hi. I'm sorry. It was a long night."

She frowns. "I thought you were done with those."

I nod. "I am. It was, uh, a different kind of long night." I open the door wider and gesture to the pillow and blanket and tent fortress.

"Ah. I see." Sheila steps precariously through the room and makes her way to the couch. "So that's Liam?"

I nod again. "Yeah. He has marks, scars, and sores. My guess is he's about fifteen pounds underweight and after seeing Carl hit him for myself, I can imagine what a typical day was like for this kid. That plus the fact that he's skittish, fixated on death, and his house is the local crack den, I'm not thinking the abuse will be hard to prove." I remember Dixie's words from the night before. "He didn't know what scrambled eggs or hash browns were. Ate like he hadn't seen food in weeks. Said he doesn't go to school much, which begs the question, how has the state not already gotten involved?"

"They're understaffed. You know this, Gavin."

I sigh and watch Liam toss and turn for a minute. "I know. Still. This shouldn't have slipped by so many for so long."

"You did," she says quietly. "When they did come to question you, you lied and made excuses. Protected her."

She's right. I did.

I still do.

"I know. I'm guessing he's been doing the same. Still . . ."

Sheila watches me carefully. "It looks different on this side, doesn't it?"

I don't answer because I don't know how to. It does seem different. Growing up, I blamed myself for the way my mom was. If she didn't have to deal with me maybe she wouldn't have gotten so bad off. But looking at Liam, I can't think of a single way what happened could have possibly been his fault.

As I got older, when I started using myself, I blamed myself for having drugs around and exposing my mom to temptation. She would always find my stash, no matter what it was. When she would get clean, I laughed at her when she told me she was pulling it together. I'd heard it so many times and it had been a lie so many times, I started being an asshole about it. That might not have caused her to fall back down but it certainly didn't help.

I run my hands through my hair and pull in some much-needed oxygen. "I assaulted his dad, Sheila. I saw him hit him and I lost it. He's still in the hospital."

The creases in her aging face deepen. "Well, that's not great, Gavin. What did you think that would help?"

"I didn't think," I answer honestly. "I just reacted."

"Time for another round of anger management?"

I nod. "Yeah. Pretty sure I'm going to get the mandatory kind, courtesy of the state of Texas."

"Could be worse," she says.

"Agreed. Can I get you some coffee?"

Sheila sets her purse down and I notice a bag with an expensive-looking camera in it. "That'd be great. Then we need to wake him up so I can talk with him and take a few photos of the marks you mentioned and document his weight."

I glance at Liam, wishing I could let him sleep more before putting the poor kid through this. "Okay. Be right back."

After I've made a pot of coffee and poured Sheila a cup, I knock on Dixie's door but don't hear a response. I push it open and she's standing there in her jeans and a bra. I turn my head quickly. "Sorry. I know it's early but, um, Sheila is here so . . ."

"I saw the car in the driveway," she answers while pulling a black tank top over her head. "Be right there."

I make my way back to the living room and lean down to where Liam is already beginning to stir. "Hey, buddy. Want some breakfast?"

He sits up, his small body wavering a little and his voice scratchy when he speaks. "Do we have dinner for breakfast here?"

I laugh at the genuine interest in his question. "Nah. I was thinking some fruit and yogurt and toast if that's okay. Miss Dixie eats kind of healthy in the mornings. I guess so she can wolf down bacon and waffles at dinnertime." I wink at her when she comes into the room at the end of my comment.

She smirks at me. "I have cereal, too, thank you very much, and oatmeal."

Liam perks up. "I like oatmeal. The kind with apples."

"On it," Dixie says, looking hugely relieved that he has a food he likes and nodding briefly at Sheila, who raises her coffee mug in greeting. "Anyone else want oatmeal?"

"I won't turn it down," I say.

"I'm good. Thank you, though," Sheila answers.

"Be right back," Dixie tells us before disappearing into the kitchen.

I help Liam out of the tent and turn to a channel I think might have cartoons. *Sesame Street* is on, which seems nuts since I watched it as a kid.

"This okay?"

He nods.

I introduce him to Sheila and his immediate wariness tells me he's met social workers before. But Sheila is a pro so she puts him at ease pretty quickly, discussing the differences between Bert and Ernie.

They chat amicably for a few minutes before Dixie returns. She hands Liam his oatmeal and a cup of orange juice, setting him up on her grandpa's chair with a TV tray.

I notice she put some fruit on both of our plates and smile as I thank her.

Sheila gets down to business pretty quickly, taking statements from Dixie and me both and getting Mrs. Lawson's info as well. When Liam finishes eating, his pace a little slower with the distraction of Big Bird, Sheila asks him if it would be okay if they spoke for a few minutes on the front porch after he changes out of his jammies. She's already coordinated with Dixie how they'll get the photos of the marks without upsetting him. Basically Dixie is going to help him change his clothes and Sheila is going to be as discreet as humanly possible.

The three of them go into the bedroom and come back out a few minutes later. Dixie's face is pale. Too pale. But Liam seems okay.

Sheila tucks her camera into her bag and nods at me as she takes Liam onto the porch to discuss birds.

Dixie takes the empty oatmeal dishes into the kitchen and I follow her. "I know this is hard on you. But trust me, he will be better for it. I imagine my life would've been a little different if someone had stepped in when I was his age."

"I know," she says somberly. "I'm trying to do that—focus on the positive. But Sheila said it could take a while to get the order in place, to make it to where his dad can't have him. What if he has to go back there, Gavin? What if—" Her voice breaks before she can finish and I wrap my arms around her out of habit. Or maybe I need the comfort as much as she does.

"He's not going back to Carl, to that house." I can't promise her much, but I can promise her this: I'll break every bone in Carl's body and put his ass in traction if I have to. Either way, he will never lay another hand on Liam. Dixie holds me around the waist for a few moments and I revel in the closeness. "I'm sorry about everything— about not telling you, about Ashley and—"

"You have to see her soon?"

I nod. "I do. I have to figure out how to pay her to defend me against the assault charges and we have to discuss my plea and what I can and cannot admit to."

Her shoulders tense and I rub my face against hers playfully. "I'm going to pay her with money, Bluebird. Please don't tense up. That way of life is in my past, where it will damn well stay. I'll pawn my kit if I have to, get her to take that as down payment, and let her garnish my paycheck from the Tavern for the rest. I'll figure it out."

"How much will it cost?"

I shrug but Dixie's eyes turn narrow. We both know this isn't my first rodeo. "Two thousand—give or take."

Before she can comment on the dollar amount, the screen door slams and Sheila and Liam return. Dixie pulls away from me and I try not to feel the sting of her absence.

We hear Sheila ask Liam to have a seat in the living room and then she joins us in the kitchen.

Dixie eyes her suspiciously. "Everything okay?"

Sheila nods. "Two things. Carl is out of the hospital and demanding to see his son, which is bad." That is bad, but it means his injuries might not be extensive enough for me to get charged with anything too terrible. Not that I wouldn't serve ten to life if it meant he never got his hands on his kid again.

"Okay," Dixie says slowly. "What do we do about that?"

Sheila's eyes tighten and I see the lines form on the edges. She's probably in her fifties but she's got tan skin, probably because she's from Puerto Rico and she seems to have stopped aging years ago.

"Right now we're going to tell him that Mrs. Lawson is lonely and truly enjoying her time with Liam and that we want to let Carl heal up a bit more before he takes Liam back." Dixie winces visibly at the last part and I drape my arm across her shoulders. "If that doesn't work, I'm going to see if I can expedite the protection order with a friend of mine at the police department."

"What if your friend can't? What if Carl shows up at Mrs. Lawson's?" The panic is coming through Dixie's voice loud and clear.

I tighten my grip on her. "Then I'll—"

"You, sir, will do nothing," Sheila interrupts, pointing a manicured finger at me. "I mean it. You are awaiting a court date for assaulting him and *his* order of protection against *you* is firmly in place."

I frown but both women give me the do-as-we-say glare and I keep quiet.

"Worst-case scenario, Carl shows up at Mrs. Lawson's and takes Liam home tonight. If that happens, we get an officer to check in regularly under the guise he's making sure Carl is safe from Gavin."

Dixie's head begins shaking back and forth. "No," she whispers until she finds her voice. Then louder, "No. You saw the marks yourself. He cannot go anywhere with him."

Sheila takes a deep breath and glances at me.

"I know it's upsetting, but Carl does have some extensive injuries and a concussion. It's unlikely he'll be getting physical with Liam."

"Unlikely but not impossible," Dixie clarifies.

Sheila nods. "Our other option is to place Liam in protective custody tonight and he can go to a temporary guardian until—"

"Can I be a temporary guardian?" Dixie interrupts. "Could he stay with me?"

I don't know why this surprises me, but Dixie never fails to do what I least expect.

Sheila explains about the necessary paperwork and background check and Dixie demands to have it all right now so she can apply. Sheila gives her a Web address and Dixie lowers herself into a nearby kitchen chair and is online before I can say my own name three times fast.

I suddenly remember Sheila said she had two things to tell us. "What's the second thing?"

"Liam needs to go back to Mrs. Lawson's as soon as possible. If Carl were to find out he was here, with *you* here"—she pauses to gesture at me—"it's likely he'd be more apt to demand his son back immediately."

I hadn't thought about that. Once again, I am the wrench fucking up the works.

"He has to go now?" Dixie looks so disappointed that I want to leave so that Liam can stay. But I don't want her here alone in case Carl does show up.

"I'm sorry," Sheila says with genuine regret in her tone. "I can see that you two are obviously getting quite attached to him and I'm glad he has you and that you called me. But these types of cases don't get settled overnight. There will be the issue of CPS assigning a temporary guardianship and then a permanent situation will have to get approved by a judge, and honestly, if Carl gets help and can convince social services he's cleaning up his act, there will always be a chance he can get his son back."

"Carl Andrews will not clean up his act. Not for social services and not for that little boy. I know his type," I practically growl.

Dixie places her elbows on the table and her head in her hands.

Sheila pats her gently on the shoulder. "Regardless, I need to get to work so I can get this report submitted. I'll walk Liam over to Mrs. Lawson's and chat with her as well. Call me if Carl shows up or you have any questions."

I nod and Sheila goes into the living room. I half-expect Dixie to break down and cry at the bleak news, but instead, she stands, eyes bright and heated.

I watch as she walks purposefully into the living room and leans down to Liam's level.

"Thank you for camping in with us," she says, smiling widely even though I know what's behind the happy mask she's wearing.

"Thanks for brinner," Liam says quietly. "I liked it."

Barely restrained pain ripples across Dixie's features but she manages. "I'm glad. I'll be right over here if you need anything. And I'll come by and check on you before bedtime. Maybe we can play Mrs. Lawson's piano for a bit?"

Liam's expression darkens. "I'm not good at it."

"That's why we practice, silly. But we don't have to unless you want to. I thought maybe we'd work on the song from the movie last night. Would that be okay?"

He nods. "Guess so."

I step over and give him a light fist bump, which he returns more enthusiastically than I would've expected. "Later, man," I tell him. "Thanks for the help with the s'mores."

We say our goodbyes and Sheila leads him out the door. Once they're gone, Dixie curls up on her couch, using my bedding from the previous night. She hugs the pillow tightly to her chest and I stand above her feeling unsure. This isn't something I can fix for her. Not really. Even as much as I wish I could. But there is a glint in her eye and a determined set to her chin and I know that she has made up her mind to handle this herself.

"I've got some stuff I need to deal with today but I can stay if you need—"

"I'm fine. I'm going to get online and see what else I can do for Liam. Go do what you need to do," she answers without looking at me.

"Bluebird . . ." This fucking sucks. Liam can't be over here because I'm here. I don't want to leave her alone in case Carl shows up here or next door. But I do need to get my kit ready and take it to the rehearsal space soon and return my boss's truck before he puts out an APB on it and me. And I need to call Ashley about payment arrangements, which is damn sure not something I want to do in front of Dixie. I meant what I said, though, and since being with her in Austin, I haven't looked twice at another woman, nor do I ever intend to.

"Go, Gav. I'm good. Promise."

She is and I know she is, but I hate not being able to be there for her when she's upset—even when she does look ready to take on Carl Andrews herself. Leaning down, I kiss her lightly on the temple. Her eyes open and flash quickly to mine and I see so many conflicted urges in them, but mostly I see a girl who needs more sleep.

"I'll stop back by later if you want me to."

" 'Kay," she mumbles while pulling her computer into her lap.

I slip out the door quietly, making triple sure my girl is locked in safe before I go.

25 | Dixie

When Gavin left this morning after the social worker visited with Liam before returning him to Mrs. Lawson, there was so much I wanted to say. All I actually said was thanks for staying and then I took a very necessary nap.

But as I start getting ready for rehearsal, I realize a few things. Some of what I have to say isn't actually for him.

So I decide to find the person I actually want to say it to.

Once I'm dressed in jeans and a tank top donning the words JOHNNY AND JUNE, I give my hair the usual college try and slip on my boots. Palming my keys, I add my cheap gas station aviator sunglasses to the top of my head and call it good.

My cell phone screen lights up as I lift it off the counter. Dallas is texting reminding me not to be late.

I swear, you oversleep one time at Austin MusicFest and your brother will never let you live it down.

I ignore his message and pull up my Web browser in search of an address. Once I find it, I type it into my navigation app.

Okay, so I might be late.

But only just a little.

* * *

Downtown Amarillo isn't huge but it can be confusing when driving. There are several one-ways going in the opposite direction and the navigation lady on my phone reroutes me more than once. Somehow I finally find the building I'm looking for and park at a meter across the street.

As I ride the elevator up to the ninth floor, where the sign in the lobby said her office was, my nerves start to play tricks on me. I can't tell if I'm angry or nervous or both but I'm something.

A potent cocktail of adrenaline and estrogen floods my system and I'm a few floors away from a full-blown anxiety attack.

The lobby on her floor is all white from floor to ceiling, with a few colorful works of art on the walls. It looks, feels, and smells too expensive to touch. Feels kind of like I might dirty up the pristine furnishings just by looking at them.

A blonde with her hair in a bun sits at the large desk with the name of the firm on the front. "Can I help you?"

I feel like Julia Roberts's friend visiting her at the penthouse in *Pretty Woman* but I suck up my feeling of inadequacy and state the name of the person I'm looking for.

"Is she expecting you?" Blonde Bun asks.

I arch an eyebrow. "What do you think?"

The woman glares at me and picks up the phone on her desk. I hear her telling someone that Dixie Lark is there to see her and asking if she should let me go on back.

"Miss Weisman is currently with a client but said she can see you in a few minutes," the receptionist tells me, her tone cold enough to give me frostbite.

"Thank you," I say evenly, refusing to let her get to me. I step over to the seating area and lower myself onto a firm white couch cushion. The magazines on the glass table all look lame so I scroll through my phone for a few minutes while I wait.

"Miss Lark," a voice calls out from behind me.

I stand and turn to see a brunette who doesn't look older than me holding a door open.

"Miss Weisman will see you now."

"Great." I follow her down the hall, listening to the beat of her heels on the shiny hardwood floor. We stop at a door on the right and she pushes it open.

Sitting in a chair across from Ashley Weisman is the last person I expected to see here.

Gavin.

My heart stutters, faltering in my chest at the unexpected sight of them together.

Ashley Weisman is stupid pretty. It's irritating as hell that she's so polished and perfect all the time. Does the woman never get frazzled? Smudge her eyeliner? Have a bad hair day? Apparently that's just too much to ask.

I wait patiently until clear green eyes meet mine. "What can I do for you this afternoon, Miss Lark?"

Gavin whirls around quickly in his chair. "Dixie? What are you doing here?"

Filling my lungs with air while attempting to smile isn't easy but I give it my best shot. "I came to discuss a few things with Miss Weisman."

She contemplates this glancing back at Gavin and then makes a face as if she doesn't see the harm in it. "Okay. As long as you don't ask me for any privileged information, I think that's fine."

"Oh, I'm not here to ask you for privileged information, Miss Weisman. I'm here to impart some."

Her eyes widen and I know my boldness might come off wrong so I ease up a little. "There are things you may or may not know about Gavin. I'm guessing you don't so I'm going to tell you because I think it is important to his case."

Gavin starts to stand when I sit. "Dixie. Don't—"

"Okay. Let's hear it." She lifts a pen and slides a notebook under it.

I lick my lips, place my hands on Gavin's arm, and begin. "First of all, Gavin didn't just attack Carl Andrews. He witnessed him hitting his kid. This is a trigger for him because he grew up in an unstable environment with a drug-addicted mother who did not provide him with a safe living situation."

Surprise widens her gaze and I know he hasn't told her about his childhood. I tell myself this is for his own good so he'll forgive me . . . eventually. His expression indicates otherwise.

"Secondly, Carl had been into Gavin's place of work with his mother before and had provoked Gavin previously."

"I'm aware of that incident," she says, but I notice she jots it down anyway. "Anything else you want to share?"

"Two more things," I say before clearing my throat. "One is that a social worker came and got some info and pictures for a report on Liam and that should be in the system soon. We can use that as evidence to support Gavin's motivation for doing what he did."

Ashley asks the social worker's name and I give it to her. "And the second thing?"

I pull an envelope with a check in it out of my small black leather bag. "This," I say, setting the envelope on her desk. "It's a check for Gavin's retainer and representation fee." I stand and watch her open the envelope. "From now on, this is the *only* type of payment you'll be receiving from him."

She arches a brow as if in challenge, but I'm prepared for that.

"And PS, if I even so much as suspect you're being anything less than completely professional with him I guess I'll just see what the bar association and the partners at this firm think about your policy on accepting alternate forms of payment." Her face pales and I smile. "Was that clear, counselor? Or do I need to put it in legal terms for you?"

"Abundantly clear, Miss Lark," she says through nearly clenched teeth. "But Gavin here just handled that moments before your arrival."

"With cash!" Gavin announces loudly. "I just paid her with cash, Bluebird. I swear."

Well, now I feel like an idiot.

I narrow my eyes at them both and Gavin holds his hands up. "I'm done with that life, Bluebird, done handling things that way. I told you that and I meant it."

"He was extremely explicit in his conditions, Miss Lark. If that helps any," Ashley says.

I sigh loudly. "Okay, well . . . good."

Ashley stands to escort us both out. "If that's all," she begins, handing me back my money, "then I really need to get to my next—"

"That's not all," I break in. "I have another legal issue I'd like your help with."

Both Ashley and Gavin appear confused by my outburst.

"Okay. What can I do for you?"

I take a deep breath and glance at Gavin and then back to her. "I want to become the legal guardian for an abused child. The one whose dad Gavin assaulted. I want to become his temporary guardian until they can find him someplace better to go. And if they can't, then I want to become his permanent guardian."

"Dixie?" Gavin gapes at me.

"Go big or go home. Right, Gav?"

26 | Gavin

EVERY MUSICIAN I'VE EVER MET HAS A RITUAL OF SOME SORT that they perform before they play. I've known some to have to drink out of certain cup, or eat a certain meal, or even sleep with a specific girl.

Ours are much less obvious, but we have them. Dallas paces. Before rehearsals and before shows. He paces and he visualizes the show and what could go wrong. I told him this was just another brand of worrying and stressing the hell out, but he swears by it.

Dixie sits and applies rosin to her bow.

Me, I like to watch Dixie while tapping out the beat of the first few songs on my knee.

I don't even know that we realize that we do it, but we do. Every rehearsal, every performance. Same drill.

Except tonight's rehearsal will be different because we're fifteen minutes into our time slot and Dixie isn't here yet.

Dallas is about two more ignored text messages from blowing a fuse when his sister finally comes through the back door.

"Sorry I'm late. Quick errand caused me to get stuck in traffic," she says while pulling Oz out of his case.

"Dixie, we talked about this. I sent you about twenty-five messages about not being late and you—"

"You want to have this fight on paid rehearsal space time, Dallas?" She lifts her bow to the strings and stares her brother down. "Or can it wait until we're finished?"

Well, then.

I don't wait for Dallas's approval. I take my cue from Dixie and count down the song we agreed on playing first at the battle of the bands.

Dallas overplays his part a bit out of anger, but by the second run-through he's calmed down.

I'm guessing we should've told him about Liam so he'd be a little more understanding about Dixie being late, but then I'm not sure it was Liam who caused her to be late. Though I suspect she was meeting with Sheila after meeting with Ashley. I guess Dallas and I aren't the only ones with secrets.

When we get to the end of rehearsal, we have to decide on an original song. There's only one I want to hear.

Dallas is getting out our list of ones we've written but I know the one we should play isn't on there.

I look over at Dixie. "Can you play the one you wrote recently?"

"The one I wrote on my arms?" She gives me a perplexed look as if I was just supposed to forget. "It's not even finished."

"Can you play us what you have so far? Maybe we can finish it together," Dallas chimes in. Clearly he's pretty curious about her burst of inspiration as well.

Dixie rubs the toe of her boot across the stained carpet. "I can. I don't know that it's much to work with, but I'll give it my best shot."

Dallas nods and we both wait patiently as she lifts her fiddle and prepares to play.

"Here goes nothing," she says softly. "I call it 'Draw the Line.'"

The room falls silent, then she begins to play Oz in a melodic trance that pulls us immediately into the music.

You say so many things. Tell me I still have to wait.
But what you don't know, is what you don't know.
No matter what you tell me to do,
I'll keep holding on to you.

I know lonely, like an old familiar friend.
I know the pain, the way you keep it all in.
I know you don't know it, but you've done your time.
We've already paid the price.
I know one day that you'll be mine,
But until then,
I have to draw the line.

You're the addiction and I'm afflicted.
You're the sand in the hourglass of time.
You're so many things,
Just say you'll be mine.

Loving someone, loving so much it hurts,
Love until you can't, love until it gets worse.
I know one day that you'll be mine,
But until then,
I have to draw the line.

Where does the line go?
Oh, I don't know. How will I ever know?
I'll just have to follow wherever it goes.

It crosses the ocean, spanning wider than the sea,
It twists and turns and always ends
Just before you reach me.

I know lonely, like an old familiar friend.
I know the pain, the way you keep it all in.
Maybe you don't realize, but you've done your time.
We've already paid the price.
I know one day that you'll be mine,
But until then,
I have to draw the line.

"So that's all I have," she announces, cutting the music off abruptly.

Dallas and I just stare at her, dumbfounded by her talent. Her words pierced the air and inked themselves onto my heart. She doesn't need either of us; this girl is a star all on her own. I don't know why she's allowed herself to remain hidden behind the band, behind Oz, but she's incredible.

And she's mine.

And I'm hers.

My pulse throbs as if the music is still playing and I am in motion.

"You should step outside, Dallas," I tell him urgently. "Like now."

I walk around my kit and make a beeline for her.

"Seriously, Garrison? What the—"

I don't hear the rest of his complaint because Dixie is in my arms and her mouth is on mine and Dallas can deal.

Dixie responds eagerly, her mouth moving rhythmically against mine before opening and allowing me inside.

We kiss until we have to come up for air. My hands wander over every inch of her skin before tangling in her hair.

"That song," I say between mouthfuls of her. "It was about me?"

"It was about us, Gavin. Everything is about us. I don't know how to make you see—"

"I do, baby," I say before trailing kisses down her neck. "I do see."

After forcing ourselves to get through rehearsal, Dixie and I end up falling into her bed.

"Tell me what you want, Bluebird," I say while looking down into her beautiful blue eyes. They are so warm and trusting as they stare unflinchingly up at me.

"You," she answers softly. "All I've ever wanted or needed is you, Gavin. Just you."

"You have me," I tell her as I lower myself down into her. Clutching her to me, I drag us both up to the head of the bed. Tongues and flesh collide as our clothes become distant memories and the promise of what is to come burns bright between us.

I lace my fingers in hers and use our hands to brace myself above her. "Oh God, Gavin," she cries out as I sink in completely.

I run the tip of my tongue up her throat. "Right here, baby. Always. I'm right here." I kiss her delicate earlobe gently and then slide several more kisses across her jawline.

"You're so deep. So amazingly deep." Her confession breaks me and I damn near lose control.

This is too important to fuck up so I hold on longer, making this last even though I have ached for it for so fucking long. My body screams at me to ram my cock inside and pound into her as hard as possible. But I don't want to just use her like that. This isn't like any of the sex I'd had before. Even with her. It wasn't about getting in and getting off. I love this girl. With all my heart. I'm not just fucking here, I'm staking a fucking claim.

I'd wanted this for so long. The number of hours we've spent apart have been a torturous waste and I was going to make up for that by making her come as much as humanly possible.

Dropping my head below hers, I allow my tongue to travel south. Sucking her sweet flesh into my mouth makes my entire body hot. Almost too damn hot.

"Please," she whimpers, slamming her knees together and clenching her thighs. I watch her squirm for a long minute before returning my gaze to hers.

"Please what, baby?"

"Um . . ." She pulls her bottom lip between her teeth and squirms some more.

I chuckle, resuming the slow, arduous path of circles with my tongue. When I reach one of her tightened nipples, she cries out.

Writhing beneath me, she thrusts her body upward and grabs my arms around each bicep. Her beautiful eyes flare brightly. "Gavin fucking Garrison, I am going to implode if we keep this up. I need you. I need all of you. I'm ready now."

After sucking each of her soft pink peaks into my mouth, I glance up at her with the most innocent expression I can manage under the circumstances.

Her hand grazes my face and traces a burning path down my chest and abs. I brace myself for her to grab my dick when she takes my hand instead.

"Ready for us," she whispers, lowering my hand with hers. "For all of us. For everything that entails and then some." The moment my fingertips touch the scorching-hot wetness between her legs, I lose my grip on logic. On reality. On myself.

Stroking her undoes me. It's everything I can do not to come apart right then.

The tight pulsing of her walls clenching rhythmically around my finger was the push I needed to back it down for a second. I can focus on her, give her this.

Sitting up on my haunches, I watch as her entire body detonates around my hand. Plunging in and out, I hold back as long as I can while she rocks her hips and moans in time. Even sex with my Bluebird is going to be like making music with her. Frantic and then slow. Amazing. Freeing. Real.

"Why are you looking at me like that?" she asks into the darkness after I've made her come and she's caught her breath. She stills completely, clamping down around the two fingers that remain inside of her.

"Because you're beautiful. Because I've wanted you, wanted this, for so long. I want to enjoy it. Memorize it. Memorize you."

"Well," she says on a breath, "how about you come here and do that then."

Slowly retracting my fingers from inside her, I give her a wicked grin before sucking them into my mouth. Her expression alone could light the entire house on fire.

She pulls me to her, and I let her. Her little tongue lashes against mine, and I tug at her bottom lip with my teeth.

Wrapping her legs around my waist, she angles her hips upward and presses against me. I groan loudly and force myself to pull back before I give in to the urge to fuck her harder. Much harder.

Her whimper of protest makes my dick throb in response.

"I'm suddenly feeling extremely hungry," I say, working hard to keep my voice even.

"O-kay," she says, eyeing me warily like I've lost my mind. "Can it wait?"

"Hmm." I let my eyes map every exposed inch of her body. "No, I'm afraid it can't. I'm starving, babe."

Before she can argue or say a single word in protest, I lower my head and lick a path up her inner right thigh. And then repeat the process on the left.

"Gavin, please," she cries out, begging and trembling beneath me. The noises she makes when I swirl the tip of my tongue around her delicate folds makes me want to beat on my chest and shout from the rooftops. She is mine, dammit. Mine and only mine. No one else will ever touch her, taste her, the way I am allowed to.

The louder her moaning gets, the weaker my self-restraint becomes. I finally lean over to reach for a condom, and she stops me.

"It's okay. Um, I'm on the pill," she informs me.

"I know this." I tear open the foil packet and sheath myself, growing even harder because she is watching so closely. The streetlights peeking in from the half-open blinds light her up like she is made of something other than skin. Something shiny and beautiful. And mine. "I'm still going to be careful with you. Always. Until . . . until you don't want to be careful anymore."

A slow smile spreads across her lips. "You're always looking out for me," she whispers as I lower myself back inside her, bracing myself above her by lacing our fingers together as I did before.

"Always."

Tangled together, telling truths and swearing never again to keep secrets, we bond in a way I never knew was possible.

Dixie Lark is as much a part of me as my past. Because she is future.

I don't know why it took me so long to see, why I got caug

the short term and failed to see how powerful what we had was, or the kind of future our love is capable of providing.

Something about her song, about the way she trusts me so implicitly, to hold her, to kiss her, to be inside her—I finally understand what an honor and privilege that is now. She bared her soul and I decided to finally bare mine right back.

"There's nothing I wouldn't trade to make your dreams come true," I tell her in bed the morning of the Phi Kap show. "You know that, right?"

"This is my dream come true," she tells me, looking up at me with those endless blue pools. "This and the band finally making it."

"Working on that last one," I say as I take her hand in mine and kiss the back of it softly.

"And . . . I want Liam to be safe. I can't stop thinking about him." Her voice lowers. "He's so much like you, Gav. And I learned so much more about you by getting to know him."

"You do have a thing for us troubled black sheep, don't you?"

"What if they give him back to his dad? What if—"

"Don't think like that. Sheila is working on it and Ashley might own us for the rest of our lives but she's going to do what she can, too."

"She will never own you," Dixie growls like an angry kitten. "I mean it, Gavin."

I chuckle lightly. "I know, Bluebird. The only one that owns me is you."

"You'd do well to remember that, Garrison." She pins me with a glare before pouncing on my chest and covering me with kisses.

"Yes, ma'am."

She collapses on my chest, both of us still too tired for more lovemaking. I think we've set some records in the past twenty-four hours. "So you never told me about your mom or what happened with the charges filed against you. I was going to ask yesterday after rehearsal, but . . ."

But we didn't exactly use words to communicate yesterday.

"Ashley was able to get Carl to drop the charges by threatening him with Mrs. Lawson's eyewitness testimony that he assaulted Liam first. I let the trailer get hauled away since my mom had stopped coming home anyway."

"About time," Dixie huffs.

"I know. I guess I felt I owed her since she bailed me out the night of the accident."

Dixie stiffens in my arms.

"I would never hurt you or Dallas intentionally. You know that, don't you? Believe me, I would rather break every bone in my own body with a crowbar than cause either one of you an ounce of pain."

She nods against my skin. "I know." Her voice is so soft I can barely hear her.

I tilt her chin to face me. "Bluebird, you are now and will always be the most important thing to me. I won't let anything jeopardize what we have, even my own stupid self."

"Promise?" She is so open, her expressive eyes pleading with me to give her everything that I am. Beautiful and perfect even though they say no one is perfect. My girl is, though. Perfect for me anyway.

"I promise. From here on out, it's you and me against the world."

27 | Dixie

THE PHI KAP GIG WAS A PIECE OF CAKE. WE PLAYED TO HUNDREDS, of drunken frat boys and their dates and the majority of the crowd was too drunk to know if we were decent or if we sucked. A few of them recognized Dallas, girls mostly, but only a handful made a pass at him. Afterward we got brinner at a nearby diner, where Robyn joined us and we had more fun than we'd had in a long time. We're a family now, the four, soon to be five, of us. It made me smile, but there was still a nagging thought in the back of my mind. I wished Liam could've been there. I could hardly eat my waffles. I didn't touch my hash browns.

I called Mrs. Lawson, who said Liam was officially in the care of Child Protective Services and that she had applied to be his temporary guardian as well in case I got turned down.

Tonight I have to put my worries aside and focus on playing. Any tension I feel or hold inside will come right out into my hands and onto Oz.

I spend the entire ride to the Tavern practicing the deep-breathing techniques Robyn has taught us all.

Dallas thinks we're ready for this. I can only hope he's right.

Walking into the Tavern the night of the competition is unreal. There are twice as many people as I expected and the energy is palpable. Despite a glarey-faced older brother breathing fire nearby, Gavin holds my hand and brushes his lips against mine several times.

Dallas will just have to get used to it. I have to watch him and Robyn practically going at it on a weekly basis.

The closer it gets to our turn, the more still we each become. None of us even speak while we're in the area behind the bar where bands are lined up. We drew number fifteen for the first round so at least we're near the middle.

Our first song is a Lady Antebellum cover called "Just a Kiss" and Dallas and I harmonize really well. Probably that whole shared DNA thing.

Next up we play a reworked countrified R&B hit that has always been a fan favorite.

We exit the stage to a wild cacophony of applause.

My nerves are shot from stress but I grin through the rest of the performances. There are only two other bands that really give us a run for our money. Still, knowing we might not win is only fueling my need for it.

We make our way back to the line, drawing number eight for round two. Only fifteen bands made the cut, so I feel like eight is a good slot.

In the second round we play a harder, more aggressive song called "Take It Out on Me," mashed up with a song called "Games," and the women in the audience are losing it. Gavin is killing it on the drums and Dallas is giving it his all. I'm singing more than I ever have before and Dallas was right, my voice does add a rich layer of depth to the band. This is us. We are on. I'm so proud to be a part of it I feel like I could burst. We've got the hometown crowd advantage for sure and our cheering section is by far the loudest.

Robyn moves through the crowd handing out drink huggers, T-shirts, and postcards with our name and social media info on them.

While we wait for the remaining bands to play, Gavin steps away to check his phone. I use the ladies' room and freshen my makeup. Butterflies come to life in my belly while the other bands play. It hits me hard during the downtime.

This is it.

This is our shot.

It's even more crucial than Austin MusicFest was because now we're actually ready for it. Dallas can't afford to keep "playing" at having a band and this is our chance to legitimize our dream as an actual career. Right here. Right now.

I feel the oncoming panic attack affecting my breathing and I need the guys to help calm my nerves. Otherwise I might float away into outer space. But I don't see either of them near the bathrooms.

Making my way through the sea of bodies filling the bar, I search for signs of either Dallas or Gavin in every small grouping of people but see neither.

Dallas waves at me from a seat where he and Robyn are talking up the Rock the Republic guys. I'm relieved to see them, but still no Gavin.

I'm drunk on adrenaline and disoriented as I continue my search.

The emcee announces that there are two bands left and I feel like I'm being thrown face-first out of a plane—with no parachute.

Where the hell is he?

I throw up a silent prayer, my last resort when I'm consumed with hopelessness.

Please don't let him choose the darkness.

Please, please, for once, for me, let him choose the light.

28 | Gavin

I DON'T KNOW IF IT'S AN INNATE THING OR WHAT, BUT I CAN LIT-
erally feel when my mom is about to come into my world and fuck it
all up.

All night at the battle of the bands I've been jittery, on edge, and
basically consumed with the overwhelming sensation of impending
doom. After round two I check my phone for news that the sky is
falling and there it is.

The trailer is gone.

I need your help.

I'm all alone.

I'm scared, Gavin. Please.

I don't recognize the number but I know it's one of the many prepaid cell phones she goes through. I resist the urge to call back until
I'm outside the bar. We've got several other acts until we go on again,
if we even make it to the finals, that is. When Dixie heads to the
ladies' room I slip outside and pull up the number.

It goes to a generic message telling me this user doesn't have voice
mail.

I wait a few seconds and sure enough, my phone vibrates in my hand.

Caller Unknown.

Except, I do know.

"Hi, Mom," I answer on a sigh.

"How could you?" her shrill voice answers back. "How could you let them take our home away, Gavin? What did I ever do to you to deserve this?"

The list is endless.

"It wasn't being paid for and you were never there. I moved out on my own like I told you I was going to. It's been gone almost a week and you're just now noticing. That should tell you everything you need to know."

A couple moves past me to go inside the Tavern and I nod and step aside.

My mom's shrieking reaches an inaudible level of hysteria as she rambles on about having nowhere else to go and how she's not safe.

"Not safe from what, Mom?" I break in. "Calm down and breathe and tell me what you aren't safe from."

"Carl," she chokes out. "No one is safe from Carl. They took his son away, said you and your friend reported him and some other stuff. He asked me where to find you and nearly strangled me to death until I told him."

Jesus.

"Where are you? And where did you tell him to look?"

She coughs her typical smoker's wheeze loudly into the phone before answering me.

"Mom. Fucking tell me where you are and where you told him I'd be."

"I-I wasn't sure," she stammers out. "I told him you work at that bar we saw you at and that sometimes you hang out at that Korean store by the truck stop. I didn't tell him anything else, I swear."

She told him enough.

"Where are you right now?"

She coughs again. "I'm at his place. At Carl's. But he's not here; he left when they called and told him he couldn't have his son back. He said he was going to find you and your friend and teach you a lesson about interfering in other people's private business."

"Great, Mom. That's great. Thanks."

"Baby, I'm sorry," she pleads. "I—he's—you're not . . . He's not a good man, Gavin. If he wants to hurt you, he will."

I breathe through my nose.

Violence.

It always finds me.

But I'll be damned if it comes anywhere near my Bluebird.

The thing about my world is that it's typically bathed in darkness regardless. People like Carl and my mother will find the darkened corners even in the bright of day. It's where they thrive.

I text Dallas that I have to check on something and that if I don't make it back in time to go on without me. He and Dixie can perform her original song acoustic-style and it will still be amazing.

I practically jog to Mr. Kyung's store, breaking into a full-out sprint when I see the flames. The scent of ash and destruction swirl in the air around me.

What the fuck?

Mr. Kyung and his wife are outside and he's shouting into the phone. I pray it's to 911 or the fire department. I run around the side of the building and grab the garden hose, pulling it as close as it will reach.

Carl set the truck on fire. The truck that *I* use sometimes.

It's a message. A warning. One I don't plan to heed. Within a few minutes the fire department arrives and begins battling the flames with much more success than I did.

I comfort Mr. Kyung and his wife, promising them both I will replace the truck and handle any damage that insurance doesn't cover. I don't know how, but I will. This is my mess to clean up.

The thought of Carl going to the Tavern and doing something similar with Dixie inside floods my mind. Mental images have me literally shaking with rage as I run as fast as I can to his house.

Once I arrive, I catch my breath and storm inside. A few junkies litter the floor in the front room and my mother sits slouched over a makeshift kitchen table made of cinder blocks and plywood.

"Mom," I say as loud as I can. "Mom, look at me." I wait until she does.

Both of her eyes are swollen and she's likely battered and high at the moment.

"Where is he?"

She's dazed, staring at me as if I'm a stranger speaking a foreign language.

"Mom," I repeat slowly. "Where is Carl? Carl, you know, your friend. Where is he?"

"Carl?"

I want to shake the answer out of her. Scream and demand she sober up and come to.

"Tell me where Carl is. Carl can help you, okay? He can help you feel better."

He can't, but this is how you get info from a junkie. Make promises of things that will never happen. The cops are especially good at it.

"Carl is . . . Carl went . . ."

She breaks out into a fit of maniacal laughter and I'm nearly losing it.

"Tell me. It's important. I'll help you feel better if you just tell me."

She sighs, then looks up at me with eyes as dark as midnight. "Carl went to get his son." She giggles again. "I didn't even know he had a son. B, B," she calls to a nearby stoner making out with some girl who looks barely legal. "B, did you know Carl had a son?"

"Where is his son, Katrina? Answer me. Where is he?" This time I do reach out and grab her.

Her attention returns to me, her eyes snapping into focus on my face. "How do you know my name?"

Fuck this.

I make my way outside, tripping over bodies and God knows what else as I go. The shadows cast by Carl's house are dark but just beyond them is the light, a glow being sent down from a streetlamp like a beam from Heaven.

"Gavin," a female voice calls from the light. "Gavin, wait."

29 | Dixie

THERE ARE CERTAIN THINGS I'VE LEARNED GROWING UP THAT have shaped who I've become.

My parents taught me about love. My grandparents taught me about patience, kindness, and perseverance.

Every moment of my life has taught me about music.

Music can seem complicated to people who don't play it. Notes and chords, scales, choruses, rhythms, crescendos and such.

But it all comes down to one

simple

thing.

The beat.

If you can feel it, you are a part of it.

The beat has always been within me, in my heart. And with every beat I have loved Gavin, have wanted and needed him.

He is the beat of Leaving Amarillo. He is the heartbeat of my existence. And I will spend my life loving him with each and every beat of my heart.

My heart will forever beat in time with his until it no longer beats at all.

"Gavin, wait."

My voice breaks the silent stillness of night and I watch him decide. He's shrouded in darkness, surrounded by the shadow of Carl's house. I knew he would come here, knew his mom would eventually pull him back in, just as Dallas predicted.

I glance over my shoulder at where my brother sits in the driver's seat of EmmyLou, waiting for Gavin to decide.

Choose us, I plead silently. *Choose the light.*

I hold my hand out, stretching my arm as far as I can until my fingertips cross into darkness.

"I love you, Gavin," I say to his frozen form before me. "I will love you in times of strength and in times of weakness. I love all the parts of you—the darkness and the light. And I will love you forever no matter what you decide."

His eyes gleam in the glow of the lamp above.

"Blue . . ."

I shake my head. "You don't have to explain. I can do the math. But here, now, Gavin, I need you to choose. I need you to pick me, pick the band, pick us, pick *this* path. I will love you forever. I choose you. But if you don't choose me, here, now, I'll have to love you enough to let you go."

Tires squeal on pavement beside us, a beat-up blue Ford coming angrily to a halt mere feet from where Gavin stands.

Carl gets out wielding a baseball bat and Dallas is out of Emmy-Lou like a genie out of a bottle.

Carl's quicker. "There you are, you little son of a bitch. Did you take my son? You and your little friend playing house, are you? Not so tough now, are you?" Carl turns to me and Gavin steps in between us.

"No," I whisper quietly so that only Gavin can hear. "He's not worth it. This is his property and he has a restraining order against you. Stop, Gav. Think."

Another man gets out of the truck that Carl was in and sneers menacingly at us. This is how it happens. This is how people with bright futures end up in comas and wheelchairs and prison—one moment, one bad decision leads to them flushing their dreams down the toilet.

"Stay away from her," Gavin calls out, walking closer to them and farther from me. "Stay away from my mom, and if you know what's good for you, you'll stay away from Liam."

"Well her," Carl calls out nodding toward me, "I could give a fuck about. But your mom can't seem to stay away from me, pretty boy. And Liam is *my* boy. You hear that, you little piano-playing bitch? *My* boy!"

I lung toward Gavin, barely catching him around the waist as Dallas wraps his arms behind his back. He's ready to fight Carl, to throw everything away for this sad, pathetic man.

"Your mom has made her choices, man," Dallas says quietly. "You need to make your own. Get in the truck and let's go back to the Tavern. Now."

Gavin doesn't budge. My stomach is hollow and my heart aches for him. This is on him. I can't save him from this. From himself. This time it has to be his choice.

"We'll be in the truck," I tell him in his ear. "You decide which you'd rather do. Spend a lifetime fighting lowlifes for your mom's sake, or be with me, with us."

Dallas gapes at me but I gesture for him to follow me to the truck.

"He has to choose, Dallas. We can't force him into our world anymore. He has to come willingly."

I kiss Gavin gently on the cheek. "I love you. All of you," I whisper before walking away.

He stands tall and unflinching and I am dying inside.

Either way, something will end tonight.

I just don't know what it will be.

30 | Gavin

I'M TORN BETWEEN TWO WORLDS, TWO OPPOSITE VERSIONS OF myself.

They say man has two basic reactions: fight or flight.

For the first time in my life I'm choosing flight.

"Go to hell, Carl." I glance up at his house. "No, wait, you're already there."

He glares at me and takes a step forward.

"Think long and hard about what you're about to do. I have witnesses this time. Lots of them."

The police I notified on my jog over from Kyung's begin pulling up with sirens wailing.

Carl glances around and curses me under his breath.

"Have a nice life, Carl. By the way, I made sure to leave the front door open in invitation so they can tally up the many kilos of illegal narcotics you're in possession of. Not to mention the underage girl inside. Take care now."

Without a backward glance, I make my way to where Dixie stands next to EmmyLou.

"What about your mom?" she asks with wary eyes as I draw closer.

"I talked to Ashley. She's going to see if my mom can get mandated rehab instead of prison time, but you were right about something."

"Oh yeah?" Dixie gives me an adorable half smile. "And what's that, drummer boy?"

"It was time for me to make my own choice, for me."

She nods with shining eyes. "And what did you decide?"

"I decided we'd better haul ass if we're going to make it back to the Tavern on time."

Dixie yelps out a small cry as I wrap her in my arms and place her in the truck. Dallas says something that sounds like "hell yeah," and we are off.

On the way to a bright new future, on the path that was meant for us, the one that began the day I met Dallas and Dixie Lark on an old, dilapidated front porch.

"One, two, one, two, three, four."
I count down the beat and we launch into the song Dixie wrote for our original performance in the battle of the bands. Dallas made a few modifications and with my beat in the background it's become one hell of a song. The audience seems to agree as we play, but we all know it isn't up to them. It's up to the competition judge's panel, which includes an executive from the record label that will be signing the winner.

My palms are sweaty as hell but I manage to hang on to my sticks. I watch Dixie as she performs, and think of how she may never realize I have been watching her, loving her, from this vantage point since we began playing years ago.

The crowd is quiet for a moment when we finish and I begin to panic. But just before I'm convinced they hated it, applause breaks out and fills the room. It's loud and enthusiastic and for a little while it feels like we already won.

We make our way offstage and head to the bar behind Dallas. He orders all three of us drinks, even Dixie, and we each take a shot of Fireball.

"We killed that," Dixie says, grinning at me after making a twisted face at the burn from the shot. "I mean, I was nervous, you know? It's a new song, we hadn't rehearsed as much as we should have, but wow. We nailed it. It was even better than I imagined it could be."

"Agreed," Robyn says, coming up behind Dixie and sidling up to where Dallas is leaning against the bar. "I'm biased, but personally I think it's in the bag."

"Might be," Dallas says before planting a kiss on her lips. "Even if it's not, it was one hell of a performance." He reaches out to fist-bump me and Dixie and we return the gesture.

"It's been one hell of a night, that's for sure." I take a long pull of the beer Jake brought me and nod toward Dixie. "Think we could catch a minute outside? Alone?"

Dixie grins at me and her smile is everything. "I think I can spare a moment for you. *Maybe*."

It takes us a while to maneuver through the crowd and make our way to the back door but we do. Amid several pats on the back and hearty congratulations we finally escape the insanity.

"That was something all right," I say once we're out back beside the dumpsters.

"Yeah, it was." Dixie leans back against the building and stares up at the stars while I stare at her. "You think everything has a purpose, Gav? Us? Our music? All of it?"

I clear my throat and glance up at the stars with her. "I don't know. I mean, I guess I hope so. It'd be nice to know someone was up there knowing what they were doing. Clearly none of us down here have it all figured out."

She laughs lightly but her smile is faint.

"Everything okay, Bluebird?"

With a heavy sigh she turns toward me. "I am so proud of you for tonight, for choosing this instead of the darkness. But I can't stop thinking about someone else. Someone else I'm afraid will forever be lost in the dark if we don't *do* something."

"You got another man on the side, Lark? I gotta say, I didn't see this coming."

She shoves playfully at my chest. "Liam, Gav. I can't stop thinking about Liam. About what he's going through and how sad he must be and confused. Scared, probably."

"Probably," I agree. "But they're keeping him away from Carl and that's certainly a good thing."

She wraps her arms around herself and I decide to wrap mine around her as well. "I know. I'm glad he isn't with Carl. I just keep thinking I wish I'd had more time with him. More campouts, more cookies to make, more music lessons to give. I . . . I miss him."

I squeeze her tightly. "I know you do, babe. And I get it. But a little boy like that, one who's had a life like mine, he's a lot of responsibility. Especially when you're a twenty-year-old woman living on her own—busy with a band and a thriving music business."

"I don't care about any of that," she bites out.

Color me surprised. "You don't care about Leaving Amarillo or Over the Rainbow? Since when?"

She shakes her head and shrugs out of my grasp. I let my hands fall to my sides.

"I do care about the band and about my organization. That's not what I mean. I just mean all the successful bands or businesses in the world won't mean anything if I have to live my life knowing that little boy slipped through the cracks."

I nod. "Like I did, right?"

She gives me a thin smile and watery eyes. "But don't you get it? You turned out okay, because you found a family to care for you. Me, Dallas, Nana, and Papa. You had us. You found love. It's why you're surprisingly well-adjusted. Why you choose the light instead of the dark. But that's why I'm worried. What if Liam doesn't ever find that?"

"There are no guarantees in life," I begin slowly, hoping a soothing tone will ease the blow of what I'm about to say. "There were none for us and there will be none for Liam. The best we can do is be there, be available to him in whatever capacity we can manage."

"That's not good enough," she says shortly. "I'm sorry, but it's not. Our paths crossed for a reason. I believe his path crossed with ours for a reason, too."

"And you think that reason is . . ." She gives me a pointed look and I place my arms back around her and pull her to my chest. "You can't save everyone, Bluebird. You can't love everyone all better even if you try your hardest."

"I don't want to save *everyone*," she says in a sexy pouty voice that turns me on at the most inopportune time. "Just you. And Liam. Is that so much to ask?"

"No, babe. It's not. I just think it might be a bit more complicated, since Liam is a kid and—"

I'm interrupted by the vibrating of her phone in her pocket between us.

"Speaking of complicated. It's our complicated blond attorney," Dixie says dazedly while staring at the phone.

"Answer it. Maybe it'll be good news for a change. Maybe she called to wish us luck tonight. Or maybe Carl reported me for violating the protection order."

She takes a few steps to the side to answer and I can barely hear her over the noise coming through the back door someone has propped open.

I walk over to close it but Dallas's head pops out before I can. "Guys. Get in here. Now. They're announcing the winner."

I glance over at Dixie, who holds one finger up signaling that we should wait while she continues her phone conversation.

"We'll be in there in just a sec," I tell Dallas.

"Hurry," he huffs out on an exasperated breath. "They're making the announcement like *right now*."

I nod. "Got it. We'll be right there."

He lets the door slam and Dixie ends her call.

She opens her mouth to speak but once again the back door opens and all I hear is cheering and indecipherable noise from inside.

"We won!" Dallas yells into the back alley while hitting the back door hard enough to bruise a few knuckles. "Holy shit, you two. Get the hell in here. We won! We're officially being signed to Rock the Republic Records. We're going on tour. Like next week! Get in here right now!"

He's practically blasting off into outer space. "Slow down, Rocket Man," I tell him. "Dix? Bluebird? You okay?" She's stoic in the face of Dallas's epic news. Not smiling. Not even blinking. "Dixie?"

Even Dallas has begun to look worried. "Dixie? Say something, please. We won."

She blinks once, then stares at us as if we're the ones who just returned to reality.

"That was Ashley. She had . . . news."

Dallas and I wait silently for her to continue. Her eyes are shining but I can't tell if they're tears of joy or sadness.

"I've just been approved as Liam's temporary guardian. Starting right now."

31 | Dixie

Nana used to say when it rains, it pours. She had a lot of sayings, but that was one of her favorites. Probably because it was one hundred percent true.

Papa rephrased it a little less gently, something about the shit hitting the fan all at once.

I am certainly finding it to be a true sentiment if ever there was one.

Rock the Republic has been sympathetic to my situation inasmuch as they've allowed us to put off touring for several months while I figure out how to manage being a part of my band and Liam's sole caregiver.

The truth is, though, I'm not the only one in love with Liam.

Dallas taught him how to play guitar and basketball.

Gavin taught him to play the drums.

Despite being an overworked and sleep-deprived brand-new mom, Robyn makes spaghetti every Thursday night because it's Liam's favorite.

Mrs. Lawson makes him cookies that he and Gavin openly admit are better than mine. And when I make brinner? Aka breakfast for dinner? They all show up. And not just for my biscuits.

Liam's laughter, Liam's smiles, they're rare—but when they're bestowed upon you, you can't help but feel special, worthy, even.

We are a family, ragtag group we may be; we are a loving unit of living, breathing people who would do whatever it takes for one another. If that's not family, I don't know what is.

But we are a family that is out of time. Rock the Republic has been generous and genuinely supportive. But they have a tour to fill, vacant concert seats that they need folks to purchase tickets for, and a whole slew of other costs dependent upon me figuring out how to be both Liam's guardian and the fiddle player and frequent vocalist in Leaving Amarillo.

I know Gavin has forced Dallas to back off on pushing me for an answer, but I also know that if I don't give them one soon, our band will be replaced on the tour by Midnight Revival—an amazingly talented duo that has been blazing up the music scene.

This morning I have to meet with Ashley to discuss my options. Turns out, she's not as much like Mandy Lantram as I initially believed. She's not a succubus in designer business suits. What she and Gavin had was a mutual arrangement between two consenting adults and as much as I hate to admit it, I would've done the same thing in her position.

Sitting across from her, I'm thankful to realize that I truly have no animosity toward her. She has been helpful with Liam and hasn't made a single pass at Gavin since we cleared things up in her office months ago.

"So I looked over everything," she tells me while taking her seat at the desk and opening our file. "And you don't have very many options, I'm afraid."

I groan because this was pretty much what I expected to hear.

'Part of me wishes Gavin were here but he's visiting his mom in rehab and I know he's where he needs to be.

"I put together your two most appealing options and obviously you need time to read over this and think and discuss with your family." She slides two typed documents over to me and I glance down at the jumble of legal-speak where most statements begin, "The guardian shall be permitted" . . . and so on.

Ashley seems to take note of my confusion. "If you need any of this clarified for you, just give me a call and I'll do my best. If I can't answer your questions directly, I'll point you in the direction of someone at social services who can."

I thank her for her help and take my documents home to read over them. Unable to wait, I read them in the driveway before going inside to where Gavin and Liam currently are having some type of epic battle on the Xbox.

Ashley was right.

I have exactly two choices.

Give Liam over to a more suitable guardian and go on the road with my band as planned.

Or find myself a career more suitable to motherhood, legally adopt Liam as my son, and fit both him and myself into a cookie-cutter life that the state deems fit.

Neither option feels right . . . or even possible.

"He's asleep," Robyn says sometime around midnight. "Denver and Liam are actually both crashed out in the spare room. I'm glad you decided to move into the bigger one so they could have that one."

I nod. "Me, too."

I glance around the kitchen table at my family, Robyn, Dallas, and Gavin, before launching into our discussion about Liam's care. We decided mutually that it would be best to discuss it without him overhearing, as he's had to deal with enough.

I describe both options, detailing the pros and cons as they were laid out to me in the documents, while passing them around for everyone to have a look. Once the papers have made their way around the table, Dallas looks directly into my eyes.

"I think it's going to be a difficult situation either way, Dix. But what's most important is what *you* want. Do you want a kid? Do you want to be solely responsible for *this* kid? And if you do, are you sure it's for the right reasons?"

I start to stand up and tell my brother he has no idea what he's talking about, but Robyn stops me with a firm hand on mine. "I think what your brother means to say is, we all want what's best for you. We just want to make sure that *you're* making the decision based on that." When I don't respond, she gives me a sad head tilt and sympathetic smile. "You can't save everyone, Dixie. And you can't save anyone if you're not taking care of yourself. Trust me, I've been learning this since Denver was born. If all you do is give and give, you will eventually hit empty and crash."

I know they all mean well, and that they all think I'm insane for wanting to adopt a troubled soon-to-be eight-year-old. But what they don't see is how Liam, Gavin and I together are . . . just . . . right. Somehow we belong together, the three of us, the same way Dallas and Gavin and I used to. We belong to each other, and that much I know to be true. But it feels like that's all I know and there are so many questions to be answered, questions I can barely comprehend in the legal documents.

I look to Gavin for his input, but he says nothing.

"A lot of these restrictions seem to be targeting single mothers. It

would be easier if you were married . . . to someone without a criminal record," Robyn adds absently while looking over the papers.
"Sorry, Gavin."

He cuts his eyes to her then meets my inquiring gaze.

"She's right, you know," he finally says. "As much as I hate to
admit it, if you married someone like McKinley or some orchestra
pit guy, you two could probably adopt Liam with the snap of a finger
and live happily ever after."

"God," I groan. "Let it go already, Garrison. I'm with you. You're
with me. Forever. Got it? No more pity parties in the peanut gallery."

Gavin gives me a half smile. "I just don't want to stand in the way
of what you want, Bluebird. Not again. Never again."

"You're not and you won't." I shuffle the papers Robyn has just
handed back to me. "But I do need help figuring this out. Will
Gavin's criminal record affect my ability to adopt Liam perma-
nently, you think?"

Robyn shrugs. "No way to know for certain. What did the attorney say?"

I sigh. "She said it depended on the judge we're assigned for the hearing. She said some judges won't make a big deal about it and some will."

"That's helpful." Robyn makes an annoyed breathy sound.
"That's like saying they're going to make the decision based on the
weather in Texas that day. So basically, it could go either way and she
doesn't know shit. Awesome."

"Yeah, pretty much."

I face-plant into the palms of my hands and try to think.

There's really only one solution and I already know what it is. I
just know it's going to hurt people I care about.

So I decide to do what Nana taught me.

I hold out for a miracle.

32 | Gavin

I'VE NEVER SEEN DIXIE AS QUIET AS SHE'S BEEN THE PAST COUPLE OF days. Sure, she's laughed and smiled and put on a happy face for everyone else's sake because that's what she does. But I know better. I know her heart and her heart is sad.

I get the feeling that she's already made her mind up about Liam and about the tour. If this were Dallas in charge of making decisions, I'd say the tour was a sure thing. But it's Dixie so I haven't even turned my two weeks' notice in at the Tavern.

Dixie is a bleeding heart determined to save the world. She can't do that just playing music on the road with her band, but she can definitely make a difference in Liam's life.

Which is why I have a plan. Granted, my plans haven't always gone so well in the past, but this time I have faith that Dixie will be open to it. At least, I hope she will. Otherwise I'm about to make a gigantic ass of myself.

The court date for Liam's custody hearing is only a few days away. And because fate is cruel, Rock the Republic has given us to the evening of the same date to give them an answer. Naturally.

*   *   *

As we dress for court in front of her bedroom mirror, I stand behind her and fasten a pearl necklace that belonged to her grandmother around her neck. She's been so busy with Liam and the band lately that I've barely had a minute alone with her. Worried blue eyes meet mine in the mirror. I place my hands on her bare shoulders and kiss her gently on the cheek.

"Whatever happens, whatever you decide, it will be okay," I whisper into her ear.

"How do you know?" Her eyes are wide and searching when she turns to face me. They examine my face as if all the answers might be written in invisible ink.

"I just know. We're here, aren't we?"

She frowns, clearly unsatisfied with my answer, but it's the only one I have right now.

I hold her hand in the car and all the way into the courtroom. I keep holding her hand while the social services resource officer takes Liam to the room he has to wait in while adults determine his fate.

I am still holding her hand when we take our seats and wait for the judge.

I finally understand what Dixie and I give one another that no one else can.

Balance. Strength. Hope.

During childhood, she provided these things for me during my weakest moments. Now I provide them for her. It's an even exchange we will continue until our last breath.

The judge takes the stand and Dixie tenses beside me.

"It's going to be okay, Bluebird. It's all going to be okay."

33 | Dixie

I FEEL LIKE I'VE SPENT TEN YEARS IN THIS COURTROOM. I'VE GIVEN my lengthy statement, Dallas and Robyn have both testified on my behalf, the lady from social services and Sheila Montgomery detailed their experience with Liam, and even Mrs. Lawson showed up to speak her piece. Just when I think the judge is going to shut it down so he can deliberate in his chambers, Ashley stands up and makes an announcement.

"We have one more statement to be read, Your Honor," she interrupts before the judge can complete his "if there are no further statements" sentence. "My client would like to be heard on this matter as he is from a similar background as the child in question."

The judge nods and I watch Gavin stand and take his place at the podium. I don't know what he has planned and I'm nervous for him. A steady tremor hums through me as he begins to address the court.

"Thank you," Gavin says in greeting, "for allowing me to address the court today in the matter of Liam's custody hearing." He clears his throat and I feel like my heart is going to leap out of my chest.

"While it may seem odd for me to speak before the court today, I would like a chance to explain why I feel compelled to do so."

Smart Gavin is blowing my mind right now. I've never heard him speak so eloquently and articulately. Just when I think I can't be any more in love with him than I already am, he goes and proves me wrong.

"As you know, I have made mistakes in the past that have placed me on the wrong side of the law. I won't deny that on paper, Dixie and I might not look like the best option when it comes to guardians for Liam. However, Dixie Lark is the kindest, most compassionate human being I have the privilege to know. And as for me, I was raised in the kind of home Liam has known for the duration of his childhood. My mother was a heroin addict—rather, she *is* a heroin addict—and moreover, she was an abuse victim and sixteen when she got pregnant with me. There was no support, no guidance, and no one around to oversee my safety and well-being." He pauses to take a breath and I wipe my sweaty palms on my skirt. I am so with him in this moment I might as well climb right inside his body. "That being said, I learned at an early age that drawing attention to the shortcomings of my living situation would only result in a tumultuous upheaval of what tiny bit of security I knew. Removal from my home and police officers and scary people in suits and then a drive to a new home, which often was just as unstable and frequently terrifying."

The entire courtroom is captivated as he continues.

"The system is far from perfect, Your Honor. I think we can agree on that. But that is not the point I am up here to make. My point is, the world looks different through the eyes of a child. And when you grow up in the type of environment that Liam and I have, you develop a certain type of survival mode. You don't think about toys or trucks or cake or playing games. You think about surviving and about getting through that day. Hiding from the dealer that kicks you

when he comes over to see mom or dad, avoiding an outraged boyfriend or friend when they're in a drug-induced rage, and scrounging
up enough foodlike substances to keep from passing out at school
because that's when they call the bad people to come take you somewhere even scarier."

I blink back the hot tears threatening to burn tracks of hatred for
both Katrina Garrison and Carl Andrews down my face. I swallow
the sob trying to escape, the audible proof of the pain I feel for Gavin
and Liam—sympathy I know neither of them wants or needs.

"Dixie and I," he says, jolting me to life with the sound of my
name as he angles himself in my direction briefly, "we've gotten to
known Liam. We've spent time with him, shown him that time with
us—whether at home or on the road—will be a time of safety, of security, and of being provided for by adults he can trust. This is rare
for a child in his situation and though we aren't married and we are
musicians who don't have the most conventional lifestyle, I can say
without reservation or hesitation that Liam needs a less restrictive
environment than most children his age. A classroom with rules he
cannot possibly keep in mind at all times will be a nightmare for
him just as it was for me. Trying to fit in and compete with children
who've had advantages he couldn't even possibly comprehend is both
unfair and unrealistic. Due to the success of our careers, we're able
to provide him an individualized education where he can set his own
pace with tutors who are knowledgeable about his situation and tem-
perament. We were also able to find a therapist who specializes in
working with children like Liam."

Gavin casts a long look over his shoulder at me and I grin big because I am so damn proud of him right now. My broody silent boy
stood up and became a man today for the sake of a child we both love
and cherish. No matter the outcome or the judge's decision, I know

we will always be a part of Liam's life and that having Gavin as a role model was part of a grander plan designed by a much higher power than us.

"Is that all, Mr. Garrison?"

At first Gav looks like he's going to wrap it up, but then he shakes his head.

"No, sir. I just want to add that when I was a kid, I thought everything was my fault. I placed the blame for my mother's behavior squarely on my own small shoulders. Meeting Liam has helped me to realize that no child is to blame or should be punished for their parents' mistakes. I don't regret the pain that I suffered growing up or carry it with me any longer because I understand that there was a purpose for it. Without experiencing it for myself, I never could've related to Liam and reached him the way that I have been able to. I consider that a gift—his friendship and his trust. I know he won't give it to many. I hope that you will look long and hard at this case, at us as individuals, Liam, Dixie, and myself, and you will see what I see. A family. One designed to be together. One that loves and supports each other. I hope that you will choose us as Liam's permanent guardians, and not because we make the most money, but because we love and care for him and understand him in a way other guardians would likely be unable to do."

The judge nods and Gavin takes one more deep breath. "That's all, Your Honor. Thank you for your time."

When he returns to his seat he reaches for my hand and I feel his trembling as much as mine.

"I love you," I whisper. "And love you."

"Ditto, Bluebird," he whispers back. His eyes meet mine and I read the promise in them.

It's going to be okay.

Gavin says we can use the broken pieces of the past to build a brighter future . . . but I'm not sure this is true anymore.

Either we lose Liam or lose the band, and I know from experience that I need them both.

Can we have both? I don't know.

All I know is that I don't want my dreams to cost me my heart.

For the first time in my life, I know I finally have the strength to hold on tight either way.

34 | Gavin

Two years later

I can't help but laugh as Dixie tries to juggle the four Grammys we won tonight. A song we wrote about Liam during our yearlong struggle to formally adopt him launched our career into the stratosphere and we still haven't come down—though we all know we will one day. For now, we keep each other grounded.

Photographers are everywhere as we leave the awards ceremony. It's a constant barrage of flashbulbs, almost like being in a club with strobe lights. Dallas has his hands full with Robyn and Denver, I'm carrying Liam, and my poor Bluebird is stuck with the relatively small but still heavy and somewhat cumbersome trophies.

"Congratulations on the twins, Dallas!" a reporter calls out. "When's the due date?"

"June," Robyn answers, glaring at Dixie, who grins maniacally in response.

"What about you two?" the same reporter calls out toward me and Dixie. "Any bundles of joy coming your way anytime soon?"

Dixie looks momentarily caught off guard so I answer.

"We have our hands full as it is right now," I tell the female reporter standing up front. Nodding to Liam, who has his face buried in my shoulder, I add, "We're focusing on our family and our music."

She takes this direct answer as motivation to push on and shoves her mic toward me. "The history with the band, how it all began, how you two ended up together and with an adopted son, it's all such a mystery to your fans. Do you ever think you'll do an exposé on your backstory? For CMT or someone else, for instance?"

I glance over at Robyn, who does our PR and marketing and typically fields these types of questions. She's busy consoling an exhausted Denver so I take a deep breath and face the reporter myself. Our backstory is messy and full of criminal records, complicated courtroom dramas, and disastrous tours in which things happened that I have vowed never to discuss. I've taken several oaths to keep specific incidents quiet—particularly those involving one band member peeing her pants and it wasn't either a child or a pregnant Robyn touring with us at the time. Dixie would kill me dead if those details ever surfaced.

"Actually, uh, we don't really have any plans at the moment as far as that's concerned. We're just kind of—"

"Moving forward," Dixie breaks in, stepping between me and the reporter. "We won't be doing any exposés on our past or our backstory because we're focusing on our future."

God, I love this woman, I think to myself while I watch her politely shield Liam and me from the remaining questions being thrown at us as we leave.

I have an amazing woman in my life and we have a son. And an internationally known award-winning band that is currently topping most of the music charts. Me, Captain Screwup, the guy who was once capable of nothing more than fucking up the one-man parade known as his life. I have everything I ever dreamed of and then some.

I was raised, I was born and bred, in complete and total darkness. Yet somehow I found the light. The same way Liam gravitated toward her, so did I. We both still do.

She is a beacon, shining relentlessly and guiding us out of the dark.

We get a lot of questions about getting married, but neither of us cares much about that. What we have is deeper than a piece of paper. Dixie Leigh Lark is my soul mate and nothing will ever change that.

Dixie glances over her shoulder and I see blue eyes full of love gleaming up at me.

"Forever," I mouth at her.

"And always," she mouths back.

My Bluebird is right. We are focusing on our future.

And what a bright, beautiful future it is.

Epilogue | Liam

"DUDE. SERIOUSLY. YOU HAVE THE COOLEST PARENTS." MALCOLM Hastings fist-bumps me as we take our spots backstage next to my cousin Denver and his grandma.

"Yeah, they're okay. I guess."

His already large eyes bulge behind the lenses of his glasses. "They're okay? We're backstage at the biggest musical festival of the year. This is freaking amazing!"

I laugh at him, no, no, *with* him. Definitely with him, because he's laughing along at how laid-back I am about the whole famous-musicians-for-parents thing. Malcolm is a unique individual and a lot of people laugh at him because they don't see the world the way he does. He actually does get laughed *at* a lot and he doesn't like it. I take special care never to laugh *at* him.

We're an odd pair. I'm a little on the stockier side in my typically solid black attire and Malcolm is tall but skinny with his suspenders and colorful bow ties. The bow ties belonged to his granddad and he gets really mad and kind of sad when people make fun of them.

He's a good guy, the kind of guy who will wake you up at a sleepover if you're having an embarrassing nightmare and will listen without laughing when you tell him what it's about. He's the kind of guy who keeps stuff to himself and my mom says it's important to have friends you can trust. Even if they wear really strange bow ties.

He's also supersmart, like, skipped two grades smart. So he's smaller than most of us in eighth grade, which is where I come in.

I'm the muscle.

After a sleepover incident in sixth grade, I decided Malcolm was my friend for life. So when some of the guys on the football team decided to duct-tape Malcolm to a toilet seat naked in the locker room, I decided I didn't like the idea too much and used my fists to express my dislike of this plan before Malcolm lost too much body hair to a roll of Kentucky Chrome.

My mom wasn't thrilled.

I was grounded for two weeks, which actually kind of sucked.

But my dad . . . he kind of got it. My dad says loyalty is important and that I get this from my mom. He said sometimes, when you learn about the world a certain way, like me and him did, you sort of learn how to deal with your problems and emotions a certain way. Doesn't mean it's the best way, just means your instincts might not always be in line with the kind of behavior that is okay with like teachers and cops and stuff. He taught me about counting my heartbeats to calm down so I can think about the possible consequences of my decisions before I act.

I count my heartbeats a lot.

Sometimes I still make mistakes, but both my parents and my aunt Robyn and uncle Dallas say this is okay.

It used to not be okay. My biological dad didn't think mistakes were okay. He punished me for them, even some that I didn't make. The dad I have now, the one who taught me to play the drums, he says sometimes grown-ups make mistakes too and that the things my biological dad did were mistakes. He's paying for them in prison, which is how I learned about consequences. And I guess how he did, too.

It took a long time for me to be okay with mistakes. Learning to play the violin with my mom and the drums with my dad taught me that sometimes something really kind of, well, beautiful and awesome can come from mistakes.

"Some of the best songs were written by accident," my mom always says. "Or from something sad or really painful."

Learning to find the good in all the bad and control yourself even when you can't—my parents say that's how you grow up and how you learn to make good decisions.

I'm working on it.

But at thirteen, I'm the only linebacker who plays violin and my best friend wears bow ties so I get a lot of practice trying to make good decisions.

It's easier said than done, that's for sure.

The music begins onstage and my heart beats in time with the drums. My dad is a pretty talented drummer and he's on a lot of magazine covers. I grin back at Malcolm, because yeah, okay, so my parents are kind of cool. For parents, I guess. They look different than some parents because they have tattoos and stuff, but most of my friends seem to think that just makes them cooler.

Tonight's concert is to benefit an organization my mom started called Over the Rainbow. She wanted to give kids like me, well, like I used to be, a chance to learn to channel stuff, which I think means deal with stuff, through playing music.

After she and my dad adopted me, some people found out and wrote an article about us and how we met. Then all these other musicians started calling and asking how they could help out. Now it's a really big deal, which makes my parents really happy.

My mom says I'm her pot of gold at the end of the rainbow, which makes me feel kind of special. I am pretty thankful that she met me and loved me and wanted to adopt me. I am also thankful she doesn't say the pot of gold thing in front of the guys. Only at night before bed.

I'm pretty lucky I guess. Not only do I have a cool mom but my dad understands how I am sometimes—even when I don't understand it myself. Through some of the events for Over the Rainbow, I've met some other kids like me, kids who had not-so-great parents or for one reason or another didn't get to know their parents. It's kind of nice not to feel alone in the world. There's this girl, Abby, she lives near me and had kind of a tough time before Over the Rainbow and she's okay. For a girl I guess.

Mom says that's what music does. It connects us, makes even the loneliest person a part of something special. It helps us to feel and to heal, she says. She's right. She usually is, but my dad says not to tell her that too much or she'll get a big head about it.

Last week at school I turned in my essay on why I wanted to be a drummer when I grow up, a professional one like my dad. My teacher, Mrs. Kingston, said music was a hobby, not a career, and that I should rewrite it.

My mom came to school and had a very long discussion with her about this. I don't know what happened during their talk because I had to sit out in the hall, but after it was over Mrs. Kingston said she'd made a mistake and gave me a hug and an A on my essay.

"Why do you want to be a drummer, Liam?" my mom asked me in the car on the way home. "Is it because you really love playing or because you want to be like your dad?"

I had to think about it for a while. "Both, I guess. And because on Career Day they said you should do what makes you feel good and what makes a difference in the world."

She smiled at me and I smiled back because she's got a really nice smile that makes it hard not to. Even if you don't want to at first, like I didn't when we first met, she will keep smiling at you until you do. "Music has sure made a difference in our world, hasn't it?"

I nodded.

When I was younger, I used to wander around town. I found my mom because I heard the music coming from her house where she gave piano and violin lessons. I don't like to think about what might've happened if she hadn't been there, if she'd been on the road with the band or away at college or at any of the other places she could've been, if she hadn't played the kind of music that brings you back again and again—the kind that makes you feel safe . . . connected. I shook off the weird feeling remembering those days before knowing her gave me and told her about how Teddy Gleason said music doesn't make a difference, that doctors did because doctors saved lives and music was "unnecessary." She rolled her eyes and said Teddy was going to grow up to live a very dull life like his dad and not to worry about it.

The song my parents wrote for me the year they didn't think they were going to be able to adopt me begins to play and I watch my parents and my uncle onstage for a few minutes. It's called "Losing Liam" and it launched their career, according to my mom. It also makes people cry, yet it was number one for like a ton of weeks. I guess some people like to cry.

It doesn't make me cry. It makes me feel . . . I don't know . . . happy, I guess, that they wanted me that much. My mom says it's important to find happiness and that not everybody's happy ending looks the same, and that's okay.

Watching them, listening to the words they wrote about me and how much they love me and how badly they wanted to be my parents, I realize that Teddy really was wrong.

Music does save lives.

It saved mine.

Acknowledgments

WHEN I LOOK BACK ON THE YEAR IT TOOK TO WRITE THIS SERIES, it feels like a blur. A beautiful, bright, neon lit blur.

I have to confess that I didn't know exactly how the Neon Dreams series would end when I began writing it. I knew the band would finally make it big. I knew that they would never want to share their backstory but that it would be a story worth telling. What I didn't know was how real their hearts and souls would become to me. While Liam may not be Dixie and Gavin's biological son, I did learn this year that family truly does come in the form of people who love and support you in both the best and worst of times and that it's not always comprised of people who are related by blood or marriage. Liam was born from that discovery.

When Dallas went on the road and Dixie stayed behind, some people were outright angry. I was. At both of them. I was confused about why this felt right. I didn't know Liam existed yet. I didn't know he was going to be wandering by an old house in the backside of Amarillo alone and afraid. I didn't realize that Dixie had to be there giving piano lessons to other kiddos so that Liam would hear and be drawn to her.

Everyone was exactly where they needed to be—even when I hadn't yet realized it.

So my first big thank you is for you, for those of you who read this series and allowed me to figure it out as I went. For each of you who leaves a review somewhere—anywhere—and tells a friend to read it, thank you times two. Times ten. Times infinity, as my daughter says.

My second thank you is to my editor, Amanda, who didn't tell me to take a hike when Liam entered the picture and it meant a rewrite of the second half of the book and that I wouldn't make my initial deadline. I love you. I thank God for you, for your always having my back and for allowing me to write the story I believed in, the way that I needed to write it.

Thank you to my agent, Kevan, for also not dropping the crazy lady who said "So . . . my life is a mess and I need this book to go a different way and I am going to hunker down in the bat cave until I get it right." Promise not to do that again . . . at least not on purpose.

To the members of CQ's Road Crew and the Backwoods Belles, you ladies have been my family this year. You have been my light in the darkness, pulling me out of one of the toughest and most devastating situations I've ever been in. I literally don't know if I could do my job without your unconditional love and support. Scratch that. I couldn't. I know I couldn't. Same goes for the bloggers who share, review, post, and rant and rave about all the book things. I love y'all. To the moon and back and around again.

To the amazing authors I am blessed to call colleagues and friends, thank you. I don't know what I did to deserve you, to even get to know you much less read your work and have my books read and loved on by you, but I'm glad I did it—whatever it was!

Lastly, to anyone who supports music and musicians in general, thank you for existing. Music matters. The epilogue from Liam is very much nonfiction in my world, and I have someone I love dearly that I believe was saved by music. You know that feeling you get when you hear that song—that one that causes you to step off the treadmill or pull the car over or freeze in place and hold your breath and strain to hear because it reaches that deep, dark, hidden place where your secrets dwell—it's a real, tangible thing, that feeling. It connects us—especially when we are positive no one else in the entire world could possibly understand what we're going through. And let's face it, life is better with a soundtrack.

Thank you to every single person who had a hand in helping this series about a small-town ragtag band become more than I ever dreamed it could be.

Thank you for making my dreams come true.

Don't miss any of Caisey Quinn's addicting
Neon Dreams series! Check out where it all began with
Leaving Amarillo and *Loving Dallas!*

LEAVING AMARILLO

Music is my everything.

After my parents died when I was a kid, moving into my grandparents' ramshackle house on a dirt road in Amarillo seemed like a nightmare. Until I stumbled upon my grandfather's shed full of instruments. My soul lives between the strings of Oz, my secondhand fiddle, and it soars when I play.

In Houston, I'm a typical college student on my way to becoming a classically trained violinist headed straight for the orchestra pit. But on the road with my band, Leaving Amarillo, I'm free.

We have one shot to make it, and I have one shot to live the life I was meant to. Leaving Amarillo got into Austin MusicFest, and everything is riding on this next week. This is our moment.

There's only one problem. I have a secret . . . one that could destroy everyone I care about.

His name is Gavin Garrison and he's our drummer. He's also my brother's best friend, the one who promised he'd never lay a hand on me. He's the one person I can't have, and yet he's the only one I want.

One week. One hotel room. I don't know if I can do this.

I just know that I have to.

LOVING DALLAS

Every dream comes with a price. . .

Dallas.

Sacrifice. I'm familiar with it.

I've had to leave behind everyone I cared about—my sister, my best friend, my band, and my high school sweetheart—in order to chase my dream of making it in Nashville.

But when Robyn Breeland walks back into my life, it's as if the universe has decided to give me a second chance. I'm just not sure it's one I'm willing to take.

Robyn.

Heartbreak. I practically majored in it.

Dallas Lark was the first boy I ever loved and the one who'd shattered my heart into pieces. But I've moved on. Working in promotions at Midnight Bay Bourbon, I'm too busy to sit around moping over my ex. But when my company decides to sponsor his tour, I'll have to face him whether I'm ready to or not. Dallas is determined to drive me to distraction, and my body begs me to let him.

Trouble is, my heart can't tell the difference between a second chance and making the same mistake twice.

About the Author

Author photograph by Lauren Perry, Perrywinkle Photography

CAISEY QUINN lives in Birmingham, Alabama. She is the bestselling author of the Kylie Ryans series as well as several New Adult and Contemporary Romance novels featuring southern girls finding love in unexpected places. You can find her online at www.caiseyquinn writes.com.